it started with a lie

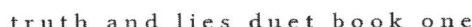

truth and lies duet book one

30/50

Kai—
can a lie become
the truth?
xo, Lisa Suzanne

LISA SUZANNE

IT STARTED WITH A LIE
TRUTH AND LIES DUET BOOK ONE

©2018 LISA SUZANNE

All rights reserved. In accordance with the US Copyright Act of 1976, the scanning, uploading, and sharing of any part of this book without the permission of the publisher or author constitute unlawful piracy and theft of the author's intellectual property. No part of this book may be reproduced or transmitted in any form or by any means, electronic or mechanical, including photocopying, recording, or by any information storage and retrieval system without the written permission of the author, except where permitted by law and except for excerpts used in reviews. If you would like to use any words from this book other than for review purposes, prior written permission must be obtained from the publisher.

Published in the United States of America by Books by LS, LLC.

ISBN-13: 978-1723082412
ISBN-10: 1723082414

This book is a work of fiction. Any similarities to real people, living or dead, is purely coincidental. All characters and events in this work are figments of the author's imagination.

Content Editing: It's Your Story Content Editing
Proofreading: Proofreading by Katie
Cover Design: CT Cover Creations
Cover Photograph: Wander Aguiar
Cover Model: Forest

ित started with a lie

books by Lisa Suzanne

It Started with a Lie
It Ended with the Truth

A Little Like Destiny
Only Ever You
Clean Break

The Power to Break
The Invisible Thread

Clickbait
Stalemate
Outwait

Conflicted

Not Just Another Romance Novel

Vintage Volume One
Vintage Volume Two

How He Really Feels (He Feels, Book 1)
What He Really Feels (He Feels, Book 2)
Since He Really Feels (He Feels, Book 3)

Separation Anxiety
Side Effects
Second Opinion

dedication

To the two boys who make me
the happiest I've ever been.

one

In my wildest dreams, I never imagined I'd be walking down the aisle with Reese's arm tucked into mine.

She's glowing today. I glance briefly at the steep curve of her stomach, and a dart of something unfamiliar pings through my chest. She's pregnant with a little girl who I know I'll love and cherish even though I don't really do the *kid* thing.

I force my eyes from the woman by my side and find my parents in the crowd. I shoot them a quick smile. My brother sits beside them, but his gaze is on the woman whose arm is tucked into mine.

As we make our way to the front of the church together, I think for the millionth time how I never deserved her.

It's probably why I didn't end up with her and my brother did.

It's also probably why the baby she's carrying will be my niece and not my daughter.

Reese Brady and Brian Fox were never meant to be—not in the way she was meant to be with my brother, Mark.

You'd think I'd have learned my lesson after what I did to her and my brother, but I didn't. It's hard to learn a lesson when everyone was so quick to leave the past behind us—a benefit of being born into the Fox family, where our parents taught us to forgive and forget.

I'm the living, breathing definition of a selfish prick, but admitting the problem's the first step, right? Only it's not a problem, and I don't plan to change any of that any time soon. I'm happy for my brother that he's having a kid with the woman we both slept with once upon a time, and I'm even happier it's not me in his position.

We approach the front of the church. Reese turns to take her place in the spot reserved for the matron of honor while I shake hands with the groom and take my place beside him as his best man.

The music changes and everyone in the church rises as they wait for their first glimpse of the bride. I keep my eyes focused to the back of the church even though I feel someone looking at me. It might be Tess, the bridesmaid who has been giving me the eye at every event we've attended leading up to this wedding.

I think tonight might just be the night to finally *break the ice* with her.

There's a few problems in our way, like the fact that she dated one of my best friends. But we're two single adults capable of making our own decisions, so whatever happened in the past doesn't matter anymore. I guess I could ask him, but I tend to follow the *apologize later* attitude.

I can't help but give myself a little pat on the back when the doors burst open and the bride makes her grand appearance. If I'd never have used Reese the way I did, we wouldn't be standing here at this wedding today. Everything happens for a reason, and as I watch Jill make her way down the aisle toward my best friend, a little part of me is even glad for everything that happened.

The physical wounds have healed—literally—and I never felt the burn of the emotional scars. I just assume every woman now only wants me because of my famous rock star brother, and I've stopped allowing that to hurt and started using it to my advantage. It only took once to learn that lesson—pretty easy when the only girl I ever really loved cheated on me with him.

People laugh and cry right on cue as the minister performs the wedding ceremony, and I'm bored as fuck and ready for the party afterward. I force myself to pay attention as we near the end of the ceremony.

"Every one of you in this room has a love story," the minister says. "Some stories are brief while others are longer. As we celebrate the love today between this beautiful couple, reflect for a moment on your own story. Grasp your main character's hand a little tighter, or open yourself up to the vulnerability that comes with finding your other half. Wherever you're at in your story, make it a good one."

What the minister failed to mention is that all stories eventually come to an end. I've already lived part of my story, and it didn't end well. Some people are meant to have happily ever afters, and then there's the rest of us. If you open your heart up for heartbreak, you're only going to get what you expect.

My eyes lock with Tess's for a beat, and I raise a brow before I look away. Staring too long at her as we stand at the front of a church during a wedding could lead her to the wrong conclusion. I'm not looking for anything more than a single night of pleasure, and I'm not too concerned with whether she gets hers before or after I do.

From what I've heard, that's how she operates, too.

She sounds like the perfect end to this night. Besides, isn't it sort of the duty of the best man to hook up with a bridesmaid?

* * *

Whiskey sloshes over the side of my newly filled glass as someone slaps me on the back a little harder than absolutely necessary. I turn around with an offending glare for the perpetrator only to find my brother, Mark.

I slap him on his back, too, a little harder than I need to in some quest to get even, a true representation of our relationship. Our parents walk up behind him, effectively ending any sort of shit we might give one another.

"So nice seeing my boys together again," our mom says, wrapping her arm around my waist.

My dad rolls his eyes and glances at my mom. "Raise your hand if you're shocked that they're standing at the bar. What did we do wrong, Diane?"

Mark laughs and mock punches my dad in the arm, and my mom looks up at me while my dad rubs the spot of his son's offense. "Everything okay, Brian?" she asks quietly. She still thinks *I* was the one who got fucked over in the whole Mark/Reese thing, and I love her for it. She's the only one who was on my side even after everything was revealed—that I was using Reese when I knew Mark had feelings for her first, that my ex, Kendra, cheated on me with my brother when he didn't know she was my girlfriend...the list goes on. It pays to be the youngest sibling, I guess. My mom's always had a soft spot for all her children, but that soft spot becomes pure cashmere when it comes to me.

I nod and take a sip of my whiskey. I look around the room and don't even realize my eyes have landed on Tess until she glances up and catches me staring. I look down at my mom without missing a beat.

"Everything's great, Mom." I give her a smile despite my lie.

She glances at Mark. "And you?"

"Aside from freaking the fuck out over this baby business, yeah, we're good."

it started with a lie

"Language!" she scolds, and Mark and I laugh like we always do when she tries to tell her adult son to watch his mouth. She lets go of me and places her hands on her hips as she glares at Mark.

"Sorry, Mother," he says.

"You better not talk like that around the baby. Not even when she's in the womb." She points to him and gives him her scariest, most threatening look. "I know you use that sort of language in your songs, but you better listen to me—"

Mark leans in to give her a hug, mostly to interrupt her, and it totally works. "Thank you. You're gonna be the best grandma this baby could ask for."

She says something that I miss into his shoulder as my dad turns to me. "How's work?"

"Fine," I say, purposely avoiding his penetrating gaze. He'll know I'm lying if we make eye contact.

Things aren't fine. They haven't been for a long time now, and that's why I need to get my brother alone this weekend.

"What's really going on, Bri?" my dad asks. He's trying to appeal to my sense of family by calling me by a nickname no one ever uses. He knows I'm lying even without the eye contact, and I hate that. My eyes land on Tess again, and this time when she catches me staring, I don't look away.

"Nothing," I murmur. I take a bolstering sip of my drink then glance at my dad. I press my lips together in a polite attempt at a smile. "Excuse me." I set my suddenly empty tumbler on the counter and stride across the room toward Tess. I'll see my family at brunch tomorrow, but tonight? I'm not talking business with my father when a hot girl has been eyeing me all night.

two

I don't have a pickup line prepared, but I'm not sure I need one. I try to come up with something witty as I approach the girl who can't seem to keep her eyes off me, but it's sort of futile. Instead of a line, I get right to the point. I grab her hips and start dancing to the rhythm of the fast song, indifferent to the fact that Jason, this girl's ex and my best friend, is somewhere in this room, oblivious to the fact that my family—my mother—might be watching. She's into it as she falls right into step with me. She glances up at me from hooded eyes that tell me the deal is already sealed.

"You better stop looking at me like that," I say.

"Why?" she challenges, one perfectly shaped brow arched at me.

"Because," I say, leaning in closer so this conversation is just between us, "if you keep giving me that look, I'll have to assume it's because you want to get fucked tonight."

I start to pull back, but she laces her arms around my neck to keep me in place. "Then I guess the look is working to my advantage."

She lets go of my neck and I can't help but wonder why this hasn't happened before.

"Now be a good boy and tell me your room number. I'll meet you up there in an hour. We can't keep dancing like this. Jason's eyes have been on us the whole time."

Another bridesmaid is dancing right next to us. To keep all suspicion at bay, I whisper my room number as I let go of Tess and grab the other bridesmaid. I start dancing with her like I just danced with Tess, and while it might be sending all the wrong signals, I act a little drunker than I am, dance a little more ridiculously than I normally would, and wait out my time.

An hour later up in my hotel room, wet lips drag across the stubbled skin of my neck, stopping briefly for a suck and the dart of a tongue as my fingers tangle in her short, blonde hair. A moan and a grunt, and it's all so predictable. I thought this might be a little different tonight, fucking a girl I already know, someone semi-off-limits because she dated my buddy and is close friends with my ex, but as I spin her around and bend her over to drive my cock into her from behind, it feels like everything else.

Don't get me wrong—it feels good, but it's further proof I'm not invested enough for this to go beyond tonight.

Tits.

I need some tits.

I grab for them beneath me, reaching around and squeezing one as soon as I find it. I want them in my face. In my mouth.

I pull out then lie down on the bed and shift her on top of me.

I bury my face in her luscious tits while she gyrates over me, and we find a fast rhythm together. As I start to come, I pull one of her nipples into my mouth and bite down. She moans as I empty myself into the condom separating us, and then she starts to really move. She thrashes around wildly, screaming in what must be ecstasy as her fingers move toward her clit. I watch for a few hot seconds before I bat her hand away. This is my one job right now—to make her come—and it'll be by *my* hands, not by hers.

it started with a lie

I thumb her clit and she cries out even more loudly, thrashes about so violently I can barely get my hand where it needs to be, but I keep at it until she falls apart. I watch as her lips fall open and her eyes close, as she grips onto her nipples while her movements slow. Her body pulses around me with shrieks coming out of her mouth as I soften inside her, and the second her shudders slow, she dismounts and collapses beside me.

She pants for a few beats as she tries to catch her breath. "Well that was fun," she says, swinging her legs over the side of the bed and standing up. She searches around for the clothes we tossed aside as we got down to business not more than twenty minutes ago.

"You're leaving?" I ask.

She shrugs. "I got what I came here for. You?"

"Well, yeah..."

"I didn't peg you to be the cuddling type, Fox."

I can't help my laugh. "I'm not. I just figured we'd have a snack and go at it again once my boys have had a chance to recharge." I gesture toward my dick, still wrapped in a condom that needs taking care of, but I'm too damn tired to get up right now after what we just did.

She picks up her bridesmaid dress and pulls it over her head. "Sorry. I have to run." She sweeps her hands down the front of the garment I tore over her head just minutes ago.

"Where are you going?"

She avoids eye contact as she pulls her shoes back on. "I have plans, okay?"

"What sort of plans?" I ask, narrowing my eyes at her. It's not my business, but she's dodging me and now I want to know.

"Look, it's not that I wouldn't do it again with you, honestly it was good for me, but I promised Reese I'd swing by their place tonight and listen to her talk about the baby. She said they're leaving tomorrow afternoon so we won't get a chance to catch up if I don't go tonight."

"You came here and had sex with me first knowing you're going to see your friend who I used to date?" I try to push the nugget of information that they're leaving tomorrow afternoon aside. I sort of want to go with her because it seems like the right time to get Mark alone while his wife's occupied, but going with her would be extending our night together when she's making it so easy for me by walking out. I'll pick my moment for a conversation with Mark tomorrow after our family brunch.

She glances in the mirror and fluffs her hair, no worse for the wear. "Figured she'd want to know for sure that you're over her."

"And what we just did proves that?"

She lifts a shoulder and shoots me a sly smile. "Well you certainly weren't *under* her, if you know what I mean."

I shake my head with a laugh.

"Bye bye, Foxy Fox," she says, and then she disappears out my hotel room door.

I don't trust easily, so I can't help but wonder if this is her thing—jetting out after sex and pretending like she doesn't care. It's not like she'd be the first woman to ever try reverse psychology on me, but I'm not buying it. If my phone rings in three days, I'll know I was right.

Either way, though, it won't matter. It's not going to change the fact that I'm not in a place where I'm interested in commitment.

three

The next morning, I'm at Mark's Vegas penthouse enjoying French toast and scrambled eggs when my phone vibrates in my pocket. I'm waiting on a new client acquisition, praying the paperwork will be signed before the end of the month but figuring it won't be.

Part of me wonders if it's Tess. After she jetted out last night, she's sort of on my mind. Maybe the reverse psychology thing worked, or maybe it's because I'm here at Mark's penthouse with his wife sitting across the table from me. I wonder if Tess told them we banged last night.

I can't help it. I pull my phone out to sneak a peek even though I'm sure my mother will scold me, and sure enough, it's the news I didn't want.

I slide my phone back in my pocket and glance at my mom. She has one eyebrow raised at me.

"Sorry," I mutter.

She just purses her lips with no words, a clear sign of disapproval, and she reduces me to a child instead of a thirty-two-year-old man.

"So, Brian, you have plans to see Tess again?" Mark asks.

The forkful of eggs I'm holding stops halfway between my plate and my lips. I force it to finish its journey as I try to come up with a witty response. His words blindside me, but I'm not surprised she told them.

"Nope," I say between the egg in my mouth. Better in my mouth than on my face, I guess.

"Sounds like she had fun with you," Reese teases.

I'm sort of surprised she's teasing me. I didn't think we'd ever progress in our in-law relationship to be able to do that, but I guess we have.

"We had a nice time." I press my lips together. "But that was it."

"Tess, the bridesmaid?" my mom asks, and Reese nods eagerly. Too eagerly. "She's very pretty," my mom adds, like it's the only worthy attribute of a woman.

"She's gorgeous, but there's nothing there," I say firmly in an attempt to get everyone off my back. "And I'd prefer if we stopped talking about this since I don't really want Jason finding out."

"Seemed like something was there by the way Tess was glowing when she came over last night," Mark says, totally ignoring my request.

"Glowing?" my mom asks, and my brother laughs.

I shake my head. We may be adults, but that doesn't mean I want to discuss my sex life in front of my mother. She's forever badgering me to settle down, just like she did to Mark before he and Reese got married. I thought when he knocked his wife up my mom would be happy and lay off me a while, but clearly I was mistaken.

"When are you two heading back to Los Angeles?" I ask, abruptly changing the subject.

"I have a private event tonight, so we're driving back this afternoon," Mark says.

"I need to talk to you before you go," I say, and I catch my parents exchanging a secret smile. "What?" I ask.

My mom lifts a shoulder and looks away like she doesn't want to ruin the secret, and my dad has a hint of pride in his eyes. I don't know what the fuck that's about, but I'm not about to ask them. Maybe Mark knows.

Once breakfast is finished and the plates are clean, Mark invites me into his office so we can have some privacy. "Is this about their anniversary thing?"

My brows furrow.

"Clearly not," he says with a laugh.

"What anniversary thing?" I ask.

"Their fortieth is this summer. Lizzie's planning something. Didn't she tell you?"

"I got a few texts from her that I ignored." I pull out my phone to check the texts from our sister, and sure enough, she asked me a month ago which weekends in July and August work best for me. I never replied.

"You're such a dick."

I read through Lizzie's messages. "She's fine and I'll be there."

"So what did you want to talk about?" he asks.

I draw in a deep breath to calm the nerves buzzing through my stomach. I hate asking anybody for anything, but I especially hate asking my brother. He has everything, and it's just further proof that I don't. "I need a small loan."

He steeples his pointer fingers in front of his mouth and folds the rest of them as he leans his elbows on his desk. He eyes me for a beat, and then he says around his fingers, "Why?"

"Why?" I repeat as my brows furrow in confusion. I don't understand what he doesn't get. There's only one reason people ask others for money…and it's because they need money. "I need money. Isn't that sort of the obvious answer?"

"Why do you need money? What happened to the money I gave you a couple months ago?"

I look away from his prying eyes. I'd hoped he wouldn't bring it up, but I should've known better. "I spent it." I refrain from mentioning I've also sunk my entire life savings back into the company. We're thriving, or at least we're on track to be thriving, but because of our quick growth, I'm spending money we don't have on employees we didn't anticipate we'd need.

"How much?"

"Fifty."

His brows go up. "Thousand?"

I nod.

"What the fuck for?"

I heave out a breath. "We're out of liquid until the end of the month because of some unexpected costs."

"What kind of unexpected costs?" He throws air quotes around the last two words.

I can't admit we've been entertaining clients Vegas-style, so instead I say, "A big client I'd been working on for months fell through. One we were depending on. I know better than to raise budgets until the ink is dry, but this was such a sure thing that I broke my own rule."

"Business one-oh-one, dude," Mark says, shaking his head.

Sometimes I really fucking hate him, but he's my only option. I don't deserve his scolding, and fifty grand to him is like ten bucks to everyone else. I wish he'd just hand it over without the side of grilling. "Look, I know I fucked up, okay? But I just need a loan to get me through to the end of the month to cover payroll. I signed three new clients this week, but our analytics team has to put in the work before we get the check from the new clients. It'll balance out eventually."

"Fucking better," he says, opening his laptop and pulling on a pair of reading glasses. "I'll get it transferred today. Should clear by the end of the day." He's a signer on the FDB Tech Corp account and has an account at the same bank, which helps move things along significantly.

He stares me down another minute. "There's two conditions on this cash, though."

I raise my brows and hold both palms up as if to say, *have at it*.

"First, I want you to know I'm investing in *you*, Brian. The real you. I know you can do better, so I'm handing money for you to put into FDB for the last time. It's not a loan. It's yours."

I nod. "Fine," I say flippantly. It's not the first time he's given me this particular speech. He'll forget and hand over the dollars the next time I ask for them, but what I told him is true. I won't need another loan. "What's your second condition?"

"I get fifty-one percent controlling interest."

I shake my head and stand up. "Fuck you, Mark. I'll figure something else out." I turn to leave, but his voice stops me.

He lifts a shoulder. "The money's yours. I'll even add ten grand more on top just to keep you ahead."

He's got me backed into a corner and he knows it. Bank loans take longer than I have. I slide back into the chair. "Why do you want controlling interest?"

"Investments." He says it so simply, yet I know there's more. "I believe in your company, Brian. I just don't think you're handling the finances in the most cost-efficient way. I want to oversee what's going on. I don't want you to ask me for more money. I want this business to thrive like I know it can."

"You've already got more control than I do and I'm the goddamn president." When my friends and I moved to Vegas to start a business, my brother came on as a silent investor. We wrote him in at forty percent, and the rest of us each got twenty.

"Co-president," he corrects. "I've only got forty percent. Round up enough to get me to fifty-one, talk it over with Jason and Becker, and then I'll push the money through today."

I glance down at the floor. "They don't know."

"You haven't explained to your business partners that you're fucking up the money end of it?"

I shake my head guiltily, and my brother heaves out a sigh as he narrows his eyes at me.

"Then give me eleven percent of your control," he says.

"That'll only leave me with nine." I know my voice is whiney, but my big brother is being a total douchebag.

He shrugs. "Should've thought that through before you started spending money you don't have."

He's right, but I can't admit that. "You're an asshole."

"This is business. If you can't handle business with family, you shouldn't have come asking for money."

I sigh. "Fine. Draw up a contract and I'll sign it before you go. I need the money yesterday, but not a word of this to Jason or Becker." With Beck getting married and Jason involved in some new projects, it's shit they don't need to worry about. It'll be over before they know anything happened anyway.

He taps his keyboard, hits print, and hands me a sheet of paper. I read it over and sign away eleven of the twenty percent of the company I own, shove it back at him, and stalk out of the room.

"Nice doing business with you," he says just before I slam the door shut behind me.

four

I gaze out my window at the view from my bed.

I guess if I'm honest with myself, I wouldn't be living here if it weren't for my brother. He's always been generous with his money, and I try to remind myself that's exactly what it is—*his* money. That's all well and fine, but he just took something that was *mine* from me, so I don't really feel all that guilty spending his money the way I always have.

Which reminds me...I grab my phone and check my calendar. I have a business dinner tonight with a local client, and this one always likes to have a good time. And by good time, I mean strip clubs with bottle service.

Thank God that money from Mark came through, and while we're being thankful for things, thank God for credit cards.

I resume my gaze out the window for a little longer. My eyes follow the peaks and valleys of the mountains, and I realize what a lucky bastard I am.

Once I get out of bed, I'll get ready to go to a job I love at a company I own headquartered a block off the Las Vegas Strip. As a kid growing up in Chicago, I always dreamed big...but I'm not sure I ever dreamed *this* big.

I finally force myself out of the comfort of the ridiculously high thread count sheets and pad naked toward my lavish shower that I had redone when I bought this place.

I looked at houses with my brother's girl back when I was "dating" her, but I didn't want to buy a place I could "grow into," as I insinuated to make her think I was ready to start a family.

I don't want to grow into anything, and it was with that thought in mind that I hired the hottest designer in Vegas to decorate this place to make it a true bachelor pad. Man cave? Fuck that noise. This is more like a man castle.

Everything is dark wood, navy blue, and added extravagance. It's more than one guy needs, but instead of rooms I could grow into, I themed them to fit my needs. Instead of separate bedrooms fit for future children, I knocked down a few walls and created a huge home office. Instead of a "family room," I have what I call my "football room." It's filled with sports memorabilia, a projector television for game day, a wet bar, and, most importantly, leather recliners and a super comfortable couch for my buddies and me to watch the game on.

I bought this place nearly three years ago, spent a few months renovating it, and have lived in it ever since, and never once have I regretted what I did to it. Never once have I looked around and thought something or *someone* was missing from it.

But I do have one hell of a good time here, and when I bring ladies back? Forget it. It somehow makes me even more attractive to them paired with my don't-give-a-fuck attitude.

Life's pretty damn good, barring the shit my brother just put me through and a few financial issues, but I'll land on my feet. I always do.

* * *

When I get to the office, it's business as usual. Becker is out of town for his honeymoon for the next four weeks. Jason sits in his office and waves as I pass by on my way to my own office. I greet my secretary, Lauren, and I think again how she just isn't as hot as my old secretary, Kelsey, and that's probably a good thing.

Kelsey and I got wrapped up in some crazy shenanigans, and ultimately it's probably my fault she quit. And when I say *probably*, I'm definitely positive of it. I didn't treat her very well, but on the other hand, she allowed it. She quit when she thought we were monogamous—something I never agreed to—and she caught me with another woman in my office. She called it cheating, but I wouldn't label it that way. Both parties need to agree to being the other's *only* significant other before it can be considered cheating, and I never agreed to it because I didn't want that with her. I haven't wanted that in a long time.

The last time I wanted it, I got burned. If there's anything my logic has taught me, it's that once you get burned, it's fucking dumb to stick your hand back in the fire.

It's a Monday morning and my brother owns the majority of this company now. I had a strange feeling something was going to be different when I walked in, and I'm relieved to see everything is the same as it's always been.

I settle into my office. The first phone call of my morning is to the vice president of one of our new clients. Ellen Howard is a cougar if I've ever met one. I met her last year at a Vegas networking event, and if I hadn't taken Kelsey as my date, I might've allowed her to work her cougar magic on me.

"I need some facetime, Mr. Fox," she says once our greetings are out of the way. "I need you to explain the newest analytics to me. I don't understand what I'm looking at with all these charts and graphs and I further have no idea what I'm supposed to do with this information."

"Let's set up a Skype meeting," I say, and she laughs.

"That's not what I meant. I mean real face-to-face interaction. You kids are always doing things over technology, but I'm old school. Take me to lunch and tell me my numbers look pretty."

"Your numbers are gorgeous, Ms. Howard, and I'd be happy to take you to lunch." I glance at my calendar. I have a meeting at one, but it's in-house with the analytics team, and I can have Lauren reschedule. "I can squeeze you in today around noon if you're free."

"I'd love to be squeezed in today at noon."

Her tone doesn't betray whether she's coming onto me or if she's simply repeating my own words, so I don't dare laugh even though it's my instinct. "Great. I can send a car for you a little before. Does that work?"

"Will you be in it?"

"I'll meet you at the restaurant. Is the one in the lobby of my building okay with you?"

"Fine, Mr. Fox. I look forward to it."

"As do I," I say, but honestly, I'm already sort of regretting agreeing to a short-notice lunch with a client whose paws I may be battling away for the duration of our lunch.

I'm late after a busy morning, but I walk into the restaurant at twelve-fifteen and find Ellen at a table with a half-drunk martini perched in her hand. One long leg is crossed over the other, and she sort of looks like an older version of a classic pin-up model dressed in a pantsuit.

"Never keep your client waiting, Mr. Fox," she says.

I run a hand along my jaw and hand her a folder. "My apologies. I won't make excuses."

"Thank you for that, at least."

A waiter comes by for my drink order. "The usual?" he asks. I come here often, obviously.

I nod my head indicating I'd love a whiskey. I feel like I'm going to need it to get through this lunch.

FDB is a predictive analytics company whose goal is to extract data and predict trends and outcomes. I show Ellen her company's latest charts and explain how the data on them can help inform her company's decisions.

"Look right here, for example," I say. "This chart shows how many clicks the links on this particular webpage received on each day of the week. You can see traffic was heavier on a Tuesday, so..." I pause as I pull another sheet out. "When we look at this graphic, you can see the direct link between when your promotional email went out and when your website got hits." I pull another sheet out. "And this graph shows your split testing for subject lines. Clearly this one—" I trail off as I feel her hand on my arm.

"Mr. Fox, this is wonderful information. Thank you."

I'm not sure what to do. She asked me to explain her data...yet she's interrupting me and making me feel like I should stop talking.

"Do you have any questions?" I finally ask.

She hasn't moved her hand.

"I do have one."

I glance up at her and arch an eyebrow, and she's gazing at me with smoldering eyes. "Is there anywhere private around here?"

I can't help my nervous chuckle. "You'd like to discuss your numbers more privately?" I ask.

She nods.

"We can go up to my office after lunch," I say. "But I do have a one o'clock meeting..."

"Then let's just forget lunch," she says, and I feel a foot traveling the length of my calf beneath the table. She doesn't stop until she finds the goods, and I shift uncomfortably.

"Oh, Ms. Howard, I don't think that would be a good idea." I'm not quite sure why I'm telling her no. I usually don't say no, in fact, but she's just so...

Old. She's old. She was probably gorgeous back in her day, but she's clearly got at least thirty, maybe forty years on me, and she reminds me way too much of my mother with her professional clothes and no-nonsense attitude.

I can't.

I don't even want to be sitting at this table with her now that I figured out why I can't, but I need to follow through with my lunch.

"Why not, Mr. Fox?" she asks, her voice suddenly sultry when it really wasn't before.

Because you remind me of my mother. I can't say that, obviously, so I lie. "I'm seeing someone."

"Oh, that's a real shame. We could've had a lot of fun." She doesn't remove her foot from my crotch despite my lie.

"I wouldn't doubt it, Ms. Howard." I shift again, and she finally moves.

Thankfully the waiter appears with some bread, so I focus on the bread rather than on eye contact with her. "Would you like me to continue discussing your reports?"

She shifts in her chair, too, and crosses her legs. "Sure," she says, and we resume the business portion of our business lunch.

When the bill comes, I grab it first and put it on the black card Mark gave me without even looking at the total. It's a business lunch and a write-off, but it's more than that. It's me being a gentleman, not making the woman pay for the meal even though she's the one who wanted to meet for lunch.

The waiter picks up the check with my card, and he returns a minute later. He looks nervous as he hands me the booklet.

I open it.

Denied.

"What the fuck?" I mutter.

"Sir, do you have another method of payment?" the waiter asks.

Right in front of Ellen.

"Can you run it again?" I ask.

"I ran it twice, sir. Same result both times."

I pull another card out of my wallet as I silently fume at the waiter. I make a mental note to let Mark know his card was denied. "I'm sorry about this," I say to Ellen. "It's really strange."

She simply raises an eyebrow just like my mother might, and I'm certain I made the right decision in telling her no.

The waiter comes back, and when I check the total, I wish I hadn't offered to pay for lunch, and especially not on my personal credit card.

It's over a hundred bucks for two people, and my mental note to let Mark know his card was denied has shifted from *letting him know* to getting ready for a fight.

* * *

I storm past Lauren and slam my office door shut when I return from lunch. I dial my brother, and as soon as he answers, I start in on him. "My card was denied at a client lunch. Do you have any idea how embarrassing that was?"

Mark sighs. "I told you yesterday, Brian. I'm not sinking more money into FDB. You need to get your shit together and you need to do that on your own dime."

"So you're cutting off my card?" I spit. I feel the heat of anger crawling up my neck.

"I put a temporary hold on spending until I get a chance to review where the hell the rest of my money has gone."

I draw in what's meant to be a calming breath because I realize he's in the power position here, but it doesn't actually calm me at all. "I have a client dinner tonight and he's expecting the same treatment he's always gotten."

"What treatment is that?" he asks, more than a hint of exasperation in his tone.

"VIP. I take him out, we talk and shake hands over a fine whiskey, that sort of thing," I say. Just for good measure, I add, "Don't act like you've never done that with your Ashmark clients."

"Ashmark is a recording label, not an analytics corporation. Rock stars get the rock star treatment, and I don't need to defend my business decisions to you." He says it in a way that clearly implies *I* do need to defend *my* business decisions to *him*.

"What the hell am I supposed to do tonight, then?" I ask.

"You're a smart guy. You'll figure it out. I have to go." He ends the call and I throw my phone down on my desk in anger. I pound a fist beside it for good measure.

Looks like my credit card will be getting another workout tonight. I double check all my balances and figure out which one has the best chance of getting approved, and then I work my ass off on acquiring some new clients to bring in more money to get me the hell out of this mess.

five

Andy and I are sitting at our usual table as a woman wearing a little less than a bikini delivers our bottle of Macallan. Her tits spill out of the thin material, and I think back to the last time I was here with him. My secretary at the time, Kelsey, came along, and after we finished entertaining Andy, we ended up in one of the private rooms in back. We watched a dancer work the pole in front of us while Kelsey stuck her hand down my pants, and then I fucked her right there in front of the stripper.

Looking back, I don't suppose it was my finest moment. It makes me sound like a total douchebag, actually, but it's hard not to look like a douche when you're entertaining clients at a strip club.

We watch the action for a bit, discuss some business, and even dig into some appetizers—bar food I wouldn't necessarily pair with the whiskey, but it's our only option. Besides, everything tastes better with a little Macallan on my tongue.

I savor the taste. It may be a while before I get to enjoy it again if I need to start watching my pennies a little more closely.

In fact, I decide to treat tonight like it's my last night out for the rest of my life. We split the bottle, we tuck twenties into G-strings, and we act like our pockets are deep even if they aren't anymore. Mark's right: I'm a smart guy. I'll figure it out.

* * *

I sit next to a brunette at the bar the following Monday. She's wearing the shit out of a dress and she's exactly my type. "I'm Brian."

Admittedly it's not my best pick-up line, but I've had just enough whiskey this afternoon that I don't care. I shrug, and she sticks a delicate hand out to shake mine. "Shandi."

"Shandi?" I ask.

"It's a family name."

"It's beautiful, and so are you."

"Now that was cheesy." She nods to the bartender to refill her glass of white wine.

White wine? Perfect. White wine drinkers are the perfect love 'em and leave 'em bait. If she'd have had a glass of red in front of her, forget it. They're only looking for relationships. They're serious. Studious. That's not what I want right now. I pull out my personal credit card when Wes hands me the bill.

She shakes her head. "That's not necessary."

"I know." I raise a brow and give her the smile that always works on women.

I chat up Shandi, who I discover is in public relations—another check in the *yes* column since I'm always looking to mix business with pleasure. That's how the saying goes, right?

By the time her glass is empty, I know her well enough to feel comfortable inviting her back to the FDB offices. "I've got a proposal for you," I say, pretending I have business in mind when my mind's not on business at all.

"Oh?" she asks, long lashes fluttering as her pupils dilate.

"We're looking for a new PR firm to handle one of our biggest clients. You interested in hearing more?"

She nods. Of course she is. "I can't come now, though. I'm meeting someone."

it started with a lie

"Is that why you're here day drinking?" I ask. I glance at my Rolex. "What time's your meeting?"

"Noon."

I glace at my watch. It's twelve-fifteen. "Business or pleasure?"

"Pleasure. A blind lunch date." She lets out a heavy sigh, and I've got her exactly where I want her. She was just stood up by some dick and here I am to save her and offer her the nice afternoon she was expecting. Plus a little more. "Where's your office?" she asks.

"We're the twelfth floor." I motion with my head upwards since we're currently on the first floor of the building. We even pay to have our name on the outside of the building, so most people in the building have heard of us.

"You're from FDB?"

I nod. "I'm the F. Brian Fox."

"So who are the D and the B?"

"My two best friends, Jason Davis and Ryan Becker."

She laughs. "Shouldn't you be working up on twelve instead of chatting me up?"

Yes, I should. Definitely. But I'm in a strange place right now as I recover from handing my company over to my brother. It's been a week, but it still doesn't sit right with me. He already owned more of it than I did, but now he has total control, and I don't like it. On top of that, it's a Monday. Payroll is cleared and I've got a little extra of Mark's money lining my pockets. Numbing felt like the right answer, so here we are. I can't say any of that to Shandi, obviously, so I go with something simpler. "I am. You're in PR, I'm looking for PR. Sounds like work to me."

She narrows her eyes at me.

"Let's grab lunch and bring it up," I suggest.

"I shouldn't..." she says, and then she takes a minute to think about it. Her eyes drift over my shoulder. "And that's him. I'm sorry. Another time, maybe?"

I nod and order my lunch after she slides off the stool to meet her late date. I'm sitting alone, checking my email for a new contract from a client I've been waiting on, when I feel a hand on my shoulder. I glance up as someone slides into the empty stool beside me.

"Tess," I say, surprised. "What are you doing here?"

"I was in the neighborhood and thought I'd surprise you with a visit."

I glance around. "Me? What if Jason sees us?"

She shakes her head. "He won't. I did some investigating and discovered he's out with a client until late afternoon."

"You *did some investigating?*"

She nods and grins. "Don't worry about it, okay? I just wanted to see you again."

This seems clingy. It seems like the exact opposite of what we agreed to over the weekend. But my decision-making skills are less than stellar at the moment.

"Have you eaten lunch?"

She shakes her head.

"Come on up to my office," I say. At least it's not a public restaurant where anyone can spot us and report us back to my best friend and business partner.

I get Wes's attention and tell him to send my food up along with something for Tess, and he nods.

We walk through the doors to FDB, and I glance around the space we created. We settled on a modern, clean look in gray, black, and white a few years ago when we launched. I lead Tess back to my private corner office overlooking part of the famed Las Vegas Strip, one of the many reasons we chose Vegas as the epicenter of our business. I'd spent plenty of time

playing out here when I lived in Chicago, so it felt right to move here.

I step behind my desk for a minute to check my email, but it's also a power move. I'm in my element back here, and I want her to see that. I feel her eyes on me.

"Take a seat," I say, nodding toward a small round table set up in the corner of my office meant specifically for entertaining clients. I sit down for a minute to respond to a couple emails needing my attention. My movements are a little slow from the whiskey, so everything's taking a little longer than it should. I glance up when the burn of her eyes on me becomes overwhelming. She stands just on the other side of my desk from me, leaning forward and giving me a great shot down the front of her dress. Her eyes are filled with lust.

"Can we talk about why I'm here?" she asks.

"Why are you here?" I ask, purposely acting like I don't know what she's talking about.

"Why don't you bend me over your desk and find out?"

Oh my.

My phone rings and my eyes flick down to where it rests on my desk. It's my brother, and he can wait. Tess, however, doesn't want to, and so she won't.

six

"Mmm, I'm coming, I'm coming," Tess moans. I hammer away at her while she comes, ready for my own release. I don't even feel a little bit close to the finish line, but then her body starts to pulse under me, proving her words true, so I reach around her dress to grip both her breasts over the material since she didn't bother to take it off.

Big tits fill my palms, and I hammer into her as I get closer to the end.

"Oh my God! I'm so sorry!"

A voice interrupts me just when I'm getting to the good part.

I glance up to see a flurry of dark locks set atop what looks like a killer body followed by the slam of my office door.

I can't help it. The exhibitionist in me lets go. Knowing someone just on the other side of the door knows what's happening in here is exactly what I need. I start to come, grunting like an animal as I unload into Tess. She lurches back against my hips as I come, and as soon as it's over, I pull out.

I excuse myself to the restroom connected to my office to clean up, and she uses it next. I draw in a deep breath as I compose myself, ready to scold whoever the fuck it was who interrupted us.

I open the door, and a gorgeous woman stands just on the other side with her arms crossed over her chest and a look of disgust on her face. She'd be much more attractive if it didn't look like she was sucking on a lemon as she glares at me.

Despite the fact that I just had sex with another woman who is still cleaning up in my private office bathroom, I can't help my immediate attraction to this woman. She's different from my usual type—maybe because she looks professional, like she's here to work, not like she came up to my office for a fuck.

On first glance, she's serious and purposeful, which is basically the opposite of the looks-like-a-good-time girl in my office.

I walk past her to Lauren, my secretary. "Did my food arrive?"

She nods and hands me a bag with a smile.

"Thank you." I walk back toward my office and give the glaring woman still standing there my most charming smile as I pretend like she didn't just walk in on me fucking Tess in my office. "Can I help you?"

She clears her throat. "I need to talk to you."

"And you thought just barging into my office uninvited was the way to do that?"

"I didn't just *barge in*." Her eyes narrow at me. "Someone said 'come in' after I knocked."

My brows furrow. "I didn't hear a knock." I think about what was going on when she opened my door. Tess may have been moaning about coming. I guess *I'm coming, I'm coming* sounds the same as *come in* when it's muffled through a door. "It doesn't matter. My secretary handles my appointments." I nod over toward Lauren. "You can make an appointment with her." I turn to walk back into my office, but she interrupts me.

"That's not necessary."

I set the bag of food on the small conference table, and the woman looks at the table and nods once.

"This'll do," she says, and she sets her purse down on the table next to the bag of food.

"Who the fuck are you?" I ask.

"Vivian Davenport." She folds her arms and looks me dead in the eye when she speaks her next words. "Your new boss."

I laugh at the absolute absurdity of her statement. "My new *what?*"

"You heard me."

I glance at the bathroom door where Tess is still putting herself back together. I can't have her overhearing this conversation, and I need to get to the bottom of what this lady is doing here.

"Is this some kind of prank?" I ask, my brows furrowed. She shakes her head.

The bathroom door opens and Tess smooths her dress back into place. "Your tacos are in the bag," I say to her, nodding toward the food on the table.

I stalk out of my office and over to Becker's so Tess doesn't overhear and gossip about whatever this delusional woman has to say to me. She follows me.

"I've been hired as a consultant," she says once the door shuts behind us, "and as much as I'm sure you won't like it, you'll be answering to me now. I've been instructed to set up shop in your office so we can work closely together." She nods back toward my office. "I assume you're not using business funds to entertain your guest?"

"I don't have to explain myself to you," I say coolly. I refuse to get defensive until I understand what's happening, but again, the whiskey is slowing my response time. "Now if you'll get the fuck out of here, my lunch is getting cold." It's probably already cold since Tess and I chose sex over food, but I fail to mention that to this woman.

"Actually, Mr. Fox, you do have to explain yourself to me."

I scoff. "I'm the boss here and I answer to my partners. No one else."

"Well, one of your *partners* hired me to oversee what's going on. Didn't Mark touch base with you?"

My mind flashes back to the call I ignored from my brother approximately twenty minutes ago.

God, I really fucking hate my brother. And so far, this woman isn't exactly on my *like* list. I heave out a sigh. "Mark hired you?" I close my eyes and rub my forehead with my fingertips. Anger is boiling my blood and I feel depleted after my romp over my desk. I really need some food to recharge. A nap wouldn't hurt, either, but I don't have time for shit like naps.

She nods. "I'm under contract with your brother."

I walk over and open Becker's door. I go to my office as *my new boss* trails behind me. "Tess, I have some work to do. You can see yourself out when you're done eating." I pick up the bag of food and glare at the vile woman who follows me around like a puppy dog. I nod toward some chairs just outside my office door. "You stay here. I have a call to make." I take my bag of food with me back to Becker's office, drawing in gulps of air as I try to process what the fuck is going on.

seven

"You thought twenty minutes was sufficient?" I take a huge bite out of my burger. The food's already helping my mood, but I have a feeling this conversation isn't going to make anything better.

My brother sighs. "You're fairly predictable, Brian. What would you have done if I'd have given you more lead time?"

"I'd have figured out a way to stop you." I talk around the burger in my mouth as I try to think of a way to stop it even after the fact.

"Exactly. I don't want this stopped. I own the majority of FDB now, something you handed over to me when you wanted my money. I'm just making sure it's being allocated correctly. Call it protecting my investments."

I hear some noise in the background.

"I have to go," Mark says. "I need you to hand over whatever she asks for. Consider me your new CEO and consider her my proxy for the next ninety days."

"Ninety days?" I practically yell. I'm stuck with this woman for ninety days?

"Three months."

"I'm not giving her private company information." My voice borders on whiney, and I hate that my first response is an emotional one. I'd like to deal with my brother in a level-headed way since clearly he's lost his goddamn mind.

"Yes, you are. That's why I hired her. Deal with it."

The fucking asshole hangs up on me. I shake my head as I toss my phone angrily on Becker's desk.

I don't know what the hell to do here. I don't want Jason and Becker to know I've blown through our profits, and I really don't want anyone to know the money I took from my brother is going straight to payroll to ensure everyone gets paid this month. It'll all balance out soon—that part isn't a lie. I really do have clients lined up, but I spent a ton of money acquiring them, and now we're hovering along the red. Mark's check was just a boost to get us back in black, but now I've got this bitch up my ass.

I blow out a breath and finish my burger. I guess it's time to face the music.

I head back to my office. Tess is gone, but the brunette sits at my conference table tapping on her laptop. I study her for a split second. Her long, dark hair cascades around her shoulders, and I wonder if it's as soft as it looks. She's focused on her screen as her fingers tap away at the keys. Slender neck, petite frame, and fuckable for sure, but she looks a little too straight-laced for me with her high-necked black blouse and her perfect posture.

She catches me staring when she glances up, and I act like I didn't pause in the doorway to check her out as I stalk into my office. I slam my door behind me, and she focuses accusatory blue eyes on me.

"I'll need your financial records dating back two years," she says. "I may need more than that, but we'll start there."

"Fuck off." I slide into the chair behind my desk so I'm back in my power position.

"Mark mentioned you might be averse to this setup." She stands and sets her hands on her hips as she squares off across my desk from me. She softens for a beat. "Look, I'm sorry I walked in on you with that woman. It was embarrassing for both of us."

"It wasn't embarrassing for me," I say, cockiness smeared in my tone.

She rests a hand on her chest in what looks like an attempt to appear genuine. She must be trying a different tack than mega-bitch, but this one isn't working for me, either. "It was for me, and I apologize. I know this isn't ideal, but I'm just here to ensure your company is thriving. You have the tools to do that yourself, but Mark is paying me handsomely to help you."

"Ah," I say, pursing my lips. "Of course he is."

She sits in one of the chairs opposite me in front of my desk. "We could do this the hard way or the easy way. Your call, Mr. Fox."

I raise a brow. "Are you coming onto me?"

Her hand flies up to her throat in shock. "No! Absolutely not! I'm a professional!"

I wink at her. This might be fun after all. "I have everything under control, Ms..." I trail off because I forgot her name.

"Davenport. Vivian Davenport."

"Right. Viv." I grin.

"My name is Vivian," she says through gritted teeth, and the fact that she corrects me tells me I need to use the nickname more often. "And if you really had everything under control, you wouldn't have hit your brother up for a loan."

I hiss through my teeth. "Look, Viv. I'll play semi-nice, but here's the thing. My partners can't know why you're really here. They can't know you're working on finances."

"You're going to lie to them?"

I shake my head. "Nah, just keeping this little detail from them. Beck's the creative visionary, Jason's the IT guy, and I'm the business brain." I feel like shit when I say the next part, but

I have a feeling my transparency will go a long way with this one. "I don't want them to think I'm having trouble holding up my end of the deal."

"They're your partners, Brian," she says softly, and she looks almost human for a beat.

"What, no more *Mr. Fox*?" I retort as I dodge the real meaning behind her words.

She lets out a frustrated breath but doesn't respond.

"Fine," she finally says after studying me for a few beats longer than necessary. "We'll figure out what to tell them later."

A knock at my door interrupts us, and before even asking who it is, I yell, "Come in!" Before the door opens and under my breath so only Viv can hear, I say, "That's how you're invited into a room."

I feel her glare on me as Jason opens the door and looks between Viv and me.

"Hey, man. This is Viv. We just started seeing each other." It's not a lie, exactly, but I'm definitely leading him into believing something other than the truth. I catch her quick gasp, and I wonder if she'll play along or throw me under the bus. I think about how grave this situation is, this shit about my brother hiring some woman to come in and tell me how to do my fucking job, and before I can stop more lies, I mutter, "It's pretty serious already."

I don't have time to consider the consequences of this declaration, but it's the first thing I could think of to explain why she's here.

"Well fuck me," Jason says. "I never thought I'd see the day a woman got this one to commit."

I glance over at Viv, scared at what her reaction might be. She smiles at Jason as he walks over to her to shake her hand.

"Nice to meet you, Viv. I'm Jason."

"It's nice to meet you as well." She smiles at him and doesn't correct him for using Viv instead of Vivian. Why's she being nice to *him* when she's such a royal bitch to *me*?

Jason shoots me a secret *nice work* look, and I put on my best show to act like I'm happy to be in a relationship with this chick. "Why didn't you bring her to the wedding?" he asks.

I push the twinge of guilt that I slept with Jason's ex to the back of my mind. "She was out of town. Just got back in last night." The lies roll off my tongue easily, just as they have my entire life.

"Hey, are you going to that gala Friday night?" Jason asks.

"Shit. I forgot about it." I shake my head. "I wasn't planning on it."

"A late client meeting came up and I can't go," he says. "They gave us two spots and there should be some great networking opportunities. Are you free?"

I glance at my calendar. "I can make it work."

"I'm sure your new girlfriend would love the spare ticket," he says.

"I was planning to spend time with you anyway, so a gala sounds like fun," she says with the most saccharinely sweet tone she can muster.

I look in horror at her and wonder what the fuck I've done with my little lie.

eight

When I walk into my office on Tuesday morning, a small transformation has taken place in the corner where my little circular table for entertaining clients used to sit. Now an elaborate desk is set up in that same corner facing mine, and a brunette woman is studying spreadsheets on her laptop when I walk in. I feel her eyes shift over to me.

I don't show her how affected I am by the fact that I went from having my own huge corner office to sharing it with a stranger overnight. I don't even bid her a good morning as I stalk over to my desk and get started on today's tasks, the first of which includes a Skype conference call with Jason's team of IT developers and one of our clients.

"Good morning," she says, attempting civility, but I ignore her as I set up the call.

"Mr. Everly," I say in a loud and exuberant greeting to the client once we're connected. "How's the wife?" I always start conference calls with something personal.

"She's great," he says. "Due any day with number four."

I whistle through my teeth and hide the horror I feel so it doesn't show on my face, and then our IT team shows up to the call. We get to business.

"Jason sent me the latest results on the attempted breach of security, and I have to say, I'm really impressed," Mr. Everly says. We've been developing cybersecurity with him that hackers can't breach for a few years now.

"I've been in touch with him regarding your numbers, and my team has been looking at the analytics." I pick up a sheet of paper on my desk just as Viv clears her throat. I glance up at her thinking she's trying to get my attention, but she's focused on her task. She taps some keys, and I lose my train of thought.

"And?" Everly asks.

"Um," I say, looking at the printout in front of me as I try to gain my footing back. "And everything looks to be on track," I say lamely. I had something to say, and now I completely forgot it because some goddamn stranger is in my office clearing her throat and tapping keys when I'm trying to concentrate.

I shake my head to clear it, and Viv opens a bottle of water and takes a sip. I glance over at her again, but she's focused on her screen. Full lips wrap around the bottle as she drinks her water, and then she sets the bottle down. She replaces the cap, and her tongue catches a stray drop of water on the side of her mouth. My traitorous dick immediately responds to the little glimpse of her tongue.

"Mr. Fox?" Everly's calling me and I'm in outer fucking space staring at this woman's mouth.

Sales pitch. I need to close this sale. I need to make this company some money. "We were able to detect and prevent every attempt at violation, and our developers have already protected several other companies during trials. We're ready for you, Mr. Everly."

He nods. "I'm ready, too. Let's meet next week to sign the papers."

Thank God. I don't say that aloud, but God, did I need this win.

We make arrangements, and as soon as I end the call, I start in on Viv. "This isn't going to work for me."

She looks up at me with brows drawn tightly together. "What isn't?"

I blow out a breath. "I need you to work somewhere else. I can't stop my brother, can't stop you, can't make this go away, but I don't have to share my office with you."

"Actually, that's not true," she says. "Mark created this setup, and I answer to him, not you."

"You're a horrible bitch," I mutter.

"Excuse me?" she asks, hand flying to her throat again in surprise. Well, baby, I'm full of 'em.

"You heard me." I stand and yank the cord from my laptop. I grab it off my desk, toss it angrily into my briefcase, and slam the lid shut. "Be that as it may, you can't force me to sit in here with you."

I stalk out of the office and toward our conference room, slam the door, and throw my briefcase on the desk. The conference room was the first empty room I could think of on short notice. Becker's office might work, too, but only for weeks he's out of town. Our space is crammed full because of all the employees we've hired over the past year. Growth has been phenomenal, in part because of ad spend.

I fish my phone out of my pocket and dial up the asshole who did this to me.

My brother doesn't answer, the little shit. I'm sure he's off being a rock star or whatever the hell he does. I leave an angry message and end with an ultimatum that it's her or me running this company, and then I set up a temporary office in the conference room.

It only works for a full twenty minutes.

Apparently the marketing team has their weekly roundtable on Tuesday mornings. "Mr. Fox, it's so nice of you to join us this morning," Marty, the head of marketing, says to me. He's clearly excited I'm here after he's invited me every week. I can't think of a good way out of it, so I'm stuck in a meeting I don't want to be in while another woman sits in *my* office running *my* business.

The meeting lasts three hours.

Three goddamn hours of my life I'll never see again.

They lose me about twenty minutes in. I act like I'm taking notes, but really I'm managing email and trying to figure a way out of this. I set up appointments and listen with half an ear as they discuss new strategies for reaching clients. Most of it involves money, so it's probably important for me to be here—or, better yet, Viv should be here.

Mark told me over the last year that I need to assemble a team for company finance because of our explosive growth, but I ignored him. I thought I could handle it.

But maybe he was right. Maybe we wouldn't be in the mess we're in if I'd have shared the plate with someone else.

I have a small team who I parcel responsibilities to: Lydia on payroll, Sam on accounts receivable, Emily on compliance, Derek on tax law. I don't have an in-house accountant because I don't want gossip in the office, so instead I pay a private accountant handsomely to keep track of our finances. He's the one who told me I overspent, but the information came a day late when I was more than a dollar short.

The interminable meeting finally ends, and when I return to my office to set my briefcase down before I head out to lunch, Viv stops me with her words.

"I need to start by going over last quarter with you," she says. "Some things aren't adding up."

I blow out a breath. This isn't good.

nine

After a lunch I eat by myself, I finally slink back into my office. She's tapping away again, but she stops once I settle in behind my desk. She looks over at me expectantly, like she's waiting for me to be friendly or issue her an apology.

She's not going to get one.

Jason appears in my doorway. He glances at Viv's setup in the corner, and he looks at me in confusion. "Does she work here now?" he asks, gesturing to her with his thumb.

I look up at her as my eyes widen. I didn't come up with a reason why her desk is in my office.

"I own a small business and he offered to let me set up shop here," she says smoothly. I wonder if it's always so easy for her to come up with a lie on the spot...and I still wonder why she agreed to lie for me when she was the one encouraging me to tell the truth. She pulls a face. "So many distractions at home."

"I hear you. I can't get anything done at home," Jason says. He looks back at me. "Not this guy, though, am I right? He's a workaholic."

She nods and gives him a look that screams *yep, sure is*, and then she gets back to work. He asks me a few questions about one of our accounts, and as soon as he's out the door, Viv looks back up at me.

"Your brother called," she says.

"When?" I ask.

She glances at the clock hanging on my wall. "About a half hour ago."

So he called her before he returned my call. Dick. "And what did my wonderful brother have to say?"

She appears to be choosing her words carefully. "He said to let you know if you were serious about the ultimatum you gave him, you won't like his answer."

I nod. He's choosing her over me, but this is *my* damn company. And it isn't just my company...it's my life. I spend more hours in this office than I do in my own home. I've closed more deals, come up with more ideas, and seen more success in the very chair where I sit right now than anywhere else in my life. I refuse to hand over what I have left to my brother, and the best way to prove that is to play nice.

But Brian Fox doesn't play nice.

He pretends to...but he doesn't.

"Fine." I force out a frustrated sigh as I pretend like I'm pushing my pride aside. I nod resolutely. "Fine," I say again. "Then let's figure out how to make this work."

A small smile plays on her lips, and I can't tell if it's victory or smugness. Does it matter? Either way, I want to wipe that smile right off her face. And I'll figure out a way to do it. I play to win, especially when my brother's got a horse in the race. "Great," she says, and then she launches into the data from last quarter that doesn't line up.

Of course it doesn't line up. When you live in fucking Vegas and your job includes entertaining clients, sometimes money gets tossed around haphazardly. My brother has never been tight with it before. It pisses me the fuck off he randomly decided to start now.

But I'll do what I have to in order to get back in his good graces, to get FDB back on track, and to get this bitch off my back.

* * *

I play nice the rest of the week, and I'm relieved when the clock strikes six o'clock on Friday. I've been listening to her crunch on dark chocolate almonds intermittently all day, distracting me from every task I'm trying to accomplish, and it's just putting me in a bad mood.

I want chocolate almonds, but I refuse to ask her for one. I want her out of my office and out of my life.

My mood turns from bad to worse when Lauren walks in and Viv offers *her* some chocolate almonds, which Lauren all too happily accepts.

I love my job and I'm one of those lucky bastards who leaps out of bed every morning because I'm excited to go do what I love.

This week, though, has been the week from hell. And it's just the first seven days out of ninety. The weekend is a welcome reprieve from the shit I've had to put up with from some woman.

It's a welcome reprieve, that is, until she asks me one simple question as I pack up my shit to head home for the weekend.

"What time should I be ready for the AceStar gala tonight?"

Fuckkkkkkkkk.

Just when I thought I was getting a break from this woman who is suddenly ruining my life, I have to take her to the event tonight all because I'm too much of a chicken shit to admit to my best friend that our company might be losing money.

I blow out a breath. "Fuck," I mutter. I check the reservation on my phone. "Cocktail hour is at seven-thirty. Dinner's at eight-thirty."

"What time do you want to arrive?"

"A little after eight is fine. It's just down the street."

She nods. "Shall we meet here?"

I slip my phone back into my pocket. It'll look weird if we don't arrive together if we're supposed to be dating. It's a front only my two best friends need to believe for the next ninety days. I'm not thrilled about the press pairing me with her, either. What if someone there catches my eye and I want to take her home? Am I stuck with Viv? Goddammit, I really need to think shit through before I allow a lie to roll so easily off my tongue. But I'm known for getting myself out of sticky situations, so this won't be any different.

"I'll either pick you up or send a car around seven-thirty," I finally say. "Text me your address."

She nods and I bolt toward the elevators as I try to push away the feeling this night is going to be awful.

The gala is black tie, and I run home to change into the tuxedo I bought specifically for events such as tonight's. This event benefits local elementary schools, and FDB has been a generous donor in the past. I just don't know exactly how that's going to look tonight since I don't really have enough money in the bank to be as generous as I've traditionally been—especially not with Viv by my side letting me know everything I'm doing is wrong.

I glance at my phone when it notifies me of a text, and when I don't recognize the number, I assume it's Viv letting me know where to pick her up. I'm ready early, so rather than send a car to get her, I jump in my brand-new Mercedes Benz E 400 Sport, click the address she sent me, and allow GPS to guide me there.

Except I don't really need GPS. The address she gave me is for the Westin hotel, less than a ten-minute walk from the office. As I pull into the valet lane to pick her up, I can't help but wonder if she lives here or if she fake-addressed me.

it started with a lie

I shoot her a text letting her know I'm in the black Mercedes, and she opens the door and slides into my passenger seat a minute later.

I glance over at her once I hear the buckle of her seatbelt, and I immediately wish I hadn't.

She's all soft, delicate curves and violet fabric that makes her skin glow. I catch a whiff of her perfume, something flowery like roses but lighter, and her dark hair cascades in waves around her shoulders in a way that tells me she cares, but she couldn't have spent hours on it because I just left her at the office ninety minutes ago.

I clear my throat and keep my eyes on the road. "Why'd you have me pick you up here?" I ask as I put the car in drive.

"This is where I'm staying for the duration of my contract."

"You don't live here in Vegas?" I ask. Not that I care. I'm just making conversation.

"No. I live in Los Angeles."

"Three months away from home," I muse as I focus on the road. I'm a little curious about what she left behind back home, but a glance at the empty third finger on her left hand tells me it's not a husband. Traffic's heavy, but it's a Friday night in Vegas and we're just off the Strip.

I see her lift a shoulder out of the corner of my eye. "No big deal."

"Don't you miss home?" I ask.

"I guess, but I travel for work quite a bit, so I'm used to it."

"You just go from business to business fixing them?"

"Pretty much," she says, mild humor in her tone. "My official title is business consultant, but insiders call me The Fixer."

"The Fixer?" I repeat.

"Yeah. I'm hired to fix companies," she says. "Sometimes when you're too close to the action, you can't back up enough to see the bigger picture or how to get out of the mess you've made. I'm not here to give you a pep talk, I'm not here to stroke your ego, and I'm not here to hold your hand. I'm here to fix the problem and give you the tools to implement your own solutions going forward. It's never easy, and it's usually not pretty, but I have a one hundred percent success rate taking companies from the red back to black."

"A hundred percent, huh?" I ask. "Pretty good odds."

"That's likely why Mark hired me." The words are arrogant, yet she doesn't come across that way. Her tone borders more on pride than cockiness.

"So you just study a few spreadsheets and tell me what to do?" I ask. We're at a red light, so I sneak another peek at her.

Bad choice. Her blue eyes meet mine. Hers are heavily made up. She went all out for tonight's gala, and she looks totally different than the pinned up, high-necked goody-goody I've been working with for the past week. This woman looks like she might even want to have fun tonight—something I'd never associate with the boring woman who has taken over my office.

"Not exactly. My work is based around three pillars. Dynamics, implementation, results. We're still in the dynamics stage. I'm researching everything I need to know to make informed decisions."

Rather than admit I'm somewhat impressed by her pillars, I go for the route of condescension. "I already know what you're going to tell me, and it's not going to work."

I shoot her a glare and she arches a perfectly groomed eyebrow.

"Oh?" she asks. "Do tell me, what will my advice be to fix FDB?"

"Stop spending money. Look, babe, I can't. I need to entertain clients."

"I'm not your babe," she grits at me.

"Tonight you are. You agreed to this fake date."

She blows out a breath. "I'm starting to wonder why," she says under her breath, and I let those words sit between us as we make our way to the gala in silence, but I have to admit...I'm starting to wonder why, too.

ten

I beeline for the first client I recognize when we walk through the doors. I don't even offer my *date* a drink first, and we don't check out the auction items or do the rounds yet. I just need to get away from her for a second, to push the smell of flowers out of my nose and look upon someone who doesn't look so goddamn fuckable in her purple dress when she's the last person in the world who I'd ever fuck.

"Mr. Chambers, so nice to see you again," I say, grateful my memory allows me to easily recall clients in settings apart from my office.

The white-haired CEO of Chamber Enterprises nods in greeting to me. "I had a quick glance at your analytics report before I left the office this afternoon, Mr. Fox, and the information is invaluable. I'll be recommending you to all our subsidiaries for future work."

"That's what I like to hear, sir," I say. I give Viv a meaningful look, as if to say, *See? I've got this shit under control.*

"This is my wife, Janine," he says, motioning to the woman standing beside him. She wears a silver dress and holds onto his elbow, and they're the picture of an elderly couple who are out for a night to enjoy themselves.

"Wonderful to meet you, Janine," I say, repeating her name as business 101 has taught me to do and grasping her hand firmly with my best toothy, businessman smile.

Viv clears her throat beside me.

"Oh, excuse me. This is my, um..." I trail off. "This is Vivian."

She rolls her eyes good-naturedly then sneaks around me to shake their hands. "Brian's girlfriend."

"Good catch," Chambers says to me, and I force a smile onto my lips. He winks at Viv then turns to me. "Now go get that beauty a drink."

Right. Because alcohol is definitely the answer here.

Maybe I'm onto something.

I smile at Chambers and turn a smirk to Viv, and then we head over toward the bar. I glance at her and raise a brow to indicate she should order first.

"Pinot noir," she says.

Of fucking course she gets red wine. It figures. I've never once found myself compatible with a red wine drinker, and clearly that still holds true when it comes to this woman.

"Whiskey," I order.

I pay our tab and make the rounds, greeting people I know and introducing Viv only when I absolutely have to. I'm sure it's getting old for her, but I don't really care. She's tagging along essentially uninvited because Jason walked into my office and asked me if I could attend this thing when she happened to be in there.

I don't want to be here. I want to be at home, sharing drinks with someone who will end up in my bed. I've never been a fan of these types of events, mostly because it feels like everyone is looking for whoever has the most money. Considering who my brother is, most people in the room eye me hungrily. It's never been an issue for me in the past, but ever since Mark decided to tighten his wallet, suddenly it is.

We sit down to dinner, and we're lucky to be at a table full of potential new clients. I immediately start networking because it's in my blood to do it. I'm always looking at every person I meet as a potential client. I'm in a room full of people who might need solutions and it's my job to sell them on my services without sounding like a greasy salesman.

"Brian Fox, FDB Tech Corp," I say by way of introduction to the woman next to me.

"Irene Banes, Jersey Group."

"Tell me more about Jersey Group," I say, and she launches into her prepared speech. I listen carefully for places where analytics like the ones we offer might come in handy for a company like hers, and by the time the salad course arrives, I've already acquired her contact information so I can send her a cost proposal on Monday.

And that's how it's done.

Viv sits quietly beside me, the perfect dinner companion, really—she's seen on my arm as a beautiful woman, but she keeps quiet as I handle the business portion. It's possibly the one thing she's done since I met her that I actually appreciate. In an effort to make it look real, I toss a casual arm around the back of her chair. My thumb accidentally brushes the cool, smooth skin of her bare shoulder. It's silky and I have the sudden urge to leave it there, to brush it again, to feel more of it.

The onslaught of blood rushing toward my dick certainly has nothing to do with *her*. It must be the rush of excitement I get as I acquire more and more potential new clients.

When dinner's over and it comes time for the live auction, I grab my paddle and get ready to have some fun. I've notoriously gotten into bidding wars in the past and always over the same thing: sports memorabilia. Every year I've attended this event, I've walked away with something incredible. Specifically, I'm a football fan from Chicago, and since one of the hugest donors to this auction is high up in the

Bears organization, I've walked away with things like signed footballs, helmets, and VIP tickets to Soldier Field.

I ignore most of the auction items. There's only one thing I want this year, and I can't wait to see what it is since I didn't have time to scout the room before dinner started.

I watch as two people carry a huge frame to the stage. The emcee announces, "The item donated by the Bears organization this year is a game worn and signed Payton jersey."

Holy shit.

It's mine. I know it's mine before the bidding even starts.

A signed Payton jersey is the holy grail of signed jerseys. They're hard to find, but a game-worn jersey is next to impossible. I've never seen one in person before, and a wave of excitement washes over me that it's even in the same room as me right now.

It *will* be mine.

"We'll start the bidding at one thousand." I raise my paddle marked with the number twenty-twelve to open the bid. A thousand bucks for that jersey? I'd pay a hundred times that.

I'm immediately outbid, and I grin across the room at Connor West, the only man who ever gives me a run for my money at these things. I assume he'll drive up the price and bow out like he does every year, but it's for charity. He raises his paddle with a sly smile back at me, and all of a sudden it's a bidding war.

I feel Viv's elbow in my side. I assume it's a slip she didn't mean since she has zero hold over me, but when Connor outbids me and I raise my paddle again, this time the elbow is more forceful.

I turn toward her with a glare. "What?"

She leans in toward my ear so only I can hear her. "You don't have the money for this."

I ignore the tickle of her warm breath against my ear.

"Fuck off," I whisper back as I raise my paddle to bid again.

"Brian, that's six thousand," she whispers. "You have to pay before you leave tonight. You do realize this needs to come out of your own pocket, don't you? I've seen the records showing your spend at these events. FDB doesn't have that much liquid in the bank."

"Actually, Viv, we do, not that I need to explain myself to you."

She blows out a frustrated breath. "No, you don't. I just looked at the account."

"Yeah, and I have that money from Mark." I raise my paddle again, forcing a smile when I want to punch the woman whispering furiously into my ear.

"The money is meant to cover payroll. It's already spent."

"Fuck off," I say again, a fake smile plastered to my lips since we're sitting next to business associates. "I've got it covered." I hold up my paddle to indicate I'm bidding twelve thousand.

"Brian, look at me." Her voice is louder and more forceful.

I finally take my eyes off the emcee for a brief second to allow a short glance in her direction, but my eyes get stuck on her face. She's serious, and she's seriously gorgeous. I hate Mark substantially more in this second for sending someone he knew fit my exact weaknesses: smart, business-minded like me, and brunette. If she wasn't such a royal bitch, she might be perfect for me.

Fuck Mark for picking *her* out of all the "fixers" he could've sent.

"What?" I finally whisper.

"Don't do this. You don't have the money for it."

"Yes, I do. What the fuck do you know about me, anyway?" We're whisper-yelling at each other now. Or I'm whisper-yelling at her and she's trying to talk me out of something that's *mine*. Something I want, something I work hard for—something I deserve.

This shit with her trying to take things that are mine is starting to seem like a real trend with her.

"You might've forgotten, but your personal financial records were in the files you gave me to review."

"Fuck off," I say for the third time. It's my go-to phrase when I'm out of words. It's childish and ineffective, but it makes me feel a little better.

The emcee's voice cuts into our conversation. "Sold for seventeen thousand to paddle number fourteen-twenty-two."

I almost yell, "No!" I manage to just barely stop myself as I seethe with anger. The fucking jersey went to Connor because Viv was distracting me from our bidding war.

"You have got to be shitting me," I mutter.

I expect a shred of guilt to cross her goddamn pretty face, but it doesn't. Instead, she has the gall to look victorious. Fucking *victorious* for distracting me long enough that I actually lost the auction to a competitor.

Fuck her.

Fuck her.

Brian Fox doesn't lose.

That was always my mantra. But ever since Vivian Davenport stepped into my life, it seems like Brian Fox can't win.

eleven

The next morning, I wake up to a woman whose name I don't remember and a fairly rough hangover. This is out of character even for me. The hangover not so much, but forgetting a woman's name after I take her to bed is not my norm.

After Viv distracted me from winning that Payton jersey I deserved, I ditched her at the table, networked, hit the bar pretty hard, and networked some more. I was giving this woman the hard sell last night, and I'm fairly certain it worked given the fact that I ended up in her hotel room. She's still sleeping. I remember she worked for Lion Group, so I quietly grab my phone and scroll their website for names that might sound familiar. I hit the jackpot when I find the directory of employees with names and photos. I eventually find that the brunette beside me is named Allison Park.

My weakness is brunettes, but I don't discriminate when it comes to willing women. She's pretty, but she looks older than my usual type. I usually go for early twenties for two reasons: one, because I can, and two, because any older than that and I start running into red wine drinkers. They want more than one fun night. They want dates and they want to be wined and dined and they want commitment. I'm not here for any of that shit.

The younger ones still know how to have some unattached, good old *fun*, and that's all I'm really looking for.

I think for a second about Viv. I can't help it. I'm still pissed at her for causing me to lose that jersey, but I suppose I sort of got back at her by ditching her last night. It wasn't really my job to entertain her.

Was it?

I shouldn't care I left without telling her, but I feel a little bad about it this morning. I wonder how long she wandered around looking for me. I wonder how she got home...or back to her hotel. I even feel a little bad she's staying in a hotel. Mark could've offered her his place, at the very least, for the duration of her stay here. She deserves to be in a comfortable place while she does things that might be a little out of her comfort zone—namely, dealing with an asshole like me.

I push those thoughts gruffly out of my mind. Fuck that. She's getting paid—apparently handsomely—to deal with my shit.

Allison shifts in the bed, and I click off her company's website and pull open my email. She flips over and opens her eyes. "Mm," she murmurs. "So it wasn't just a dream."

Ah fuck. That's not good. That means she's going to want more—another date, another night, another whatever. They all do, but I'm in my early thirties and having fun playing the field. It's just easier this way.

Kendra flashes through my mind again.

She was so much more than her job as a model. She was smart and funny. She was fun to be with, and she was one of the only people who could ever really get me to open up. She was everything I ever wanted in a woman—the total package...until she just wasn't anymore. Until I found out the real reason she was even with me.

If I'm honest with myself, and I mean *really* honest, the truth is I prefer playing the field now because of her. She was the one woman who ever stole my heart, and just when she held it

it started with a lie

in her hands and I had a perfect future planned for us that included everything—kids, the house, the dog, even the goddamn white picket fence—she shattered both my heart and my dreams when she slept with my brother.

He claims he didn't know she was my girlfriend. They were both drunk, and he'd never met her. It turns out she was using me the whole year we dated just to get to my brother, and I exacted my revenge when I went after the girl he had feelings for. But that's a long story.

It's in the past, and it shouldn't matter anymore, but it does. And every time a girl looks at me with a desire for more, I crawl back into my shell as I remember the devastation of trying to pick up the pieces of the heart Kendra broke. I'm not the same man I was when I was with her. I used to be good. I used to tell the truth. I used to look out for more than myself.

But she did what she did, she broke me, and I'm this new person who lives in the shadows of the walls I've built around my heart. I refuse to give it away again.

"I need to go," I say in response to her *not a dream* statement.

"So soon?" she asks. She throws in a moan for good measure as her hand starts skating down my torso toward the goods.

I throw my legs over the side of the bed and stand up before she has a chance to get to her goal. "I need to head into the office today," I lie. Putting work as a priority over a woman tends to turn most women off, and it also hits my goal of proving how dedicated I am to my job—the perfect combination of what I need right now since last night I came so close to getting this woman on board for a seven-day trial of FDB's newest models for predictions. Our newest products sell themselves after the trial.

"If you stay, I'll sign up for that trial," she says.

I refrain from expelling the sigh I want to heave out.

On the one hand...we need the business. I don't want FDB to tank because I couldn't gain new clients.

On the other hand...I have my morals, my ethics. I can't just sleep with a woman to get new business.

I laugh to myself before I even finish that statement in my head.

Of course I can. Ethics? Morals? Yeah, I don't have those—not when it comes to business.

"Okay," I say. I climb back on the bed and hover over her. I lean down to nuzzle her neck, and just as my lips meet her skin, the vivid image of Viv's bright blue eyes ambushes me.

Usually it's Kenda whose face comes to mind in these situations. Seeing Viv where Kendra usually resides is out of context and it happens when I least expect it, but those eyes looking at me with a glare invade every corner of my mind. The sweep of her dark hair around her creamy shoulders, the gentle smell of roses, the gorgeous curve of her body in that violet dress, beautiful and unending violet...it bombards me from every angle.

I grab a condom and shove my way into Allison purely to try to get Viv out of my mind, but it's fruitless. As this woman writhes beneath me only as a means to an end for me, I'm not having sex with a stranger as part of a business deal. In my mind, it's Viv, and as I shove harder and harder into Allison, I'm revenge fucking another woman in some futile attempt to give her everything she's got coming to her.

twelve

I have a Monday morning meeting with a client, so it's after lunch when I finally head into the office. I feel a sense of dread as I take the elevator up, and it only gets stronger the closer I get to my floor. I shouldn't dread going into my own office, and I never did until I was forced to share it with that devil-woman.

The truth of the matter is I feel like an asshole for ditching her at the gala. She came along as my date after I sprung that little lie on her, and I should've at least extended the same respect to get her home.

She's studying printouts when I walk in. She wordlessly holds up a manila folder that blocks my way into my own office. I grab it from her hands and toss it on my desk, somewhat tempted to forget my heartfelt apology at her cold greeting of holding a folder in my way.

I sit down, but before I power on my laptop, I say, "Sorry for the prank I pulled. You didn't deserve it."

She just raises her eyebrows, as if to say it wasn't a *prank* at all and I'm a total asshole. I brush it off. I gave my apologies, so my conscience is clear.

I have double the normal amount of Monday morning email to go through, in part because it's Monday afternoon and also because of the networking I did on Friday. I spent Saturday and yesterday emailing proposals to everyone I came in contact with at the gala, and today I have a ton of replies and interest in what we can do to provide solutions for a whole bunch of new clients.

I'm excited about all these new opportunities, and I'm even chewing on the idea of hiring some new employees to help us out with all the new work we'll be acquiring when Viv clears her throat.

I glare in her direction and catch her looking at me. Actually, she's standing just in front of my desk with her hands on her hips, and she looks pissed.

I fold my arms across my chest. "What?"

"I need to go over the information in that folder with you."

I turn away from her and read the next email in my inbox. "I'm busy."

She ignores me and charges on. "I've proposed several cuts to your current budget, and I just need your approval."

I snort. I can't help it. "Good luck with that."

She blows out a breath. "If you don't want to go over them, you lose your chance for compromise."

My head whips in her direction. "What the fuck's that supposed to mean?"

"It means your brother has full control over your company, and therefore I do as his proxy."

I fold my arms across my chest and open my mouth to respond, but she interrupts me.

"I can and will freeze spending in several areas if that's what you want." She folds her arms over her chest, and I can't tell if it's to mirror me or if it's because she's uncomfortable having this conversation. I hate that a small part of me is enjoying the challenge of figuring it out. "Mark has instructed me to work this out with you until we reach a happy middle ground, but if you're unwilling to negotiate with me, the cuts start immediately."

We glare across my desk for a few beats, her with her arms folded as she stands and me with my arms folded as I sit. I have a feeling this is another fight I'm going to lose—not because I'm giving up, but because I don't have a choice. I gave up my ability to choose when I signed the majority of my company over to my asshole brother.

"What cuts?" I finally ask.

She picks up the folder I tossed haphazardly onto my desk and hands it to me. "We start with cutting ad spend. You don't need to advertise as much as you are when you can cold call and network. It's a waste of money and if you took a look at your own predictive analytics, you'd know that."

My glare at her deepens as I narrow my eyes at the insinuation I'm not on top of my own company's analytics when that's what we sell other people. "Fine. Cut ad spend."

"Travel expenses are out of control."

"We have to go to the clients sometimes, Viv." I set the folder back down.

"Vivian," she corrects through gritted teeth. "And be that as it may, you can take care of a lot of those with Skype calls. You don't need to fly first class, and you can certainly cut accommodations. I've never seen such a high per diem in my entire career of studying budgets."

I roll my eyes. "Cut accommodations?"

"You've been staying at some of the most expensive hotels every time you travel. Ever heard of the more budget-friendly ones? Plus a lot of those budget hotels have continental breakfast, so you can cut breakfast from your per diem."

"Fuck off," I say with a smirk.

She charges forward again. "Your entertainment budget will be cut into a quarter of what you're spending now with my option of lowering that at any time."

I shake my head. "Nope. We can't cut that budget. It's how I connect with clients."

"Then find another way. You don't need to wine and dine every time. Keep doing what you're doing or let me get you out of the red. Your choice."

I heave out a frustrated sigh, snap up the folder from my desk, and stalk out of the room just to get away from the source of the headache that's suddenly pounding in my head.

She won't let me get away, though. Her persistence is one part annoying as fuck and one part hot as fuck. She follows me into Becker's office. I collapse in the chair behind his desk without flipping on the lights.

"Can't I just have five goddamn minutes alone?" I mutter. I rub my forehead with my fingertips and squeeze my eyes shut as I will her to go away.

"No, Brian, you can't. My job is to stay on top of you until everything's fixed."

My eyes pop open and I notice she flipped the lights on. She's standing on the other side of Beck's desk, so we're basically in the same spots we were in back at my own office. She's too close, yet she's too far away. "On top of me?" I ask, giving her my laziest grin as my eyes fall to her chest. I arch a brow as my eyes move back to hers. "I didn't realize that was part of the job description."

Her face turns red, and I get a front row seat as I watch the red rush into her chest. Her hand flies to her neck, and she gives me a really special glare before she turns and bolts out of the room.

I stay behind in Beck's office for a few minutes just to give her some recovery time—gentlemanly of me, I know. I finally open the folder, and I hate that she actually has a lot of good ideas in there. Some are easy cuts, and some are harder, but I've been spending money like I have it because I always did. I

it started with a lie

don't understand why suddenly Mark decided he doesn't want to help my business financially anymore, and maybe it's a conversation I need to have with him.

Whatever the case, I realize as I'm sitting in my best friend's office...I sort of do need her. If Mark is cutting me off and I want to keep this minor financial blip under wraps, I'm going to have to listen to some of her ideas.

I head back to my office to tell her I'm willing to play nice, but my door is shut—odd considering it's *my* office and I didn't shut it. When I get close enough, I can hear her voice through the closed door. I can't make out her words, so I rush back to Becker's office and listen through our phone system. I don't make a sound as I pick up the line and quietly dial into my own office.

Her voice fills the room. It's soft and distant, but I can make out the words. "I can't do it. He's just so difficult." I think she might be crying, and my heart squeezes.

My heart squeezes?

Why the fuck would my heart squeeze?

I shake it off. I wish I knew who she was talking to—my brother, I assume.

"I know. Only eighty more days, it's a great problem to solve, the money is good. You can keep reminding me of all those things, but none of it makes this easier."

I suddenly feel bad. I feel bad listening to what she thinks is a private conversation. I feel bad I've been treating her like shit. I feel bad I insinuated she wants to sleep with me when clearly that's not the direction our relationship will *ever* take.

I hang up the line and wait a few minutes. When the muffled voice through the wall quiets, I finally call my brother.

"Are you playing nice with your new boss?" he answers.

"You should know since she just ran to you with the report."

"She did?" he asks. He sounds confused.

"Weren't you just talking to her? Wasn't she telling on me and whining about how she can't do this anymore because I'm too difficult?"

He laughs. "That doesn't ring a bell."

If she wasn't talking to him...who was she talking to?

I sigh. "Why, exactly, are you doing this to me?"

"Hang on." He clearly sets the phone down to go do something, I hear some commotion and then a loud crack, some light clapping, and then a louder cheer. He returns to the phone. "Sorry."

"Where are you?"

"Celebrity golf tournament." I hear the crunch of gravel under what I assume is a golf cart. Bastard is playing golf while I'm holed up in my partner's office.

"And you answered my call?" I ask.

"Call it curiosity. Plus I have a pregnant wife, so I always have my phone handy. What do you need?"

"I need to know why you cut me off and pulled my business out from under me." I blurt out the questions that have been preying on me.

"I already told you." He sounds annoyed.

"Explain it to me again, then."

He lowers his voice. "Look, rich people aren't rich because they waste money, Brian. You're wasting all the money you've made. Your business won't last until the end of the year if you keep spending the way you have been."

"I just needed one small loan," I say in protest.

"That's where it starts. If I don't cut you off somewhere, you'll be back next month for another. And then another." He pauses and says something to whoever he's with. "It snowballs, and frankly I have a kid coming any minute. My priorities have changed, including my own fiscal responsibility."

"You're cutting me off because you're having a kid?"

"No. I'm cutting you off because you spend like a fucking moron and I can't continue to support that. Are we done here?"

"Can you at least tell her to back off a little?" I ask.

"If anything, I'll tell her to make it even worse for you. I have to go putt." He hangs up, and as much as I hate what he just told me, a tiny part of me can't help but think he's right. And I *really* hate when my brother's right.

thirteen

When I go back to my office this time, the door is open and Viv is scrolling through files on her computer. She doesn't say anything when I walk in, and I stand in front of her desk expectantly waiting for her to look up. When she doesn't and continues to ignore me, I finally say, "Viv."

Her eyes whip to mine, and hers are full of fire. "It's Vivian," she grits. She's scary and viciously beautiful like this.

I close my eyes for a beat, mostly as a way to reign in my frustration with her correcting me when I'm trying to give her a damn apology. "Why do you hate it so much when I call you Viv?"

She purses her lips but doesn't reply, and I decide to get to the point.

"I'm sorry for what I said, *Vivian*. It was out of line."

She looks back at her screen rather than at me. She doesn't accept my apology and doesn't say a word; instead, she merely gets back to her work as she puckers her lips at her screen.

I feel like a jerk as I slink back to my desk. I open the financial reports that need my immediate attention as I feel uncomfortable in my own damn office.

I've always made no apologies for who I am, so it's strange for me to feel bad right now.

I'm about to open my mouth to say *something* to get her to speak to me again when Lauren buzzes into my office. "Call on line four," she says.

"Who is it?" I ask.

"Someone from Desert Lights High School," she says.

The memories start to hit me. Mark's wife used to work there before she became Mark's wife. I used to date her when she still worked there, and she once had to come to this very office to ask me for a donation to her school. I gave her a shit ton of money and got her to agree to a date with me. It wasn't easy finagling my way into that particular situation, but when you want something bad enough, you'll do whatever it takes to get it.

And I wanted revenge on my brother bad enough.

I'm sure the school is calling to hit me up for more money. They call every year around this time, and I always give them at least a little bit. It's the least I can do as penance for my sins.

"Brian Fox," I answer on speaker.

"Just calling to see whether you've had a chance to recharge and you're ready for another round." The unmistakable sultry voice of Tess comes through my speaker, loud enough for all ears present in my office to hear…which normally wouldn't be an issue, but I've never had to share my office with someone else.

My eyes widen and I quickly take the call off speaker while I glance over at Viv. Her lips are pursed and one brow is arched, but she doesn't look away from her computer screen.

"When my secretary said it was someone from Desert Lights High School, I really never imagined it would be you," I say.

"I figured if I identified myself as Tess, she'd direct the call to Jason. You're the FDB president I'm interested in talking to, though."

"Oh?" I ask, injecting as much flirtation into that one little syllable as I can possibly muster since Viv's clearly pretending like she's not listening to my conversation. "And why's that?"

"I can't stop thinking about our night together or our subsequent romp in your office. Are you sitting at your desk now? The one you bent me over the other day?"

I clear my throat as those particular memories hit me and all the blood in my body seems to rush to my cock at once.

"It was fun, wasn't it?" I ask. "But I think it might be too complicated." I blurt the words before I can stop them, not because I haven't had a great time with Tess, but because it's just supposed to be sex. Repeating the act more than once or twice in a few weeks seems like it's making it something more than that, and our history is too woven together. I like her, and we had fun—and the sex was great—but I'm really not interested in anything more than getting my crank yanked again, and if I'm going to betray my best friend by sleeping with his ex, I feel like I need to be invested. I'm not.

"You're probably right, but something about complications makes me all sorts of turned on."

I laugh. "I can't disagree there, I guess."

"I'll be drinking whiskey at my place tonight at ten. Naked. Be there. Naked."

"Awfully demanding for someone who already got hers," I retort.

"We'll both get ours twice now. I won't even care if you stay the night."

"What is this, Tess?" I ask, my voice softening a little as I turn away from Viv in some futile attempt at privacy. "Why are you asking me to do this?"

"It's just for fun, I swear. I don't want something serious, and I know you don't, either."

"Promise?" I ask.

"I promise."

I blow out a breath. "Not a word of this to anyone."

She laughs. "You, either. This is just two people getting theirs in secret."

"Fine. Text me your address and I'll see you tonight."

"I don't have your number," she says. "It's why I called your office."

I give her my number even though a tiny voice somewhere way in the back of my head tells me not to.

"Oh, one more thing," she says.

"What?"

"Bring whiskey."

I laugh, and as soon as we hang up, I look over at Viv. "I assume you signed some sort of NDA?"

"A non-disclosure agreement?" she asks. "I did for your brother. Not for you."

I sigh and open the NDA file on my computer I've always had my secretaries sign. I change a few names, print it, and set it down on her desk with a dramatic sweep of my arm.

"Don't worry, Brian. Whatever that was...it's not my business and I wasn't listening."

I give her a tight smile. "Be that as it may, it's a matter I need kept private, and a good businessman doesn't leave anything to chance."

She nods, reads it over, finds that it's all standard legalese, and signs with a flourish. She writes something next to her name and then hands it back to me.

"Thanks," I mutter as I grab for the paper. It's stuck, though, as she holds firmly onto her end.

"I'll hand this over on one condition," she says, leaning over her desk to hold tightly to the paper and giving me a shot right down her shirt.

It takes everything in me not to shift my eyes down there.

I didn't think she had it in her, to be honest. She's a feisty one, and a traitorous part of me likes that in her. She holds my fate in her hands. I need to know what we talk about stays between us. I need to know Jason and Becker can go on doing their jobs without worrying I'm not doing mine. And I guess I need Jason to believe I'm dating Viv, no matter how repulsive the idea sits with me.

"What's the condition?" I think of all the possible things it could be, from cutting my travel expenditures to getting Viv her own corner office, but I'd have never guessed her actual condition.

"You deal with the fact that I'm your boss and you stop treating me like dirt. And if you can't do that, as I wrote next to my signature, then this contract is invalid. I hold no loyalties to you, and I won't hesitate to out all the lies you're telling your partners."

"I can make an attempt at being a little nicer," I say.

"Don't make an attempt. Just do it," she hisses, and truthfully she's a little scary like this. I can't stop myself anymore. My eyes dart down to the creamy globes hidden beneath a silky bra. I play it off like I'm looking away from her since she's more or less scolding me, smoothly averting my eyes to the floor on my pass by her tits.

I ignore the pang in my chest at the perfection I saw there, and I finally say softly, "Okay. Fine."

She hands over the paper, and the two of us return to our respective desks to get back to our respective work.

Something changed in that little exchange, though. Somehow she went from this monster trying to take over my business to an actual human being who's here to help me.

I don't want her help. But I'm starting to think I do want *her*.

Jason walks through the door just as I'm filing the NDA in the only drawer of my desk with a lock. He collapses into one of the chairs facing my desk, greeting Viv with a hello on the way. She smiles at him smoothly, and I wonder why I don't get the same treatment.

Maybe because I don't give it to her.

"Are you two busy tonight?" he asks.

I glance over at Viv as part of the act like I'm checking with my girlfriend whether we're busy. She's shooting me a look that clearly says *I've got plans*, and I clear my throat. Technically I have plans tonight, but I'm sure Tess wouldn't mind if I had to postpone the evening because of business. "What do you have in mind?" I ask before I answer his actual question.

"Ever since the wedding, I've been thinking about Tess. I thought we could grab some drinks, just the four of us."

Tess.

I glance at Viv again, and I see the light of understanding dawn there.

Shit.

I'm caught. She just overheard a phone conversation with a girl named Tess. It's too coincidental for a fairly uncommon name. I'm sleeping with my best friend's ex, and he wants to get back together with her and go on a double date. And Vivian, my pretend girlfriend who I actually loathe, looks like she knows everything.

This can't be good.

"Vivian has plans tonight, right Vivian?" I say.

Jason's head swings in her direction. I try to shoot her a look of desperation, but she ignores it as she shakes her head and smirks at me.

"Nope. Free as a bird."

I shoot her a glare before Jason turns back to me.

"Great, then," Jason says. "I'll set something up with Tess. Let's do dinner, too. Jack's Steakhouse at eight?"

"Fine." I keep my focus on the papers in front of me rather than on my friend. I've perfected the act of manipulation, yet he knows me better than most.

"While I'm here, can you send me the analytics report on Timber Ridge?" he asks.

I click a few buttons on my computer and attach the file to an email to him. "Done," I say.

"Thanks. I'll let you know when I touch base with Tess." He leaves, and I blow out a breath.

"Same Tess, I take it?" Viv asks quietly once he's gone.

"Would there have been any other reason I had you sign an NDA?" I shoot back.

"You mean aside from the fact that you're out of money and I'm part of the cover up?"

I clench my jaw tightly, and I feel an angry tick working my jaw. It's not worth getting into another round with her when I'll have to play nice with her tonight, so I keep my mouth shut.

A text comes through from Tess not five minutes later.

Tess: *You agreed to a double date?*
Me: *I was backed into a corner.*
Tess: *How awkward. I didn't know you were seeing someone.*

I glance at Vivian, those milky white hills still peeking out the top of her shirt. I need to get laid, and despite knowing it's a total betrayal to my best friend, I write her back.

Me: *I'm not.*
Tess: *Then are we still on for afterward?*

I only have one condition to that. I absolutely refuse to sleep with her if she has any intention of getting back together with my friend. I have to draw the line somewhere, and I will *never* be party to cheating. Not after what happened with Kendra.

Me: *Are you getting back together with Jason?*
Tess: *Nope.*

Me: *Then we're still on for afterward.*

fourteen

I pick Viv up from the front of the Westin so we arrive for our "double date" together. A weight of guilt presses on my chest as I realize all the lies I'm telling the guy I call one of my best friends. It's not just the relationship with Viv, or the fact that I'm sleeping with his ex...it's his livelihood. I'm fucking up the very thing we quit our jobs in Chicago for, the very thing we moved to Vegas for, the very thing we put all our hard-earned savings into. I didn't set out to hurt the guy, but at this point, I've got so many lies stacked up I don't even know how to keep them all straight.

Once Viv fixes FDB and goes on her merry way, life will be back to normal.

It's just my luck that goddamn Vivian has to look like a fucking goddess as she waits in front of the hotel. She's wearing a dark red lipstick that makes her lips look bigger, and my mind first goes to the most obvious place: what they'd look like wrapped around my cock.

She slides into the front seat and I breathe in her soft, flowery scent. She's wearing a modest black dress that could go either way in terms of dressy or casual, but she looks like an elegant queen in it, and I hate her a little more for it. She's not showing enough skin in my humble opinion, not that it matters—but if I'm trying to get my best friend to buy that she's my girlfriend, it sort of does matter. I normally wouldn't date someone like Viv, so we're going to have to come up with some reason why the two of us are together.

Rather than telling her how lovely she looks once we're on the road, my first words to her are, "How'd we meet?"

"Uh, your brother hired me to fix your company. Remember?"

I huff out a sigh of exasperation. "I mean in our little pretense."

"Oh." She's quiet for a few beats, and then she says, "Online."

I shake my head. "I wasn't looking for commitment when I ran into you. Jason wouldn't buy online. It would have to be out somewhere. A work event or a bar. Something like that."

"So basically you work and drink?" She laughs. "What kind of person am I fake-dating?"

"The kind who works and drinks. You're a little more uptight than the woman Jason's used to seeing me with, so let's say a networking event."

"Uptight?"

I sense the indignation in her tone with just that single word. "You know what I mean."

"No, actually, I don't. Care to explain?"

I glance over at her. Her arms are folded over her chest defensively and her brows are raised at me.

"I just mean you're a workaholic like me," I say, poorly covering up my word choice. "Look, we don't have much time to kill to get our stories straight. We met in February at the Ellsworth Creek Luncheon. You were at my table and we just got to talking."

She sighs, and I'm not sure if it's in agreement or not. I don't bother to ask.

it started with a lie

"I asked for your number and called you later that night because you were so intriguing. The rest is history." I hit the brakes for a red light.

"Why don't you just tell him the truth?" she asks softly.

I glance over at her, but I look back at the road when I answer. It's my single vulnerable spot, and she just pressed it. "Because I can't admit my brother's coming to my rescue again, okay?"

My tone comes out rougher than I intend for it to, and the two of us are quiet for the remainder of the short ride. Once I pull into our parking space, I feel the weight press more heavily, but I leave it behind me as I get out of the car.

I spot Tess's yellow hair first, then Jason sitting beside her. They're already at a table.

I grab Viv's hand as we walk toward them to make it seem like we're an actual couple, and her small hand is ice cold in mine. I have the sudden urge to wrap my arms around her to warm her up, and I have no idea where that thought comes from. I fight against it with everything I have, just as I fight against the urge to squeeze her hand before I let it go.

I fight even harder against the urge to pull it into mine again once we're seated and the introductions have been made.

"Good to see you again, Tess," I say, pretending like the last time I saw her was at Becker and Jill's wedding.

"You too. You guys hear from Becker about the honeymoon at all?" she asks.

"I last saw Tess at our friends' wedding," I say to Viv. She smiles and nods, playing the part, and then I say, "Beck sent a few emails checking in, but otherwise he's pretty much been off the grid."

"Good for him," Tess says. "So how did you two meet?" She directs the question at Viv, as blunt as ever, a firm reminder as to why I like to fuck her but wouldn't want anything more than that. I wonder if Tess recognizes her from my office the other day.

"At a luncheon," Vivian says with a smile, and I can't help but hang onto her words. "He slid into the seat next to me and talked my ear off the whole time."

Jason and Tess both laugh at her assessment while I pretend to join in on the fun with a fake smile. I'm riding a weird line here—acting like she's my girlfriend for one person at this table while I don't really want the other one thinking I'm in a committed relationship with someone. I take a sip of water since the whiskey I ordered isn't here yet, and then I say, "She was just so intriguing I couldn't help myself."

Viv glances over at me with a fake smile, and I wonder if either of the two of them catch it.

I doubt it, though. We're pretending we're on the love side of the razor-thin line, but passion is passion whether we're talking about love or hate.

"How did the two of you meet?" Viv asks Jason and Tess.

They glance at one another and burst into laughter. "Long story," Tess says, "but actually one of my best friends, Reese, used to date Brian."

Viv raises an eyebrow as she looks in my direction. "Reese as in Mark's wife Reese?"

"You know Mark?" Jason asks. I appreciate my friend for asking since he knows the history of my sordid relationship with my brother.

"Not really," Viv says smoothly. "Just what Brian has told me about him."

Jason raises an eyebrow and lets out a low whistle. "Must be really serious if he told you about his brother."

Viv glances over at me, and I pull out a smooth answer that's vague enough to make everyone at the table happy. "I trust her."

it started with a lie

* * *

I've got whiskey in hand when I knock on Tess's apartment door a little before midnight.

After the stress of what was just supposed to be a night out with friends, I'm ready for something to help relax me.

Putting on the act with Viv was harder than I thought it would be. I found myself torn between hating her because of why she's here and wanting to get to know more about her.

She didn't say much during the meal, but she didn't have to. Tess is one of those people who steals the conversation, so we let her. It took the attention off us, and because of that, it also meant we didn't have to keep lying. Not out loud, at least.

When Tess opens the door, she's naked as a jaybird, and I push all the random thoughts of wanting Viv that've been plaguing me all day to the back of my mind.

I don't *want* her. She's the opposite of what I want. She's straight-laced and boring and intrusive. She's buttoned-up and high-necked and proper.

The hot, naked girl opening her door and immediately lunging for the bottle of whiskey in my hand with the promise of no commitment?

Now *that* is what I want.

I hold it just out of her reach, and I step into her apartment as I slam the door behind me. She arches a brow at me, and I grin.

"I held up my end of the bargain," she says. "I said I'd be naked."

"Before we get started here, I just want to reiterate sleeping together again doesn't *mean* anything."

Her brows draw down. "No shit, Fox. Now hand over the whiskey."

I laugh.

"Jason never finds out about this," I say. Even though she told me she's not getting back together with him, I just want to verify he won't get hurt if we do this again.

I shouldn't be here. My conscience is trying to tell me not to do this.

But I'm here, and she's naked. Lust wins tonight, no matter how wrong it is.

She nods. "Who was that girl tonight?"

"Does it matter if this is just casual?" I ask.

She shakes her head. "You're absolutely right." She grabs the whiskey out of my hands and unscrews the cap. She helps herself to a shot directly from the bottle before passing it back to me. I chug more than my fair share, slam the bottle on the counter, wipe my mouth with the back of my hand, and pull the very naked Tess against my body, my eyes right on her gorgeous tits through the entire process.

"You ready to get fucked?" I ask, my voice husky.

"I've been ready all day. Sitting through dinner was torture." She doesn't mention she was sitting with my best friend, and I don't mention I was there with someone else, either. She doesn't say a word about whether she might get back together with him, and instead, she reaches a finger down to her pussy. When she pulls it out, she pushes it into my mouth. "See?" she asks, her lips pouty and her voice sultry as I taste the very wet tang left behind on her finger.

Jesus Christ.

I twirl my tongue against her finger for a beat before I pull it out from between my lips. My mouth crashes down to hers as I guide her hand down to my very erect cock.

She moans when she feels how hard I am, and then she grasps me over my pants. I grunt into her mouth as I thrust my cock against her hand. I'm horny as fuck after dealing with the woman taking over my office for the last few days. I've been putting in so many extra hours I haven't had much chance for the sort of relief I'm about to get, and thinking about Viv and her perfect breasts isn't helping matters.

And there she is again in my thoughts. I let her linger there for a beat as I recall her sweet floral scent. I let myself pretend just for a second it's her touching me, that we're in my office together and the door's closed and we can do whatever we want. I realize I don't really know a single thing about her apart from the fact that she's from Los Angeles. I don't know why I suddenly want to know more.

When Tess reaches her hand into my pants and starts stroking my cock, I draw the line. I push Viv out of my head because even though this is just a casual fuck between friends, Tess deserves to have me here with her...and Viv doesn't deserve to have me defile her, even if it's just in my head and even if I want to bend her over my desk after I spend some time luxuriating in those perfect, creamy tits.

I force that thought out. That's not what I want. I'm not even attracted to her. I hate her with a strange sort of passion. She's here to ruin my life, and she's masquerading around like she's here to help.

And there she is again.

I can't seem to stop thinking about her.

I force my focus on Tess. I nip at her neck, kiss her skin, trail down my mouth to her breasts. I nuzzle them and grab them, lick them and tweak them, pinch them and suck them. They're bigger than Viv's. There's nothing soft or subtle about Tess.

She lets me know she's having a good time with loud and enthusiastic moans, and I can't help but think Viv would never be that loud. She may be firm and direct when it comes to business, but she seems so much more demure than Tess.

She'd give me soft purrs and kitten moans, not loud shrieks of pleasure.

I think I'd like the soft moans more.

Tess is almost riding the line of going overboard, and as I prepare to fuck her by sliding my finger inside her, I wonder if she was this loud with Jason. She's a good fuck, wild and crazy, but I'll never see her as anything more than a good time.

Viv, though…

Viv.

I don't finish that thought because Tess is lowering my zipper and kneeling on the floor and pulling my dick into her mouth. She sucks me in so far I'm going down her throat, and she doesn't even gag. Her eyes don't water. Her lips are wrapped around me, and all other thoughts leave at that point. I don't even have to force them away. They magically disappear on their own.

My balls tighten, and I pull myself out of her mouth. No coughing or choking—this girl has clearly done this before, and she's damn good at it.

I grab the condom from my back pocket and secure it. I figure she'll lead me to the bedroom or the couch, but she doesn't. Instead, she pushes me toward the door, laces her arms around my neck, hooks one leg around me and then the other, and I shove my way into her as we fuck right in her entryway.

My hands move under her ass, and she cries out so loudly I think she must be having an orgasm. She isn't contracting around me, not yet, and I try to get on board with the enthusiasm. I try to match her screams with grunts of my own, but I'm no match for her brand of crazy. She's staring at my face as I drive into her over and over, and it's too intimate for someone who's just supposed to be a fuck buddy. Besides, I can't come standing up like this—it's too much of a workout as I try to hold her body up and thrust into her at the same time. I'm in good shape, but even I have my limits.

I finally let go and set her down. "Bend over," I say, and she follows directions as she grabs her ankles. This is a much better angle for me, and this way I'm not staring into her face. This way, I can pretend she's whoever I want her to be, and she can pretend I'm whoever she wants me to be, too. Maybe she's pretending I'm my brother. It wouldn't be the first time that's happened. She could be pretending I'm Jason or one of her other exes. Or it's possible she's not pretending at all, that she's present in the moment with me even though we agreed it's nothing more than sex.

I can't say the same, though.

It's not Tess's face in my mind when my thrusts slow and my balls tighten and I let go as I finally blow my load.

I just wish it wasn't Viv's.

fifteen

When Friday rolls around, I'm ecstatic for a few days away from the woman who has taken over my office and seemingly my life. I'm ready for the weekend, but first I have to get through the day.

It's just about lunchtime and I'm nearly finished looking through the newest data for one of our clients when she walks through the door. A few beats later, my email pings with a new one from Lauren. It was sent to my whole in-office staff.

Employees of FDB:
Enjoy the free lunch in the breakroom, and Happy Friday!
Lauren Weller
Administrative Assistant to Brian Fox

I glance over at Vivian. "Free lunch?"

She nods. "Little bags from Panera. Sandwiches, chips, that sort of thing."

"From you?"

"Well, from *you* technically, I guess."

My brows furrow. "What are you talking about?"

"It's always a good morale booster to surprise everyone with lunch."

"You bought lunch for my staff?" I ask.

She lifts a shoulder. "I know you don't want anyone to know about me, but I still have a job to do here. Since I'm acting for the co-owner with the biggest stake in this company, part of that job is to take care of my staff."

"You're not a co-owner," I grit out. "And it isn't your staff." It marks yet another time she's treating other people with a congeniality I don't always seem to receive, but it isn't just that. It's the fact that she did something nice for my entire staff I never once thought of doing.

She clears her throat. "I don't mean to be blunt, Brian, but when you signed enough of your stake over to Mark to give him fifty-one percent of this company and he hired me to fix it, he hired me on as acting CEO."

I blow out a breath. Fuck her, fuck this lunch, fuck Mark, and fuck my life. I don't respond, and I certainly don't take part in the free lunch she provided for my staff.

* * *

"It's five," I say when the clock strikes the magic number. "You can go back to your hotel now."

She glares at me as she packs up a few folders and her laptop. She moves quickly as she sticks her things in her bag, yet she lets out a long sigh before she responds. I briefly wonder if the sigh is in relief that she gets to spend a few days away from me. Probably not, I realize with some degree of arrogance.

"Just for the record, I'm not leaving because you told me to," she says.

I raise a brow as if to tell her to explain why she's leaving. As if I care.

"I'm leaving because I'm heading home for the weekend and my flight takes off in under two hours."

it started with a lie

A strange sensation rushes through my chest, something I can't quite identify—but it's definitely at odds with my brain rejoicing that she won't even be in the same city as me.

Disappointment? Is that what that was? It couldn't be. There's no possible reason I'd be disappointed she'll be gone for a couple of days. I'm thrilled to be away from her, thrilled to have some of my privacy back even if it's just for a few days. Shit, maybe I'll stay at the office all damn weekend just to remember what it's like to be alone in here. I can jerk off with my door shut and no one would care.

I certainly can't do that with Vivian Davenport sitting a few feet away from me.

"Safe travels," I say, averting my eyes to my phone as if I'm disinterested. I want to ask more, like why she's going home and whether there's someone there waiting for her, but I keep my mouth shut. She doesn't say another word as she finishes gathering her belongings and walks out the door.

I at least expected her to bid me a good weekend. She seems like she has manners.

She must really hate me, which is fine since the feeling's mutual.

A short while after she leaves, Jason saunters into my office. "Big weekend plans?" he asks.

I shake my head. I thought about calling Tess again, but I don't want to initiate it. There's less guilt that way. "Work, probably. You?"

"Hanging out with Tess tonight." He slides into the chair opposite my desk, and that weight of guilt presses on me again. "You and Viv want to do another double date?"

"She took off to Los Angeles for the weekend," I say.

"Why?"

"Family stuff." The lie is instant and automatic, and I wonder when it became so easy for a lie to roll off my tongue.

"And you didn't go?"

"Too much to catch up on here." I click around on my laptop for a few beats to prove my point, and then I glance up at him. "We're not really at the meet the family stage yet."

"But you're at the share an office every single day stage?"

I lift a shoulder. "She needed a space to work." I glance around. "This office is huge, and you can't beat the views."

He nods. "True story. How are things going with you two?"

"Fine." I throw the ball back in his court because I don't really want to tell more lies. "How about you and Tess?"

"I haven't stopped thinking about her since Beck's wedding. We just sort of drifted apart the first time, you know? I wanted more, she didn't. I'm hoping she's in a place where she does now."

"Do you think she does?" I ask, fully knowing the answer to that.

He shrugs. "She seems open to it. She didn't say no. It was a little strange she went home alone after our double date the other night, but maybe she's just playing it slow because she wants something less physical and more meaningful this time around."

I fail to mention the reason she didn't go home with him is because I met her at her place. I don't know what to say, so I try to steer the conversation so it's clear I think we're done talking about this. "Good luck, man."

My plan to end that part of our talk doesn't work.

"You think she seemed into me at dinner the other night?" He's vulnerable, and I'm not used to seeing him like this. She's knocked him down a few pegs, shaken his confidence. He's always had a pretty easy game when it comes to the ladies, but something's different where Tess is concerned.

I need to stop sleeping with her. This entire conversation is evidence that even if she doesn't want more, he does, and it's not right for me to stand in the way when all I want with her is a roll between the sheets.

"Yeah. I think she did." Another lie to add to the list.

"For the record, I really like Viv. You two are good together."

"I'm glad you approve." I don't know what else to say, yet I'm sort of left wondering if he's right. Would we be good together?

I may hate her, but I haven't loved *or* hated so passionately since…

That's when it dawns on me.

Since Kendra.

Since the girl who used me for a year to get to my brother broke my heart.

Love turned to hate when I found out what she was doing, and I can't help but wonder one thing.

Can hate turn to love this time?

sixteen

I'm trudging carefully through revising a contract on Tuesday morning when Lauren walks into my office holding a Starbucks cup. I feel a rush of relief that my secretary knows me so well. I'm just about to thank her for a cup of salvation when she sets the cup on Vivian's desk.

I glance at Lauren's hands to see if she has another cup that might be for me, but they're empty.

What the fuck?

"Payback for those two you brought me last week," Lauren says with a smile.

"Oh, you didn't have to do that!" Vivian says. She stands and gives Lauren a hug.

A fucking *hug*.

What the hell am I missing here?

Why is she so nice to everyone around me but she's such a goddamn devil to me? How does she know Lauren's Starbucks order, and how does Lauren know *hers*?

Lauren is *my* secretary and I don't even know how she takes her coffee. Both of them are all smiles this morning while I try not to seethe behind my desk. And that's when something sort of clicks in my mind.

Is it just me? Am I the problem?

She obviously cares enough to get to know Lauren. She bought lunch last week for the entire office. Everyone seems to love her, and they don't even know the truth that she actually does work here. Maybe my employees are treating her with kindness because they believe the lie that she's my girlfriend and think being nice to her might get them into my good graces.

But somehow I doubt that.

I'm starting to piece together the real issue here, an issue I'm neither ready nor willing to admit, when my phone interrupts my thoughts with its jarring ring.

I blow out a breath as I glance at the screen, and it's a client. This particular client tends to be fairly needy, and he always wants me there in person and on short notice. It used to be fine when we were just starting out and he was my biggest client, but now I've added more to the table. I was busy back then, but I'm even busier now. My entire life is this company, all day every day, and I really don't have time to take a business trip on short notice.

But I will. I always do, because the number one rule in good business is to keep the client happy.

"Good morning, Paul. How's the weather in Miami this morning?" I answer. I put the call on speaker so I can keep shuffling my paperwork as we talk, an old habit that dies hard. It's still my office, and I'm not going to bend over backwards just because some chick thinks she can set up shop in my territory.

"Humid, Mr. Fox. Humid."

I give him the fake laugh he always buys, and then I ask, "What can I do for you today?"

"Our contract with Schneider Technologies ends in a couple weeks, so we'll need you back here for renegotiations sometime before then."

If he wasn't the president of Porter Electronics, I'd tell him where he could shove his renegotiations. I take a quick glance at my calendar. *Thanks for all the notice, asshole,* is what I want to say. *Didn't you know this expiration date was coming?*

I study my calendar. I have a local conference I'm presenting at on Friday, and I was going to use most of Thursday to finalize my presentation. I suppose I can put in a few extra hours each night this week to make it work, and the thought of getting away from Viv for a few days has me feeling lighter somehow. I need this. I need a few hours away to do my work without someone breathing down my neck, clearing her throat, smelling like roses, licking her lips, and interrupting me every three seconds.

I need to get away from her and her goddamn distractions.

"As it happens, I'm heading to Florida tomorrow evening," I say as a way to appease him.

"You are?" Viv murmurs loud enough for me to hear but quiet enough that Paul doesn't catch it.

I ignore her. "I'd be glad to meet with you on Thursday."

Viv starts shaking her head in the corner, and I ignore her.

"Thursday works for me," Paul says. "It might bleed into Friday."

"Unfortunately I'm presenting here in Vegas at the Vegas Business Con, so I can't do Friday. But I'll be there first thing Thursday morning," I say, and Viv's violent headshaking becomes a little more vehement.

He sighs heavily, as if the fact that I'm only clearing *one* day for him just isn't good enough. I can't afford to lose him as a client, but I can't afford to give him any more than twenty-four hours this week. "Fine," he finally agrees.

We discuss a few more details, and when we hang up, Viv glares at me. "You don't have the budget for a last-minute flight to Miami."

"That's what plastic's for, babe." I shoot her a grin and dial Lauren's extension even though she sits literally twelve feet outside my office.

"I'm not your babe." I hear the angry words come from the corner of my office, but I take the high road as I choose to ignore her.

Rather than put Lauren on speaker so Viv can overhear all the details of our conversation, I pick up the line. "Book me the redeye to Miami this Wednesday."

"Same accommodations as usual?" she asks.

The usual is the Ritz. The budget-friendly hotels Viv mentioned a few days ago flash through my mind, and I shake my head. Fuck it. "The usual," I say, and I cut our call.

Viv blows out a breath and shakes her head while she closes her eyes.

I arch a brow at her. "What?"

She stands and walks toward my office door. "Mark specifically requested I accompany you on all business trips to track spending."

My chest tightens and my stomach turns on me. I can't fucking get away from her.

She heads out to talk to Lauren for a minute, and when she returns, she sits back at her desk like everything is back to normal.

"What did you just do?" I ask.

"Gave Lauren my credit card number to book me on the same flight as you. Oh, and also, the hotel's on me."

"On you?" I ask. She doesn't seem like the generous type.

"Okay, on your brother. He gave me a card for my expenses."

"He gave *you*, a stranger, a card, but he's essentially putting a freeze on my own spending?" I ask.

She nods and presses her lips together, and then she sits. "That about sums it up." She opens her mouth to say something else, but I'm already storming angrily out of my office, so I never get to hear whatever it was.

As I stalk past my secretary, she stops me. "The red eye is full, Brian," she says. "I can get you on at twelve-fifteen Wednesday afternoon. You'll land a little after eight at night."

"Fine," I say. Can't one damn thing go right?

* * *

We never discussed going to the airport together, and I don't even really think about it until I'm getting in the line for security and see her just making her way through the metal detectors. I barely recognize her since she's not wearing her usual professional attire, but the gorgeous dark waves cascade around her shoulders in a flurry just like they always do, and that's what calls my attention to her.

I go through the precheck line since I travel for work often. I'm through security and catching up to Viv in record time. "Hey," I say, tapping her on the shoulder.

She whips around. "Oh!" she says, her hand flying up to her throat. "You scared me."

Something's off. She looks far less put together than usual—a strange sight to behold considering I have yet to see her as anything besides perfectly poised. Her eyes are red-rimmed and she's wearing jeans paired with a giant gray Raiders sweatshirt that's unfortunately covering the delicious body I know she has under there.

Raiders?

She's a Raiders fan? I didn't know those existed. I always thought that was some kind of unicorn.

"What's wrong?" I ask, my brows furrowing.

She shakes her head. "Nothing. I'm fine." She keeps walking but stumbles a little. I grab her and lace my arm around her waist before she trips as something unfamiliar filters through me: worry.

"Vivian, what's going on?" I ask.

She squints up at me, and she's more vulnerable than I've ever seen her. "I took my sedatives a little too early I guess."

"Sedatives?"

"Yeah," she mutters. "I hate flying and I hate you, so the pills were meant to calm all that anxiety. I still can't believe I'm going to one of the most romantic cities in the United States with *you*." Her face twists with disgust as she admits truths she clearly wouldn't say if she wasn't high on sedatives.

I hate you.

Those three little words plow into me with the force of a tornado. It's one short phrase that sticks in my brain, twists into my guts, and pushes a violent ache into my chest.

She *hates* me. She had to take drugs to calm herself since she has to sit on a flight beside me.

How many other women have I done this to—make them feel so shitty about themselves they had to get drugged up just to spend time with me? I let go of the fact that she also hates flying because in this moment, it doesn't matter. I'm part of the equation, and I suddenly feel horrible for every mean thing I've ever said or done, for every lie I've ever told, for every heart I've ever stomped on.

But most of all, I feel horrible for the way I've treated her.

It's like her words flip a switch in me. They shouldn't hurt me—not if I hate her, too. But it's in that moment I realize I *don't* hate her. Quite the opposite, in fact.

Regardless of what those thoughts mean, she deserves to be treated better, and it's time for me to step up and be a better man.

it started with a lie

"Why are the hot ones always such assholes?" she mutters as we walk toward our gate, and I can't help but think *this* is a Vivian I like. This is one I can get on board with. She's funny, she's candid, and she's finally letting go of the professional demeanor she wears like a suit of armor.

I don't answer as I hold onto her, her flowery scent winding its way into my nostrils. It's some sort of calming scent, or it's something about her being in this vulnerable position. She needs me to get her on that plane, and I'm the one who didn't even want her here in the first place.

And it doesn't escape my notice she called me one of the *hot ones*.

I let it go for now, but I'm sure those words will replay in my mind as many times as *I hate you*.

We find a couple open chairs when we get to our gate, and she closes her eyes and rests her head against my shoulder. "Thank you," she murmurs, and then I'm pretty sure she falls asleep.

The flight starts boarding, but I let her sleep on my shoulder even when they call our row. I let her sleep all the way until the gate agent says, "Flight seven-sixty-two to Miami is now boarding all rows."

I gently shake her arm, and she shifts with grogginess. "We need to get on the plane," I say loudly, trying to wake her up.

"Mm," she moans, and she leans back into my shoulder.

"Come on, Vivian, it's time to board." I shake her shoulder some more, and she reluctantly sits up and rubs her sleepy eyes. Make-up smears onto the skin beneath her lids, and it's instinctual to reach up with my thumb to help wipe it away.

Her eyes focus on me, and I see a split second of horror before it smooths away thanks to the calming effect of whatever drug she took.

She finally stands, and I wrap my arm around her waist again to help her to the plane.

"Is she okay?" the gate agent asks as she scans our tickets.

I nod. "She was nervous about the flight," I say, and the agent nods in understanding.

I help her onto the plane and direct her toward our seats, her in the middle and me on the aisle as I always request. Some stranger sits by the window and doesn't even acknowledge us as we slide into our seats. Her head falls back to my shoulder, and I have to actually buckle the seatbelt around her waist. The back of my hand accidentally brushes against one of her breasts, and my dick hardens in response. I pull my hand away quickly like I just touched fire.

I didn't touch fire, but I'm pretty sure this girl can still burn me straight down to the ground.

seventeen

The flight is about four and a half hours, and she sleeps through the whole thing. I don't move her from my shoulder, but I do manage to fish out my tablet to put the finishing touches on Friday's presentation. I go through my slides and memorize the material, and then I work on a few contracts and review my notes for tomorrow's meeting.

We've always hired Schneider Technologies in Germany as a third-party contractor who designs the model we've used with several of our clients, but I'm starting to wonder if we should cut Schneider out of the deal and move it in-house. We didn't have the means to do that when we first started our company in Vegas because we didn't know what we were doing, but now that we're more established, I'm certain we could hire contractors that work for us rather than paying the astronomical fees associated with a third-party. I can't help but think Viv would be proud of me for attempting to save some money, but I just don't have enough time to check in with Jason and Beck *and* be sure we have someone lined up before our meeting with Porter. I do, however, think we could manage it for next year.

Before I know it, the wheels are touching down and we're in Miami, apparently one of the most romantic cities in the United States. I'm afraid to wake her, afraid the nap she took on the plane will force the sedatives out of her system and I'll have the old Viv back—or maybe afraid that *won't* happen.

Even though I like drugged up Viv, I need regular Viv to return to me. I need to see how she interacts with these new thoughts swimming through my brain as they turn into feelings starting their descent toward my chest.

"We're here, Viv," I say softly as I shake her shoulder. I'm pretty sure the dude by the window is itching to get out of our row, but we're all stuck for the moment as we wait for the flight attendants to open the door.

She finally sits up. "Dang, those pills worked *good* this time," she says. She's much more lucid after her nearly five-hour nap, and I can't help my chuckle at her use of *dang*. I realize for the first time I've never actually heard her use a curse word. She's the consummate professional, so seeing her drugged up on sedatives has actually been sort of entertaining even though she slept through most of it.

"You didn't move the entire flight," I say.

"I tried a new kind," she admits. "Plus I took two even though the directions only recommend one unless one doesn't work."

I laugh. "Maybe just one for the return flight."

She nods and seems to retreat back into herself as she realizes she's playing nice with me, and I feel a sudden sense of loss as the professional shield moves firmly back into place.

My new goal for this trip is to get her to lower it again.

We take a cab to the hotel rather than the chauffeured car I usually have Lauren arrange, and when we pull up in front of the hotel after we've only been traveling a few minutes, I discover why she offered to pay for our accommodations.

The Ritz is twelve miles from the airport—usually at thirty-minute drive. This couldn't have been more than two miles.

The bright lights of the hotel that's so budget friendly it doesn't even have a brand name, it's just called the Miami Airport Hotel, twinkle in front of me.

it started with a lie

"You have got to be shitting me," I say under my breath. "Is this a prank?"

She glances over at me with a raised brow and shakes her head. Maybe it's all in my head, but her eyes seem to twinkle with excitement, and I think she's starting to enjoy tormenting me—especially since she's got me under her thumb after the whole NDA thing. "Don't you love the red and green flashing lights? It's like Christmas in the spring."

"Christmas in the spring?"

"Sure," she says with a grin. "It's my favorite holiday. Isn't it everyone's?"

I heave out a heavy sigh. "This is silly. The Ritz is right on the beach and it's a few blocks from Porter. We're gonna end up paying the same in travel expenses to and from Porter as we'd pay just to stay on the beach."

"That's not exactly true. I price compared, and your hotel is about three times more expensive than staying here."

I roll my eyes. Of course she price compared. Do I even know who I'm dealing with here?

No. The answer to that question is a firm and heartfelt *no*.

"Why are you enjoying this?" I ask after the cab driver pulls our bags from the trunk and we're heading toward the reception counter.

Her grin widens. "I think I'm still a little drugged up."

She gives the reservation number to the clerk.

"I have two nonsmoking rooms with a request for king beds," the clerk says. She taps some keys.

"That's right," Viv says.

"Unfortunately we're packed full this week with a textile convention in town and we only have double queen rooms left. Will that be okay?"

"It'll do," Viv says.

I huff out a frustrated breath. It has to do, I guess, but I'm not happy about it.

The clerk taps some more keys then hands us each a little booklet with our keys tucked inside and our room numbers written on the outside. I'm in one-twenty-seven, and she's in two-thirty-two. We're not even on the same floor, and that's just fine by me.

I'm hungry, I'm tired, I'm confused, and I just want to get away from her. There's a restaurant across from the lobby, and I decide that's where I'll be having my dinner. "Have the bellhop bring my luggage to my room," I say to the clerk. "I'm going to get dinner."

"Um, sir, this is the Miami Airport Hotel. We don't have bell service."

"Fucking figures," I mutter, and then I grab my suitcase so I can haul it to my room as I leave Viv standing there by herself.

I let myself in my room and use the restroom. I'm looking at myself in the mirror as I wash my hands, lost in thought over what the hell I'm really feeling for Vivian. I shake the excess water from my hands and glance down to grab a towel when I spot it.

"What the fuck!?" I practically yell as my heart races and my eyes fall onto some sort of terrifying creature sitting right there on the towel.

And it's not just any creature. It's big and it's ugly and I'm not sure if it's a bug or a frog or some sort of mutant.

It's fucking enormous and there's no way in fuck I'm staying in this room.

My heart pounds in the way only a life-threatening predator could make it pound as I grab my bag with wet hands and haul my ass back to the front desk. Someone's checking in, and I wait my turn like a good boy.

it started with a lie

"There's a giant bug in my room," I hiss to the same clerk who checked us in once it's finally my turn. It wasn't just some little bug. It was a fucking mutant. I refrain from saying that to this clerk.

"I'm sorry, sir," she says, and I can tell she's trying to cover her laugh, but fuck her because she didn't see it and didn't just have the shit scared out of her by some alien insect when she just wanted to dry her damn hands. What if I'd have taken a shower in that room? I shudder at the thought. Housekeeping would've found my lifeless body, naked and wet in the shower the next morning. I've never seen a thing like that at the fucking Ritz, that's for goddamn sure. "I'll be happy to send someone down to take care of it."

"I don't want someone to take care of it," I nearly yell. That fucking bug nearly gave me a heart attack. I draw in a calming breath. There's no use in yelling at this lady. "Well, I do, but I also want a new room."

"Of course." She taps her keys and the light smell of roses attacks my senses. I glance up and find Viv beside me.

"Is everything okay?" she asks. She looks a little worried. "Are you switching rooms?"

I don't embarrass easily, but telling her I found a bug in my room sounds totally ridiculous. I'm a man. I should've killed it myself.

But, fuck, it was huge, and it wasn't just my imagination. That thing had to be hopped up on some radioactive fluids or something. Jesus Christ.

"He said there was a bug in his room," the clerk says, and Viv clearly tries to hide a smirk. The clerk looks back up at me. "Unfortunately, we're booked solid tonight."

"You two can stop laughing now," I say, embracing the situation. "You didn't see it. I'd be happy to show both of you if you don't believe me."

Viv lets out a howl she clearly tried holding in, and the clerk makes some sort of snorting noise she doesn't cover very well. "Screw both of you," I say, and I stalk off back toward my room as I leave my bag at the front desk. I take a deep breath as I pause outside the door, and then I open the camera on my phone. I enter the room, run into the bathroom, and snap a photo of the thing now crawling along my sink, and then I run out of the room like a child. With a better view, I think it might just be a little frog, and I think I might've overreacted a little. My heart pounds again, but this time I take my time getting back to the front desk. Viv and the clerk are still laughing when I return.

I flash the photo to both of them. "Brian, it's just a little frog," she says, her eyes still twinkling with merriment.

"Oh my God," the clerk breathes. "That's a Marine toad."

"A what?"

"A Marine toad. It's poisonous." She makes a face of disgust as she looks away from my screen. "Oh, God, what if there's more?" She slaps at her own arms like there's one hopping up her skin. "I feel like it's on me. Is it on me?"

"It's not on you," I say, shaking my head and rolling my eyes. "But it *was* in my room. What are you going to do about it?"

"I'll send an exterminator right in, but my guess is you won't be able to stay there. We can give you a voucher for a return trip, but we're out of rooms."

I huff out an annoyed chuckle. "There are two things wrong with that statement. One, I won't need your voucher for a return trip as I never plan to stay here again," I say, glaring at the clerk. "And two, I need a fucking room."

"Brian, calm down," Viv says beside me. "Just stay with me. My room has two queens."

I look down at her. She's tall, but I've got an easy six or so inches on her. My eyes catch on hers, and I notice for the first time how long her lashes are. Thick and dark and lush. It's a strange thing to notice, but it's also very pretty, and it somehow has a calming effect on me.

"We can't do that," I say in protest. "It's not *professional.*"

She rolls her eyes. "It's not ideal, but it's just two colleagues staying together because one has poisonous toads in his room." She tries to hide her laughter at my expense. "It's fine."

I finally huff out, "Fine. Lead the way."

She nods and I follow her to her room.

eighteen

"This doesn't have to be so bad, you know," she says. "I'm really not that horrible of a person."

I glance over at her in the small elevator car as we travel to the second floor. "I value privacy, and I've had very little of it since the day you walked into my office."

"I'm sorry, Brian. Really, I am. About the toad, about barging into your office when you weren't expecting me, about everything." She's letting down her guard, and I'm not sure if it's because of the toad or because of the sedatives, but I feel like I'm hanging on her every word. "I'm sure this can't be easy for you, but I promise I'm only here to help. I'm only doing the job I was hired to do."

"That doesn't make it any better," I mutter petulantly.

She nods and doesn't say anything else. I should be nicer to her given the fact that she's sharing her room with me—and I signed a contract that says I agreed to be a little nicer to her—but this whole thing is throwing me off balance, especially the part where I suddenly can't stop looking at this chick's eyelashes. What the fuck? I don't think I've ever noticed *eyelashes* on a woman before, of all the stupid things.

"I'm going to dinner," I announce once I've set my suitcase down. Maybe a little food will ward off the anger and the annoyance. I think I might just be *hangry*, as my sister calls it when I get so hungry I get angry—and then mean. "Alone."

I don't wait for her to tell me to order the cheapest thing on the menu, and I don't bother to look at her as I channel all my frustration into heavy steps as I stride toward the door. It latches shut behind me with a click that echoes down the empty hallway.

I lean against the wall beside the door for a beat as I try to gather my bearings. I close my eyes and draw in a deep breath, and as I exhale, I try to breathe out all the exasperation she incites in me. It's useless, though, and as I walk down the hall toward the elevator, I can't help but think it's because part of me wants a large king bed in that room instead of separate queens.

I order a steak because it's the only thing on the menu that looks appetizing. I check my email and see some new ones from both Jason and Becker, which tells me Beck's working on his honeymoon. He shouldn't be. We all agreed he'd be out of the office and away from work for the duration of his vacation, but we all love this company.

That's the thought that sends a dart of guilt through me.

What am I doing?

Jason and Becker love FDB as much as I do. If they knew we were barely hanging on by a financial thread right now, what would they have to say about that? And worse, if they knew I signed my stake of the company over to my brother so the three of us don't even actually have majority ownership of our own company, what would they think?

The steak is chewy and the potatoes are cold. The wine is bitter. *At least the company is first rate*, I think to myself as I eye the empty chair across from me.

What would Viv have ordered? She seems less like a red meat kind of gal and more like a chicken eater. Red wine for sure, though I almost wonder if she'd skip the alcohol altogether at a business dinner. She didn't at the gala, but that was different—and she only had one. Before I ditched her, at least.

I hate that I'm thinking of her as I cut into my steak. I hate that I feel guilty for leaving her in the room we're sharing as I came down here to eat alone.

I especially hate that she's not down here eating with me. That's on me, though.

I have got to get this chick out of my head, and the perfect distraction comes through just when I need it to in the form of a text message.

Tess: *You free this weekend for some more fun?*

Me: *I knew you'd come crawling back for more. They always do.*

Tess: *That's because you're good in bed. No other reason.*

Me: *I can't deny that. And to answer your question, I'm free late Friday.*

Tess: *Perfect.*

Me: *Should we plan on ten, naked, whiskey, your place again?*

Tess: *You bring the whiskey. I'll take care of the rest.*

Me: *Deal.*

I set my phone down and glance up just as dark, wavy hair catches my eye as the host leads her to a table. A rush of emotion pings through my chest when our eyes meet, mine still twinkling from my conversation with Tess. A little smile tips Viv's lips as she thinks the twinkle is directed at her.

I blow out a breath. That tiny smile on her face brightens the entire room. How can I keep being the guy that wipes it away?

I can't. Not anymore. Not after her vulnerability at the airport and not after she confessed she hates me. Not after she offered up the spare bed in her toad-free hotel room and not after I saw the long lashes framing the blue eyes I want to keep seeing look upon me with something other than disapproval.

I nod toward the empty chair across from me, and she pauses.

"I thought you wanted to eat alone," she says, her tone full of surprise.

"I do. Did. I've eaten half my steak alone, so this is my way of compromising."

"I don't want to bother you. I'll just get my own table," she says.

"Stop," I say. My tone is firm, and I don't want it to be. I want her to have the option, so I soften my next words. "I'd like for you to join me."

She predictably orders grilled chicken and steamed vegetables with a glass of red wine, and once I'm finished with my meal and she's waiting quietly for her food, I think it's time to get to know her a little better. I'm not sure if that's a good idea or a bad one, but suddenly I feel like I want to know everything.

I start with what I know we have in common. "So how did you meet my brother?"

"I've actually known him for a long time. My cousin is Vick," she says, naming my brother's band's assistant. "She invited me backstage ten or so years ago after a show in LA and we got to talking."

"You didn't sleep with him, did you?" The question blurts out before I can stop it. It wouldn't bother me, exactly, if she did, but I'd force myself to lose interest if she had some flame burning for him. I can't go through that shit again.

Her eyes widen and her cheeks grow red. "No!" she exclaims, as if she's offended I'd even think that. She averts her eyes to the table. "But I almost had a thing with Ethan."

I laugh and shake my head. Both men have historically been known as womanizers in the press, and they didn't earn their reputations because they're virgins. "It's always either the singer or the drummer."

She lifts both shoulders. "It's not that I wasn't attracted to Mark, but Ethan got to me first."

My chest tightens at the mention of her attraction to my brother.

"One of their bets?" I ask.

She rolls her eyes. "Vick filled me in later. Ethan got fifty bucks for getting me in his dressing room before Mark did."

"And you still decided to work with him?" I definitely didn't peg her as the type to let something like that go, let alone get involved in a professional relationship with someone who did that to her. More proof I really don't know anything about her, I guess.

"It's ancient history, and a little embarrassing if I'm honest. But nothing happened with either one of them, and I've met them lots of times since then. They've both apologized to me, and we've all moved on. Besides, Mark's offer was one I couldn't refuse."

"How much is he paying you?" I realize it's not my business, but the question is out before I can stop it.

She looks uncomfortable for a minute as she takes a sip of her wine, but she answers anyway. "Sixty."

"Thousand?" I ask as I try to hide my surprise.

She nods. "Plus expenses. He said he gave you that fifty you asked for plus ten extra, and he wanted to match that. He said it would be the last money he ever put into FDB."

I press my lips together as I think how nice it would've been if he'd have discussed this with *me* first rather than tossing Viv on me and my company.

"Sixty thousand for ninety days of work," I say. "Not too shabby."

"Not the least I've made, but not the most." She says it confidently, and for as demure as she paints herself sometimes, she's also a fierce businesswoman. Yet another question for the what's-that-like-beneath-the-sheets list.

"Do you have other projects you're working on while you're in Vegas?"

She nods. "You're my nine-to-five, sometimes six. I have to do something to keep myself occupied after that."

"What are your other projects?"

"They're confidential," she says, and of course they are. I feel a little stupid for asking, but I'm suddenly curious about what her life is like when she's not sitting in my office.

"You just work at your hotel?" I ask.

"You're full of questions tonight." She eyes me suspiciously.

"Just making conversation." I say it like I'm defending myself, but I shouldn't have to. I wish I would've come across a little differently from the start if she feels like I might have ulterior motives in a simple conversation. It forces me into the realization that maybe I was the one who made the bad first impression—not her. I was so blinded by my anger she was even here in the first place that I never gave her a fair chance.

"Let's talk about something other than work, then," she says.

"That's pretty much my go to topic since I've dedicated my entire life to it."

"Do you ever wish you hadn't?" Her voice is soft when she asks the question, and I run my finger around the rim of my glass as I try to imagine what life might be like if hadn't gone headfirst into growing FDB after my last real relationship.

I shake my head to answer Viv's question. "No. I love my job. I love FDB. I love calling the shots. And that's why I've been such an asshole to you."

She looks surprised by my admission. She opens her mouth to say something, but I charge ahead before she can with more truths I never imagined myself admitting to her.

"My friends and I started FDB so we wouldn't have to answer to anybody else. It's a fuck ton of work to own your own business, but it's been beyond worth it to have something that's just mine."

"And then I came along," she says softly.

"It was stupid of me to let it get as far off track as I did. If Mark hadn't given me that money, I'm not sure what my next step would have been." It's something I haven't admitted to a single soul—something I've barely come to terms with myself. I never thought it was something I had to worry about since my brother always took care things for me, but I've spent it all and now I'm cut off.

"You know this already, though, since you've studied the reports," I say. "I made the situation seem like no big deal to Mark, but it's actually been pretty dire."

She nods. "I didn't want to overstep, but if you need help budgeting your personal finances, too, I'm at your disposal. It's all part of my contract with Mark."

My brows shoot up. "My personal finances are part of your contract?"

"Not in so many words, but anything that could affect the finances of FDB is under my jurisdiction, and if you've been pumping your own money into the company, I can help you figure out how to make it back."

"You just wave your magic wand and fix it all?" I ask.

"Not exactly, but...yeah. Pretty much."

I laugh and shake my head as the waiter drops Viv's grilled chicken in front of her.

"Okay," I finally say. "Let's do it."

She takes a sip of wine, and I swear I hear her mutter, "*That isn't part of the contract*" before she digs into her chicken.

My phone notifies me of a new text, and when I pick it up, I find it's one of my Miami friends replying to a text I sent earlier.

Dan Shipley: *Does The Cork tonight at 9 work?*

I weigh my options. Nights out with Danny used to be fairly epic, but he's settled down quite a bit since he got married and started a family. It might not be as wild as the old days, and that might not be a terrible thing since I have an early morning.

Me: *I'll be there.*

"Who's that?" Viv asks after she swallows a bite of carrot.

"My buddy Danny," I say, surprised she asked but feeling a little closer to her after our conversation. "He lives just outside Miami in a little suburb called Coconut Grove."

"Doesn't that sound kind of magical?" she asks, her eyes suddenly turning a little dreamy. I look away from her, but not before the image burns itself into my memory. "You going to see him while you're here?"

"Tonight at nine. Want to come?" I ask. The question is out before I can stop myself, but I suddenly find I *want* to spend time with her. Maybe I'm just finally getting used to her being around all the time.

"Oh, no," she says, waving her hand. "I wouldn't want to impose on your boys' time."

I shake my head. "It's not like that. He's bringing his wife along. A night away from the kids and all that."

"Okay," she says, nodding. "It could be fun. Better than a night alone in my hotel room, anyway."

"Our hotel room," I correct her.

She laughs, and I wonder if I'll ever get used to the rush of emotion I feel when I hear that sound.

nineteen

We Uber our way over to The Cork since it's right next to the Ritz. I didn't have the balls to confess the truth to Danny about the Roach Motel, so I let him think I'm staying where I usually do.

I didn't realize when I asked Viv if she wanted to come that this would feel sort of like a date. I don't want it to. I don't even like this woman, yet she seems just a little more human to me. She took sedatives for a plane ride. She nearly hooked up with Ethan, the drummer in my brother's band. She's not perfect. She's a workaholic like me, but from everything I gather, she's savvy enough to have some money in the bank—not so much like me.

She didn't do anything different, really—just freshened up while I waited in the lobby for her—but she looks gorgeous. I can't exactly pinpoint what changed, but something did.

She hates me.

She told me when she was hopped up on her sedatives, and maybe that's what changed. I don't want her to feel that way about me because even though I should hate her for what she's doing, she's only doing it because she was hired to. She's just fulfilling the contract she signed so she can collect her paycheck. This isn't her fault. It's my brother's. Maybe his own way of getting back at me—putting this ridiculous temptation in front of me.

We're twenty minutes early, but I did that on purpose. "Want to take a quick walk?" I ask after we're out of the car and standing on the sidewalk.

"Sure," she says.

I remind myself this is nothing more than two colleagues on a work trip together going for a romantic walk by the marina.

Oh shit. I'm fucked, aren't I?

I fall into step beside her, that floral scent drifting up toward my nose. Her heels click on the sidewalk, and I can't help but glance at her shapely legs. They're all sorts of calf muscle gorgeousness, probably because she works out or runs and wears heels all day every day, and now I can't get the image out of my head of her legs wrapped around my neck with her feet planted firmly in those heels.

We get to the dock, and the first row of boats are the yachts for sale. The fence in front of them holds paperwork showing pictures of the interiors along with their price tags.

"Four million?" she says, eyeing the Sterling hundred-thirty-eight-footer in front of us. "Looks more like a three and a half."

I laugh, and we walk to the next one. "I'll take two of these," she says. This one is bigger, newer, and about eight times the price.

"My brother has one sort of like this down in Mexico," I say wryly. "I think he's selling it if you're interested."

"Why's he selling it?"

"Same reason he won't continue to fund FDB," I mutter.

"The baby?" she asks.

I look over at her with a furrowed brow. "He told you that?"

She shakes her head. "My brother-in-law did the same thing when they got pregnant. He put a halt on all spending. I think

it started with a lie

it's just the typical man response, you know? Women start nesting, men start saving."

I shrug. "Mark has more money than he knows what to do with," I mutter.

She glances up at me. "That doesn't mean it's smart to throw it away."

I look away from her before our eyes have a chance to lock, because once they do, I'm pretty sure I'll be done with the whole *pretending I don't want her* ruse. I start a lazy stroll toward the next boat. "You have to defend him. You're working for him."

We both look at the price tag, and when she looks up at the boat and starts talking, her voice is soft and gentle. "I think what you don't realize, Brian, is that I'm also working for *you*. I may technically be your boss, but once this contract is up in ninety days and I'm gone because I've waved my magic wand, as you put it, it's up to you to keep everything afloat. Mark won't hire me back again. He'll just shut down FDB if you run out of money, and then your best friends will certainly learn your secret."

She says the last part like she doesn't approve of me keeping information from my partners, but it's not up to her to judge. It's how I've decided to run my portion of the business, and I have a contract saying she agrees to keep my secrets...provided I keep up my end of the bargain. I feel like I'm off to a better start playing nice since dinner, but that's also the time I can best pinpoint when things started to change for me.

When I started seeing her as someone more human even though I don't want to.

When the ache in my chest and subsequently in my cock started becoming unbearable.

When I realized I want her in my bed tonight. Or, given our situation, I want to be in *her* bed tonight.

"We should probably get over to the bar," I finally say, choosing not to acknowledge her words about my company.

She nods and I fight the urge to grab her hand and clutch it in mine as we walk toward The Cork.

I glance around the bar when we walk in. It's crowded, but I spot Danny as he waves me over toward his wife.

"You're my girlfriend and you came with me on this business trip," I murmur in Viv's ear as we make our way toward my friends. She nods to indicate she heard me but doesn't otherwise respond—except I swear I hear a little gasp as I set my palm on the small of her back and guide her to my buddy's table.

"Fox!" Danny exclaims when we're close.

"Shipley!" I yell back in the same tone, and he stands and smacks my back in a bro hug. I hug his wife, Carrie. I was in their wedding five years ago, back when Danny and I both still lived in Chicago.

A lot has changed since the good old days.

"This is Vivian," I say, nodding toward the woman standing beside. "We just started seeing each other."

Carrie's eyebrows shoot up and Dan's jaw gets stuck open.

I narrow my eyes at both of them. "Don't say anything stupid."

Dan's jaw snaps shut in an attempt to ward off the words on the tip of his tongue, but Carrie manages to find her voice. "It's lovely to meet you," she says. She leans in conspiratorially. "Brian's just bounced around so much over the past few years that it's sort of hard to believe."

"That's exactly the sort of thing I just told you not to say." I roll my eyes, and Viv laughs.

"I'll tell you all my secrets about how I got him to commit, but I'm gonna need some wine first," Viv says.

Carrie nods. "Yep. I like her already."

We sit and a waitress comes over to take our drink order.

"So how did you two meet?" Carrie asks Viv just as Danny turns to me and asks, "How's business?"

I want to hear Viv's answer, but I have to play the part. I'm here to catch up with Danny, so I'm going to allow her to handle it.

"Everything's great," I lie, because that's what we all do when we're catching up with an old friend, isn't it? "I acquired four new contracts just this week. Beck's off on his honeymoon and Jason has been busy with the IT team developing even more innovative ways of tracking data." I leave out the part about suddenly finding myself in debt up to my ears. I glance over at Viv as I try to catch the end of what she's saying, but I miss it as Danny asks me another question.

"How long has this been going on?" he asks. My chest tightens. Shit. Does he know about the debt?

I glance up at him, and he nods toward Viv. A rush of relief darts through me.

"A couple months," I say. "It's new, but it's good."

"You seem different." He says it quietly, almost like he doesn't want the two ladies at the table to hear him.

"How?" I ask. The waitress drops off my whiskey, and I take a grateful sip.

Danny keeps his voice low. "The way you keep looking at her."

The way I keep looking at her?

How am I looking at her?

I choose to change the subject. "How are the kids?"

He closes his eyes for a beat like he hasn't slept in months—or years—and then he grins. "Amazing. You two gonna have some?"

I choke on my sip of whiskey. "It's been *a few months*, dude. We're not even at the point for discussion yet."

"You're in your mid-thirties, aren't you?"

"Early. Don't confuse me with my older brother."

He laughs. "Don't wait. Take it from me. I'm forty and I have three kids under six. I understand now why people have kids in their twenties."

"Why's that?" I ask.

"Because I'm old and real fucking tired."

Carrie laughs beside him. "You telling him why you should've had kids fifteen years ago?"

He nods sagely, as if it's a story he's told lots of times, and she mock rolls her eyes. "I've heard the story a hundred times, but the ending never changes. He's still an old man." She elbows Danny, and he chuckles. Their easy demeanor is contagious, and it's a natural reaction when I drape my arm across the back of Viv's chair. Her shoulder bumps near the side of my chest, and a waver rolls down to my stomach.

The waver turns into an actual throb that darts to my cock when she glances up at me and our eyes meet. Her tongue peeks out to wet her lips, and I can't help but watch as my cock responds with a healthy appetite for her.

It's fake, this act we're putting on, but there's something real there. I see it in her eyes, too. She's looking at me differently. She can't possibly deny it.

She looks away first and goes right for her red wine, and I feel like that's the signal I'm in. If she needs relief after her eyes met mine, if she feels thirsty and needs to be sated, if she's turning to alcohol to solve that thirst...it doesn't make any sense she'd be doing any of that if she didn't feel it, too.

With my arm around her chair, I allow my fingertips to graze her bare shoulder. Her head whips up toward me, and this time there's a question in her eyes. I'm not sure what she's asking—it might be something along the lines of *what the hell are you doing*, or it might be something much deeper than that.

A carnal question of desire, a question asking if my fingertips grazing her soft skin means more than the act we're putting on for the world to see so I don't have to admit the truth.

She doesn't move her arm, doesn't wriggle away from my hold, but her attention returns to Carrie and their conversation, and my attention returns to Danny. We talk a little business so we can make sure to write this one off. The old Danny starts to emerge a bit when our second round of drinks makes its appearance, and by the time our third round comes, Carrie and Viv are laughing like old friends and Danny isn't hiding the fact that he wants to get his wife home to fuck her. In fact, I'm fairly certain he isn't going to wait until he gets home.

Even as I think it, I realize how much I want that for Viv and me, too. Not marriage—that's not something on my radar, certainly not with her, but the sex. I want her, and now that I've stopped denying that, it might be time to let her in on the secret, too.

The more drinks Viv has, the more I see her relax right before my eyes. Her posture sags a little, the pinched look on her face that she always turns in my direction softens, the red of her wine creeps into her cheeks, flushing her face. A wisp of hair falls over her eyes, and she tucks it back behind her ear with delicate fingers as she giggles at something Danny just said. I didn't hear it, though, because I'm too focused on staring at Viv as the transformation takes place right before my eyes. She's no longer the uptight, straight-laced, annoying woman sent to tell me how to do my job.

Now she's the gorgeous woman who's my date for the night—the woman whose bed I plan to share tonight.

I feel a little looser after a few drinks myself, and when she looks up at me with those gorgeous blue eyes, my lips tip up into a secret smile. She grins back at me, and just like that, the wall between us starts to come down a little. I don't know her at all, but I intend to change that. Just sitting here tonight beside her, laughing with her and acting like we're actually on a real date, it's enough to tell me I *want* to get to know her.

It's with that thought in mind I brush my lips across her temple in an unexpected and totally involuntary move.

The light scent of roses fills my nose as I breathe in her hair, and that's when I know I'm a goner. I heard years ago that women emit powerful sexual chemicals from their hair and that men fall in love with a scent. I don't know if it's true, but I've always believed in the danger that comes with smelling a woman's hair. Proof of the theory came when I first smelled Kendra's vanilla hair and again when I smelled Reese's strawberry hair.

And now roses?

I don't know if I'll ever look at the stupid flower the same way again without thinking of Viv and the soft scent enveloping her.

My lips drop from her temple and she looks up at me. I see the confusion written there—I see the questions.

Is this for real, or is this just part of our act?

The lines are so blurred that I'm not sure anymore, but I'm ready to drop the act.

I grab for the bill as soon as it comes, and the pinched look is back on Viv's face. I check her wineglass to see if it came with a lemon since it looks like she just sucked on one by the way her face is puckered in my direction.

It's not just a write off, it's a habit. I always foot the bill, and besides, we talked business, so it's a business meeting. I forgot for a minute I'm not supposed to be paying for shit like this, and as I catch sight of the total on the bottom of the bill, I realize why.

I pull out my personal credit card again since the black one is dead to me. With the way Viv's eyes are glued to me, I almost think she's going to pull the check out of my hands and pay for it herself, but she doesn't. In fact, she doesn't say a word at all.

"She seems like a keeper, Bri," Carrie says quietly to me as we hug goodbye. "Treat her right. I'm happy for you."

I press my lips together in a small smile and nod.

I don't know if she's a keeper. I don't know if we'll have anything beyond the rest of the ninety days she's with me to fix my company.

But what I do know is if she'll let me, I'll treat her right for tonight.

twenty

"Can we walk by the boats again?" she asks. I'm ready to take her back to the hotel and get her naked once we leave the bar, but it appears she has other plans. "It's just such a nice night and I don't know the next time I'll be back in Miami."

"Sure." We make our way toward the marina. It's in the upper seventies, but it's dark and the air cools the closer we get to the water. We walk and look at the boats in peace, neither of us talking but neither of us wanting to break that silence, either. It's comfortable and tranquil, and I have the impulse to show her just how romantic this city really is.

I don't, though. I'm trying to work out the best way to play this to move past the professional relationship and let her know I'm interested in something more. I usually have so much more confidence when it comes to women, but this one throws me off my game.

"Do you live by the marina in Los Angeles?" I ask, finally breaking the silence once we find ourselves halfway down the pier.

She shakes her head. "Landlocked in Tarzana."

"I don't know where that is," I say. "My brother's place is in Malibu."

"San Fernando Valley. An hour northwest of LA with no traffic, like that's a real thing." She gazes over at the boats, and I battle the instinct to toss an arm around her shoulders. "My sister and I used to love my dad's boat when we were kids."

It's the single most revealing sentence she's given me since I met her. She has a sister and a dad and they had a boat.

"Do you have any other siblings?" I ask, suddenly curious about every aspect of who she is.

She shakes her head. "I did."

"You did?" I ask before I can stop myself. It comes out more insensitively than I mean for it to.

"I had an older brother." Her voice gets quiet as she slips into her memories. "I was only seven when he passed away."

"Oh." It's all I can think to say. "I'm sorry," I add.

She stops in front of a huge yacht and we both stare at it. "Thanks," she murmurs. "It's been a long time now."

This time I don't fight the urge. I wrap my arm around her shoulder and pull her closer in to me.

She doesn't wrap her arms around me, doesn't give into the comfort. Instead, she simply allows me to comfort her for a few seconds before she turns and starts walking. I drop my arm back to my side once she ducks out from under it. "He was ten and shouldn't have been riding his bike in the street."

"God," I murmur. "That's horrible."

"It was hard, but I was seven, you know?" She doesn't stop walking as she muses quietly beside me. "I didn't really get it. I always sort of thought he'd come walking back in someday. Even now, I let myself think that sometimes. I wonder what sort of relationship we'd have today."

"You'd probably be bossing him around," I tease, trying to lighten the mood.

She looks over at me and I prepare for a glare, but instead I'm met with the tip of her lips and just a touch of merriment in her eyes. "He always hated playing school with me. I'd always get to be the teacher and he'd always go whining to our parents that I was being too bossy."

it started with a lie

I raise a brow, and she looks back out over the boats. "Some things never change," I murmur.

She chuckles. "When do you think kids develop those qualities that stick with them the rest of their lives?"

"I think they're born with them," I say without missing a beat even though I have no real idea. I've never even thought about it before.

"Sorry for getting philosophical on you."

"Don't apologize," I say. "I'm enjoying this side of you."

She glances over at me and moves her gaze quickly back to the boat in front of us, and I wonder what that was all about. Is she enjoying it, too—but she doesn't want to admit it? Or is she scared to ride the line between business and pleasure?

"Do you have any siblings other than Mark?" she finally asks.

I nod. "A sister. Mark's the oldest, then Lizzie, and I'm the youngest."

"Ah," she says. She moves away from the boat in front of us and stops in front of the one next to us. "That explains a lot."

"What does?"

"That you're the baby. You're so reliant on Mark to get you out of trouble that it's no wonder he cut you off."

My brows furrow. "We were having such a nice time and then you had to go and say that."

She lifts both shoulders. "I didn't mean anything by it. I'm simply restating the facts. I ran a study for a course in my master's program and found a lot of stereotypes to be true."

"Like what?" I brush aside the fact that she has a master's degree for now, though I'm curious what exactly her degree is in.

"The youngest learns through imitation. You've seen your brother spend without limit, and so you've learned that behavior." Before I can interrupt to tell her she's wrong even though if I dig deep enough I can see the truth in her words, she continues. "The youngest is generally well-liked and has a big social circle. True of you from what I've seen, though I can't say I really like you all that much."

"That's just the red wine talking."

She laughs.

"What else?" I ask.

"The youngest is charming but also a manipulator, and he almost always gets his way," she says. She moves onto the next boat while she leaves me wondering what that's supposed to mean.

"Do you see me that way?" I ask when I catch up with her.

"Abso-freaking-lutely," she says, and I chuckle at the closest she's ever come to cursing in front of me.

"Give me one example," I say as I glare at her.

"Charming the pants off women since the day I first walked into your office, manipulating everyone around you by lying about the two of us, and getting your way...yeah, you tend to just power through to get whatever—"

I can't help it. She's so passionate as she talks about all my worst qualities that it's a total turn-on. I cut her off mid-sentence when my mouth comes crashing down to hers.

She gasps at my sudden movement, like she's in total shock I'd kiss her. The gasp gives me an opening into her mouth, and suddenly my tongue is dancing with hers in a violent tango of aggression, like we're kissing each other for our very survival. I give her the kind of kiss she can live off forever as I thrust my hands into that gorgeous rose-scented hair. It's softer beneath my fingertips than I imagined. I keep one hand planted in her hair as I hold her face to mine, and the other hand trails down and lands on her hip. She relaxes into me as our bodies meld together on a pier in Miami, and I jerk my hips against hers to let her know just how fucking wild she's driving me.

I need more. I need all of her, need her naked body beneath mine, need to sink myself into her warmth, need to feel her soft skin. I wish she wasn't wearing a dress so I could trail my hand under her shirt to feel the warm skin of her back. I wish we were naked at the Ritz together. I wish for so many things, but right at this moment, the one thing I seem to have been wishing for since the day she dropped into my office—that she'd just go the fuck away—seems to have disappeared from my list.

When she moans softly into me, that's when I stop everything. I can't keep kissing her on a pier like this and hold it together. So instead, I back away from her. She gazes up at me from hooded eyes, her lips red and swollen in the soft light of the moon and coming from the boats around us. She's always beautiful, but like this she's simply stunning as her chest heaves from exertion like she ran a marathon, not like she was just kissing me.

"Jesus, Viv," I exhale as I try to catch my own breath back, too.

"It's Vivian," she says through gritted teeth, and she's angry with me.

Because I called her Viv after I kissed her?

"What the heck was that?" she hisses.

"It was a kiss," I say flippantly as I find myself back in control.

Control with this one never lasts for very long, though.

"Well it was inappropriate. Take me back to the hotel," she spits at me.

I'll take her back to the hotel, but I'm afraid that in her anger, she's forgotten one important detail.

We're sharing a hotel room.

The Uber ride back to the hotel is silent. The stalk through the small lobby and subsequent elevator ride is quiet. She doesn't say a word to me, just silently fumes, and I'm not sure if it's because I called her Viv or if it's because I kissed her. Either way, the cut of rejection is fresh in the air.

"I'm sorry," I finally say as she rummages through her purse for the hotel key outside her room.

"For what?" she mutters. She finds the key and shoves it into the door, and the green light lets us in.

"For calling you Viv. For kissing you. For whatever got you so mad at me."

She sighs and tosses her purse on the dresser with deep scratches on its top. "Look, I'm not mad at you. I'm mad at myself. And a little bit at you. I don't mix professional with personal, and we crossed a line. And now I can't even be mortified in peace since we're sharing a room."

"You don't have to be mortified. I kissed you. It was wrong of me, but it didn't feel very wrong, Vivian." I use her full name to try to get back into her good graces, and then I take a step toward her. I seem to lose control of my limbs as my arm reaches out toward her and I tuck some hair behind her ear. "Sometimes these things are beyond our control."

She takes a step back so she's out of my reach. "This isn't one of those things. I'd like to get ready for bed. If you'll excuse me, I just need ten minutes."

I nod. "I'll give you some privacy." I pick up the key she dropped on the dresser and head down toward the lobby as disappointment sits heavy in my gut.

twenty-one

I've never really considered myself an angry person, but suddenly I feel like punching a hole through the wall.

Even though I'm short on cash and it's eleven miles back the other way, I call up an Uber to take me to the beach. I need a walk. I need to feel the sand between my toes and breathe in the salty ocean air. I need it to clear my mind and help me figure out what the hell I'm doing.

The driver is close by and traffic's light, so I'm back near the Ritz in no time at all. I'm not sure what I'm doing here, not sure why I came here—something just called to me, and just like that, here I am.

As I walk through the familiar lobby, I think about the toad back at the roach motel and the woman I'm sharing a room with. I wish we were here together—this feels so much more like my home turf, like I might actually have a chance of getting on her good side in a place where I'm comfortable.

I walk through the hotel and out to the path I know leads to the beach, and I walk like I belong here. I *do* belong here.

I kick off my shoes and leave them on the sidewalk just before the beach. The sand is cool in the moonlight, and I make my way through the sugary softness down toward the water.

I stand with my feet in the water as I stare at the reflection of the moon. It shimmers as the waves roll in and out, and the soft lapping of water on my bare feet brings back a sense of calmness as I feel the anger start to dissipate.

Viv was upset we crossed some imaginary line she drew, and I suppose I can understand that. Tonight just felt like it brought us closer together, and I was expecting it to go somewhere. Instead, I find myself alone after I gave in to all the realizations I wanted to be with her tonight—and maybe beyond.

Maybe Mark knew what the hell he was doing when he sent her. I'm starting to think it wasn't just for the company. Of course he wants his brother to be happy, and what type of woman is more suited for me than someone as savvy—and sexy—as Viv?

I draw in a deep breath. I haven't been near the ocean in far too long. I love Vegas, but I'm landlocked in the desert there. I was born and raised in Chicago, which had awful beaches compared to this, but somehow sand and sun has always been a soothing balm to my soul.

My phone rings, the sound both shrill and unexpected in the stillness. I grab quickly for it for no other reason than to quiet the loud shriek breaking the quiet of night, and I'm shocked when I see Viv's name flash across my screen.

"Hey," I answer, my voice surprisingly warm.

"Where are you?" she asks.

I glance around as I wonder how she'll take my answer. "The beach," I finally admit.

"I was getting ready for bed and, um..." She takes a deep breath and then she blurts, "One of those huge toad thingies was in the shower."

I want to say *I told you so*! I want to say *that's why we don't stay at the roach motel*! I somehow manage to refrain when I hear her sniffle.

I think she's crying, and my chest tightens with concern. "Oh, shit. I'm sorry, Viv. What do you want to do?"

"I don't want to stay here. I called Mark and he's in the process of unfreezing your card. He approved wherever you choose for tonight."

A rush of relief filters through me.

"Our bags are still in the room and I'm not," she says. She says it in a way that tells me she's not going the fuck back in there with whatever the hell that mutant toad is.

"I'm already at the Ritz." I start walking up the sand back toward my shoes. "I'll head up and reserve a couple rooms and then come get you."

"You're at the Ritz?"

I clear my throat but don't answer. "I'll be back soon, okay?"

"Thank you, Brian." She says it with so much gratitude that I can't help but want to run over and hold her in my arms.

Wait.

Hold her in my arms?

That's new.

Fuck her, sure. Kiss her like we did on the pier again—of course.

But *hold her*?

That's the sort of relationship shit I've avoided since the day I found out my girlfriend was only with me because my brother was famous.

I trudge up to the reception desk as I wonder what the hell I'm getting myself into here. I ask for two rooms, and the clerk with a shiny gold nametag that says *Rebecca* on it shakes her head. "I'm afraid we're nearly at capacity tonight due to the textile convention. I don't have any of our regular rooms available, but I can offer a two-bedroom suite instead."

I think about it for all of a half a second before I agree. "That'll be fine." After the roach motel, we deserve some pampering. I hand over my license and the black card I kept in my wallet for old time's sake.

"Welcome back, Mr. Fox," Rebecca says as she taps the keys.

I give her a tight smile and a nod, and then my phone starts ringing again. I figure it's Viv calling me back to check where I am, but it's not. It's Tess.

I send the call to voicemail and get two room keys from Rebecca. I call for a driver since Mark's footing the bill, and when I'm comfortable in the back of a town car, I check my voicemail.

"We've got a problem." Tess's voice is urgent through the recording. "Call me as soon as you can."

I dial her back.

"Jason wants to get back together," she answers. "He wants something serious with me."

"So?" I'm confused here as to why this is a problem for *us*. Besides, I sort of already knew.

"So I'm fucking you!" She says it like the answer's obvious.

"Three times," I remind her.

"We just made plans to fuck some more this weekend!"

I school my voice to calmness. "Have you been drinking?"

"A little, but that's beside the point."

I chuckle. "It's exactly the point. Look on it tomorrow and it won't seem like that big a deal. Look, what we have is casual. If you want to get back with Jason, I won't stand in your way. In fact, we should probably just cancel our plans and keep what happened between the two of us." Sleeping with my best friend's ex wasn't the smartest move in the first place, and besides, the more time I spend around Viv, the more I think I want to try to pursue something with her.

"Three of us. Maybe four."

"Who else knows?"

"Reese. I told her. And she probably told Mark," Tess says. Each word is a little more frantic than the last. I don't mention Vivian also knows since she walked in on the two of us her first day at FDB.

"It's fine. Jason never has to know."

"God, I don't know what to do," she says. "Maybe I never wanted it to end with him in the first place, and now I've slept with his best friend."

"Is the guy you're casually screwing really the right person to discuss this with?" I ask. She's quiet in response, so I continue. "I won't tell anyone if you won't. If you want to be with Jason, be with him. Have fun. He could use the brand of excitement I know you can give him."

She lets out a long breath, and then she finally says, "Okay. Thanks, Brian."

My chest puffs with pride as I hang up. I feel a little like a superhero. I'm saving women left and right and I'm back on top of my game with unlimited spending at my disposal and the Ritz in my rearview.

When we pull into the Miami Airport Hotel, I immediately spot Viv. She's standing out front in slippers and apparently what she wears to bed—a white tank top and black shorts that are so short her ass cheeks are practically hanging out. Her hair is twisted up off her neck and her arms are crossed over her chest. I can vividly picture very hard nipples poking through the incredibly thin material of her shirt despite the way her arms are crossed.

I stare at her unabashedly from the back of the car as the driver puts it in park, and I leap out of the car as soon as it's safe.

I'll admit I like seeing her like this, but that doesn't mean I want the entire world to.

"Oh, thank God," she says, and I feel a rush of desire bolt through me as she drops her arms to her sides. Sure enough, her hard nipples are right there for me to stare at. My eyes flick down automatically, but I focus them purposefully back on her eyes.

"Is our shit still in the room?" I ask.

She nods. "I abandoned my toiletry bag in the bathroom."

"Would you like to get it or would you like me to?" I ask dryly.

She shakes her head. "You."

I nod. If I hadn't seen one of those same toads myself in my own room, I'd be rolling my eyes. But that fucker was huge and scary, and I'm not about to abandon Viv in her time of need. "I've got this."

"Thank you," she whispers.

My eyes flick down to her chest again and it's exactly the sustenance I need to get me through this task. "Now get your half-naked ass in the back of the car before I..." I trail off. Before I what?

What am I going to do? Take her right here in front of the hotel?

"You gonna finish that sentence?" she asks as she raises an eyebrow.

I grin at her before I turn to go into the hotel. "Use your imagination."

I stop at the front desk first. "We'll be expecting a full refund for both rooms," I announce. Some people standing in the lobby look over in my direction as they wonder what the issue is, so I don't beat around the bush. "The poisonous toads we found in two different rooms are disgusting and I'll never stay here again."

it started with a lie

The desk clerk mumbles an apology, I give him our room numbers, and then I head up to Viv's room to battle whatever mutants are in there so I can get our stuff.

twenty-two

"Did you see it?" she asks after I return to the car. Her eyes are wide with worry. "Was it bigger than the one in your room?"

I chuckle as I hand her my suit jacket—it's the only warm thing I have with me on this trip, and further, it's the only thing within reach that can provide some coverage for her.

"I didn't see it. Your screams must've scared it off." She narrows her eyes at me in a glare, and I laugh. We're both quiet for a beat as she wrestles into my jacket, and I finally glance away from her as I mutter, "I'd like to hear those screams."

She shakes her head as she rolls her eyes. "You have got to stop."

My jacket is big on her small frame. Her torso is entirely covered, but my eyes land on the curve of her neck for a beat as I wonder what it would feel like beneath my tongue. She gave me the sweetest preview earlier with that kiss, but I need more. I suddenly *crave* more with a voracious appetite I'm not sure how to control.

I sigh. "I feel like if you *really* wanted me to stop, you wouldn't be in the back of this car with me right now. You'd have figured out your own solution rather than calling me."

She's quiet, and I know it's because I've cornered her. She could've called the front desk to get her stuff, but she didn't. She called *me*. She wanted *me* to come save her. And here I am, her knight in shining armor, ready to battle the toad and get our bags and provide her with my jacket in the way only a real, true superhero can do.

I might be giving myself more credit than I deserve...but I need the confidence boost. She manages to knock me down another peg every time I'm around her. Being able to do something for her this time pushes me almost back to an even playing field.

Almost.

I have a feeling I'll never *really* be on an even playing field with her, but I haven't exactly figured out why just yet.

"Your bags were in there, too," she mutters. It's a weak defense and we both know it. She ran into a crisis and somehow she chose me to be her savior. If she hated me like she claims she does, she'd have ditched our room and my bags and gotten herself some new digs.

But she didn't.

I don't respond as that thought settles between us. When we get close to the Ritz, she digs through her bag and finally pulls out some clothes. "Turn toward the window," she says, and I wonder for the first time why she pulled my jacket on when she had her stuff inches from her feet.

I do what she says, and I watch the landscape as it passes us by. It's dark in the back of the car, yet a light from outside draws my attention to her silhouette in the reflection of the window.

She bumps into me as she wrestles out of her shorts to pull on her jeans. I catch a glimpse of panties—they're dark, and I can't tell the color or the pattern, but my dick hardens painfully as I imagine their soft silkiness beneath my hands as she's climbing on top of me.

I close my eyes for two reasons. She asked me to turn toward the window, and a dagger of guilt pierces my gut as I watch her when she asked me to turn away.

The very idea that I feel guilty watching her change tells me she's changed me already.

In the past, I wouldn't have cared. I'd have turned toward her in the middle of her changing and openly ogled her. I don't want to do that with Viv, though. I respect her privacy. I respect *her*, and I don't even know when the hell that happened.

But I also want to give into the image in my mind for a beat. I'm only snapped out of it when she says, "Okay, I'm decent."

I open my eyes and turn from the window, and she's wearing jeans and the same Raiders sweatshirt she wore on the plane earlier. She looks different—younger, more innocent, not quite as hard and proper as I'm used to seeing her, yet that image of her in that white tank top and tiny black shorts is seared into my mind.

"I liked the other outfit better," I admit.

She giggles as she hands me the suit jacket. "I didn't think it would be appropriate for waltzing through the Ritz."

"Neither's the Raiders sweatshirt."

She narrows her eyes at me, but before she can retort with some witty comeback about how great her team is, we pull in front of the hotel. It's late, and suddenly I'm exhausted. It's been a long day, and tomorrow won't be any better since we have an early morning, but at least I got my way.

"They didn't have two single rooms, but I got us a suite with two bedrooms since my brother's footing the bill," I say as I help her out of the back of the car. She opens her mouth to protest, but I cut her off. "It's one night and it won't even dent his checkbook. Trust me."

She closes her mouth and nods, and I feel like I've sort of won this particular round.

We make our way through the lobby and toward the elevators, leaving our bags with our driver, who will work with the bellhop to get our stuff to our room. This is the life I'm used to, and I enjoy the look of appreciation on her face at the opulence of the lobby—the stately mahogany columns are a far cry from the Miami Airport Hotel we just left.

We take a semi-private elevator to the eighteenth floor. I haven't stayed in this particular suite before, but I know this hotel and I know our room faces the ocean. I walk through the sitting area and open the doors leading to the balcony. The air is thick with salt and humidity, and I collapse into one of the chairs out there. I need a few minutes of listening to the waves lap at the shore to clear my mind—especially after that tank top and especially knowing she'll be wearing it just one bedroom away from my own tonight.

She slides into the chair beside me a few minutes later. "Our bags are here. I see why you like this place," she says.

I glance over at her with my lips tipped up, but I don't respond as I turn my attention back to the moon's reflection on the water again.

"I'm sorry, Brian."

Her voice is soft beside me, and I'm surprised at her words.

"For what?" I ask.

She blows out a breath, and I keep my focus ahead to allow her to get out what she's trying to say. "For choosing that hotel, for making this trip harder than it needed to be. Mark gave me free reign to choose any hotel I wanted, but I was trying to prove a point. I guess I was wrong."

I finally turn toward her as I allow my tone to soften. "You couldn't have known about the poisonous toads, Viv. I'm sure that hotel is fine to stay in and it was just a fluke."

She shrugs, and I notice she doesn't yell at me for calling her Viv. "I was sure it was fine, too."

"I get what you're trying to do...what you're here to do."

"Do you?" she asks, her voice full of genuine curiosity.

I nod. "Yeah. I need help. I've gotten myself into quite a mess, and I'm finally ready to admit you're the one who can straighten it all out."

I'm shocked at my own words. They tumbled out of me without censorship, but regardless of that fact, they're true. Maybe it's the whiskey from earlier getting me to speak the truth, or it could be the magic of the ocean air—or it could just be the woman sitting beside me. Maybe she makes me want to admit the secret truths I do my best to hide.

It's with that thought that I finally stand. I draw in one more deep breath of ocean air, and then I glance down at her. She stares straight ahead silently like she's shocked by the words I just spoke.

"I'm gonna call it a night," I say. "We've got an early morning with Porter. Meet me in the sitting room at six-thirty, okay?"

She nods and stares ahead at the water. "I'm gonna stay out here a few minutes longer," she says. I open the door to head back in, and just before I close it behind me, she says softly, "Goodnight, Brian."

I fight the urge to kiss her. I did it once tonight already, and I don't want to end the night on a note where she feels like we've done something wrong. Not after I just saved her.

"Night, Viv," I say, and I hear her annoyed chuckle just as I close the door.

twenty-three

Viv is tapping away on a laptop in the sitting room when I emerge the next morning a little after six. It's too goddamn early and I haven't even had a cup of coffee yet, but she's back to perfect in her professional little skirt and blazer combo. Her hair cascades around her shoulders again, and she reaches for the paper coffee cup beside her that tells me she's already left our room this morning.

I, on the other hand, haven't even showered yet. I wipe the sleep from my eyes. I didn't put on a shirt—just a pair of basketball shorts I packed—because I didn't think she'd be up and at 'em this early. I just came out here to make myself some coffee because I'm useless before I've had my first cup. I watch for a beat through bleary eyes as she pulls the cup to her lips, and I find myself jealous of a stupid coffee cup.

"Good morning," she says when she lowers the cup. She finally glances away from her screen and up at me, and I'm instantly grateful for the time I've spent on sit-ups recently. A small gasp falls from her lips as her eyes land on my half-naked form and the abdomen I've given up pizza and French fries for.

I strut over to the coffeepot on the counter to set myself up, acting like I don't feel her eyes on my backside as I walk past her. "What are you doing up already?" I ask once I've poured the water in.

She clears her throat. "I, um, always get up early. I went for a run on the beach and grabbed myself a coffee."

"Sleep okay?" I ask. I look over at her, and I have to look away before I do something she'll regret later.

She shrugs. "The bed was comfy."

"That's not an answer." I walk over toward her and sit on the couch across from her while I wait for my coffee.

She glances away from me and back at her screen then clears her throat. "I haven't been sleeping well recently."

"Sorry to hear that. As soon as my head hit the pillow, I was out." If I would've known she was having trouble sleeping, I could've helped. I could've massaged her shoulders or fucked her into relaxation or simply held her in my arms before she dozed off.

I don't say any of that, obviously. Instead, I just sit with arrogance on the couch across from her as she presses her lips into a tight smile and keeps her gaze fixed on whatever she's working on. I wonder briefly why she had trouble sleeping. Did it have anything to do with me? I've read that anxiety can cause insomnia. Am I stressing her out? If I am, I need to work harder on changing that, especially after the way we unexpectedly connected last night.

"Have you considered bringing the work you're subcontracting to Germany in-house?" she asks.

"I thought about that just yesterday," I say. The coffeepot beeps, signaling that my salvation is ready. I stand and pour in some sugar and a packet of powder cream. It's not the most appetizing thing in the world, but beggars can't be choosers and right now I'm desperate for coffee. "I didn't think I had enough time to touch base with my partners to ensure it's a good fit."

"You made time to drink at a bar with your friend and kiss me on a pier," she says, and my head whips toward hers in surprise as my brows furrow.

She looks shocked that she said the words. Her hand flies up to her neck in some attempt to disguise the red embarrassment creeping out of the cleavage of her blouse. "I'm sorry," she says. "I just mean if it's important enough, you'll make time. And this is important enough." She's rambling to cover up her embarrassment. "I've run the numbers on it and if you can get someone permanently on staff, it'll actually be a huge cost savings even with benefits and salary. You could hire an entire team for what you're paying Schneider."

I clear my throat and try to hide my smile behind my coffee cup. She's feisty, and I like it. I like it so much, in fact, that I'm not really sure the thin fabric of my basketball shorts is hiding my total infatuation with this girl. "I know. I've run the numbers, too, and I don't disagree with you. We haven't had the resources to pull what they do in-house, but I think we're there now. The problem is that Becker's on his honeymoon and who the hell knows what Jason's up to while I'm here in Miami. I didn't have a big enough window to work this out earlier."

"Can you do a shorter-term contract so you can work out the details?" she asks.

I take a long sip of coffee and give a little *ahh* as the hot liquid burns down my chest to awaken my senses. "I can offer a one-month extension to their current contract, but I don't think that's something Porter would be interested in and I don't want Schneider to know I'm considering pulling my business from them. I can't afford a half-assed product from someone who knows their time is limited with me."

She nods and gazes thoughtfully out the window. Her lips twist as she obviously concentrates on working out details in her mind, and it's too early for me to be having a business conversation. It's not just my first cup of coffee; I haven't even showered yet. I need a burst of cold water to calm down the boy in my pants and help snap me awake.

"What if you email Becker and Jason and find out if they'd be on board? Maybe they'll get back to you before we get to the meeting."

"Jason's three hours behind us, so it's three in the morning back home." That also explains why I feel so tired. Well, that and the fact that we were up far too late last night. "And I have no idea where Becker is, but we were given strict instructions not to bother him on his honeymoon."

"Try anyway. It's important."

I shake my head. "It's fine, Viv. We'll work out the terms and pull from Schneider next year."

She gives me a look like that's just not good enough, and she's probably right. I'm not in a position to throw money away right now, and if bringing more work to FDB is part of the solution, I need to figure out how to accomplish that. "What if you just can't come to an agreement today?" she suggests.

"That's not really my style. Don't worry, Viv. I'll think of something." I finish my first cup of coffee and get another one brewing, and then I head toward my shower.

* * *

I'm off my game during the meeting with Porter, mostly because fucking Vivian is completely distracting me. She sits in the corner taking notes like she's my secretary, but she's not. She's my boss, and it's not just that.

She's this powerful woman who creates all these conflicting feelings in me. I want to fuck her and I want to kick her out of the room. I want to impress her but I don't care what she thinks of me. I want to be her savior at the same time I want to let her fend for herself.

I don't understand what's happening to me, but when she's in the room, she becomes the center of my attention. With every deal I try to make, I glance her way to gauge her reaction. With every business tactic I try, I look her way for her nod of approval. With every joke I tell, I check to see if she's laughing.

It's just a crush. I'm attracted to her. Of course I am—why wouldn't I be? She isn't just delicate and kind and beautiful. She's different than the women I typically bed. She's smart and savvy, and she can hold her own with me. She doesn't just agree with everything I say to impress me. In fact, it sort of feels like the opposite half the time.

Plus there's the rejection side. She let me kiss her last night, but then she told me it was a mistake.

I always want what I can't have. It's why I slithered my way in front of the woman my brother eventually married and got her into my bed before she knew I was related to the god of rock, Mr. Mark Ashton. It's why I manipulate and lie, and it's why I work my ass off to make the things I'm not supposed to have mine anyway.

I just need to figure out how to do that with Vivian Davenport.

"With the short notice on renewal, Mr. Porter, I need to discuss the terms with my partners and get back to you," I say. "I'm suggesting a one-week extension on the terms of our deal with Schneider. I'll come back to sign a brand new contract next week. I think you'll be pleased with our newest offer. What I have in mind will be lucrative for everyone."

Viv shakes her head at me like it's a bad idea to plan a return trip to Miami, but fuck it. If I can get her back to the beach—and for more than a single night next time—I'll get her in my bed, and that's a promise I'm making to myself. We'll walk the pier, look at the boats, and I'll kiss her again.

I can't believe my motivation behind my current business deal is based on how to bed the girl, yet there it is.

Paul sighs. "Fine, Mr. Fox. I'm not entirely thrilled with the idea, but I understand the need to discuss the renegotiation with your partners."

"I'll be honest with you. I didn't expect Schneider's rates to skyrocket this quarter, and it'll take some convincing on my part to ensure my partners are still on board." I'm bullshitting now. It's probably wrong to begin a sentence with *I'll be honest with you* when the words that follow are anything but honest...but I need to buy a week to figure out how to bring the work a company in another country is so adept at doing back home into our offices. I need to make sure it's something we can even logistically do, that it isn't just a good idea but something we can actually put into action.

Paul stands. "We'll see you in a week, then," he says, and he reaches out his hand to shake mine. I stand, too, and then we bid our goodbyes and leave.

The entire meeting took fifteen total minutes.

It was a complete waste of time, money, and resources to travel across the country for that, yet I can't help but feel like the whole trip advanced my relationship with Vivian.

I can't help but think she doesn't hate me anymore after getting to know each other just a little more—and especially not after that kiss last night.

twenty-four

The flight home is sort of like the flight there, but with one major difference.

Viv sleeps on my shoulder after pounding her drugs while I try to get some work done as I keep my arm as still as possible—just like the flight out. As I review my notes for tomorrow's presentation, though, I realize what the difference is.

She doesn't hate me.

She didn't admit it, per se, but the way her eyes fall upon me tell me a different story than they did when we boarded the plane from Vegas to Miami. Now that we're headed back to Vegas, my mind wanders to what will change.

Not to *whether* things will change, because I know they will.

I feel differently about her now than I did yesterday. It seems like a lifetime ago when I hated her just like she hated me, when we were forced to work together because of my brother. As I think toward what it'll be like sharing an office with her, a sense of anticipation darts through me rather than dread.

Now I just have to figure out how to make *her* see that things are different, too.

I'm not sure the next time she'll allow me to be so close to her, so I close my eyes, turn my head in her direction, and breathe her in as we start our final descent. I memorize her rose scent as I tuck it away for later. I think about the kiss we shared last night, and I give into five short minutes of a strange type of relaxation I don't know I've ever felt in my life.

Once we land, the tranquil spell is broken. I shake her awake, and her blue eyes are sleepy when they come into focus on me. She runs an embarrassed hand over her hair and tucks some behind her ear.

"Sorry," she mutters. She runs her fingertips under her eyes to catch any stray make-up, but she's perfect. She's always been perfect, I think, but I'd been too blinded by anger at my brother to notice.

"For what?" I ask, looking away from her and focusing on putting my tablet back into the laptop bag.

"Using your shoulder as a pillow again."

I finish what I'm doing and pull the bag onto my lap, and then I finally look over at her. "Best five hours I've spent in a while," I say softly.

Her brows draw in as if she's some mix of surprised and confused by my words, but we don't have time to analyze them because the door opens and people start making their way for the exit.

We both carried our bags on, so once we're off the plane and near the terminal, I ask, "Do you need a ride back to your hotel?" *Or to my place?*

"I was just gonna grab an Uber," she says, avoiding eye contact.

"I really don't mind." *It'll give me a few extra minutes with you.*

"If you're sure," she says.

I nod and we walk together toward my car. I count this as a major victory because if she really did still hate me, she would've opted for the Uber.

But she didn't. She opted for the leather passenger seat of my Mercedes, and after I toss our bags in the trunk, I open the door for her. She slides in, and I wonder if my car will forever smell of roses. I gaze at the beauty in my front seat just long enough to keep us both comfortable. As I walk around the car to my own seat, a feeling that's completely foreign washes over me.

I've never lacked self-confidence, but that's what this is. I'm unsure and doubtful of my next move, and that's territory I've never navigated. I always know what to do when it comes to women. It might not always be the smartest choice or the most honorable way to go, but I do what needs to be done.

With her, though, it's different. We're already faking a relationship. Why can't it turn into something more?

Viv tries to hand me money for the parking attendant, but I wave her off without a word as I pull my wallet out of my pocket. I may be short on cash, but I remember with joy that my black card is all thawed out.

As I hand over the card to the attendant, I realize the only roadblock standing in our way of giving this a try is her little thing about not wanting to cross the professional line, but surely I'll come up with something to combat that. We're only working together for ninety days, anyway, and we're already a few weeks in. If I have to wait for her, then so be it.

Wait a minute.

Wait for her?

I'm willing to *wait for her?*

The thought crosses into my mind so naturally it momentarily floors me when I realize it.

"You're quiet," Viv says once we're out of the parking lot and on the back roads toward her hotel. It's a Thursday night, a popular night for people to arrive in town for their What-Happens-in-Vegas-Stays-in-Vegas getaway from reality, so traffic's heavy.

I pretend like that's what has me distracted since I can't exactly admit I'm thinking about her. And it's not just getting her into my bed anymore. There's something else there, something in my chest that tingles in an unexpected way, something unfamiliar and, if I'm being truly honest with myself, it's more than just a little terrifying.

"Sorry," I say. "Just paying attention to traffic."

I feel her eyes on me, but I don't look over at her. It's not that I think she'll be able to read my feelings on my face—I've perfected the mask and the act so women never *really* know what I'm thinking, but I know making eye contact with her in this moment might be dangerous. It might make me blurt something out she's not ready to hear.

Or maybe it'll lead me right to her bed—the exact place I want to be tonight.

I pull up to the Westin, all the while debating whether I should park the car and walk her up or just let her out. Before our trip to Miami, I would've just let her out. But now...things have changed. I don't want her to see me as a jerk. So with that thought in mind, I pull up in front of the lobby and drop her off.

"Wait!" she yells as I pull away. I'm sure she's trying to stop me from driving off with her bag, but I pull into an open parking space, grab her bag out of the trunk, and meet her by the doors.

"I thought you were taking off with my suitcase," she says, laughing.

I shake my head and give her a wry smile. "I suppose ditching you at the AceStar gala might've given you the impression I'm much more of a dick than I actually am."

She raises a brow, but her eyes twinkle. "Might've?"

I lift a shoulder. "I'm sorry. I acted like an epic douche that night, and you deserved a better date. Can I make it up to you?"

She narrows her eyes at me and spins on her heel. I follow behind with her suitcase.

"How?" she asks.

"There's a charity ball next Friday."

She stops at the reception desk. "Checking back in," she says to the clerk, and then she turns toward me. "Yeah?"

"Go with me."

She blows out a breath. "I don't know, Brian," she says.

"Come on. It'll be fun, and besides, you know the deal with Jason."

She looks me over, and before she can answer, the clerk interrupts us. "I've got you in the same room, Ms. Davenport."

I glance over at him, and he gives me a grin. The asshole knows I'm waiting for her answer.

"That'll be perfect," she says to him. He taps some more keys, and she looks at me. "It's not the fact that you ditched me, Brian. I don't care. It's your life and your business, and if you think leaving with that woman was a good idea for you personally or professionally, then that's on you. What bothered me was how you treated me before that. Like I'm less worthy than the dirt on your shoes, because at least the dirt is on *your* shoes."

"Here you are, Ms. Davenport." The clerk hands her a key and a booklet and shoots me another sly smile. I want to punch it off his smug face, and I'm not enjoying the fact that he's overhearing this private conversation. "Enjoy your stay."

"Thanks," she says, and she turns toward the elevators. "I can take my bag from here," she says. She moves to grab it from my hands, but I pull it back.

"Let me take it up for you," I say.

She rolls her eyes. "Fine."

We step onto the elevator, and the tension feels thick. Thoughts of my lips moving over hers as we stood on a pier less than twenty-four hours ago attack my memory.

I stare straight ahead, but I allow myself a tiny glance of her in the mirrored doors of the elevator.

She's looking at me. My eyes catch hers, and neither of us looks away until the elevator lands on her floor and the doors slide open.

It was just one simple lock of our eyes, but it told me everything I need to know.

She wants me, too, but something's stopping her. I just have to figure out if it's the professional relationship thing or something more.

"Let me think about the ball," she says once we're stopped in front of her hotel door. She slides the key in and avoids eye contact with me as she says it.

"Okay," I say, and that's when I know for sure tonight's not our night. If I want to get onto her good side, part of that will include treating her the way she deserves to be treated and respecting her wishes.

Once we're in the room, I set her suitcase on the dresser for her. I glance at the bed as every thought about what I want to do there with her flashes through my mind, but I quickly avert my eyes back to Viv. "See you tomorrow," I say.

She presses her lips together and nods, and then I see myself out.

twenty-five

Friday morning comes too quickly.

After I left Viv's hotel and came home, I went over my presentation for today a hundred more times, making sure everything's perfect. I present at nine, and between getting home late, unpacking, and prepping, I'm running on caffeine, two hours of sleep, and the hope that Viv decides to come with me to the ball next weekend so we can turn our fake relationship into a real one.

I get to the office at six. The presentation is at the convention center just a few blocks away, but after being out of the office half the day Wednesday and all day yesterday, I can't afford another minute away. There's too much at stake here—and impressing Viv by working hard to get FDB's finances back on track is certainly not the least of it.

The presentation is ready, but I need to keep myself busy for the next two hours before I head over to the convention center. On the plane yesterday, I put together a proposal for Becker and Jason with my idea to bring the Germany work in-house, so I send that email off. I catch up on other correspondence and clear half the paperwork off my desk, and at seven-thirty, a gorgeous woman walks into my office looking refreshed and ready for the day ahead.

"Good morning, Vivian," I say.

Her lips tip up in a small smile of victory, likely because I used her full name this time and didn't need the reminder. "Good morning, Brian. Did you sleep well last night?"

I laugh. "For about two hours. You?"

"Two hours? Why?"

I shrug and shuffle some papers around. "I had work to do."

"Workaholic," she mutters.

"You're the one prancing in at seven-thirty," I say.

"Yeah, and you're the one who's probably already been here at least an hour."

I grin. She's got me pegged. "You give any thought to the charity ball next weekend?" I ask.

She nods, and just when she opens her mouth to respond, Jason walks by my office door. He stops and leans on the doorframe. The laptop bag on his shoulder indicates he just got in. "How was Miami?"

"I postponed signing the contract. I sent you a proposal this morning for bringing the Schneider work in-house."

Jason raises an eyebrow as he looks up at the ceiling in thought. "I have two or three guys I think would be able to head that up." He thinks another few beats. "We'd need at least three minimum, I think. One to head it up and two support. Where are we at on hiring?"

"Frozen," Viv says.

I glance over at her with a glare, and her eyes widen as she realizes her mistake.

"Sorry, that's what Brian was talking about a little while ago." Her attempt at a cover is weak, but Jason buys it.

"For how long?" Jason asks, looking at me.

I shake my head. "It's not frozen. Ignore her. If you need to hire three new guys, let's get a panel together for interviews.

it started with a lie

I need the team assembled before I try to talk Porter out of Schneider next week."

"You have time today for interviews?" he asks.

I shake my head. "I've got Vegas Con today." I glance at my calendar. "I can do this weekend or Monday, though. Porter wants me back within a week to sign off on our new deal. I didn't mention bringing the work here."

"You hear from Beck on it?"

I shake my head. "Doesn't matter," I remind him...even though it *does* matter.

We wrote a policy into our bylaws that if forty percent of the stakeholders vote on something, it passes. It can only be blocked by a fifty-one percent vote. If I had my twenty percent stake, which I don't, I wouldn't need Mark *or* Beck on board for our final decision.

But I don't have my twenty percent, so I need to figure this out. I'll email Beck one more time.

Maybe Jason deserves to know the two of us can't make these big decisions together anymore, but it's my stubborn right to keep it to myself. I remind myself I'm working on it, and he doesn't need to worry about it. The justification is weak in my own mind, but I brush it off as I glance at Viv.

She shakes her head. She's Mark's proxy, as she's reminded me numerous times, and she's saying no, he wouldn't be on board with this decision. Instead of listening to her, though, I say, "We've got it covered."

Her jaw opens a little at my clear defiance. I'm supposed to be turning over a new leaf, but she's supposed to be pretending like everything's fine. If she can fuck things up for me, I can do the same right back to her.

As soon as Jason's out of sight, she glares at me. "What was that?"

"A chat between co-presidents."

She stands up and strides over to the other side of my desk, and my eyes take in the full view of a woman in a black dress on a mission. "I'll tell you right now you don't have the money to hire three new employees. Even if you get a wave of cash at the start of the month, you still won't have enough in the bank. What are you doing?" She's hissing at me, and it's hot.

"I've got a beautiful woman here to help me figure it out." She rolls her eyes at my words. "Look, Viv, we're saving money if we cut ties with the third party out of the country. We'll get the work in-house, and it'll take a few months to balance, but we'll get there."

She thinks about it for a minute—really thinks this time, and then she finally says, "Fine. But you're just making this harder on me."

"That's why you're getting paid the big bucks."

Jason's head pops into my doorway again, and I wonder how much he might've overheard. From the look on his face, I'd guess none of it, but I need to be more careful about closing my door when Viv and I have these chats.

"Hey, you going to the Delnore Charity Ball next weekend?" Jason asks just as I take a sip of coffee. "I asked Tess to come with me, and she's in."

Tess, right. The girl who called me in a panic last night because Jason wanted to get back together...the girl I completely forgot about as all thoughts of Viv began to invade my every waking thought—and even my sleeping ones, if you count the sex dream I had about her last night during my brief window of sleep.

I manage to hold myself together. "Yeah, we'll be there," I say absently, and I hear Viv's sharp intake of breath at my words. I keep my eyes trained on Jason even though I feel the daggers she's shooting at me from across the room. "And we can't wait." I shift my eyes over to her. "Right, Viv?"

"We're just so excited," she grits out between a locked jaw and a glare in my direction.

"Great. See you there. Knock 'em dead on the presentation this morning, all right?" Jason says, and I nod.

As soon as he's out of sight, my grin at Viv is met with a glare.

"That was rude," she says.

"Admit it. You were gonna say yes. I just made it easier for you."

She rolls her eyes and averts her attention to her laptop screen, but I don't miss the tiny tip of her lips upward even though she tries to hide it.

* * *

I'm tackling the most intricate part of my speech during my presentation, the one I had to go over a few extra times to ensure I had the numbers correct, when she walks in.

And just like that, I'm not in front of four or five hundred business men and women. It's just Viv and me in the room now, and when her eyes find mine after she slides stealthily into a chair in the back of the room, I catch a glimpse of guilt despite the distance between us. I'm not sure if it's because she's late or if it's something else, but it does have the effect of shorting out my brain for a few beats.

I pause as I collect my thoughts, and then I steal a glance at the slide behind me to try to get back on track. I have to pretend she isn't here. I have to get through this.

I have to really sell our company today. If I can't do my job and we don't acquire some new blood, we run the risk of bankruptcy.

It's with that thought in mind I draw in a deep breath and pull myself together.

"As you can see from the data on this slide, our predictive models can help you attract and retain your most profitable consumers. FDB is committed to seeing your business grow."

I continue with my presentation, and when I'm done, I know I knocked it out of the park. A long line of people forms beside the stage as individuals have personal questions related to their own companies, and I stay behind to answer all of them. This is where I make the hard sell. These are warm leads, people who are already interested, so now I just have to give them a little bit of my attention and make them feel like they'll fit in with the FDB family.

I can't help it when my eyes keep edging over to Viv, but I do my best to focus on the people in front of me.

I'm talking to the fifth or sixth person in line when I glance at Viv again, and her gaze is intent on me.

Fuck it.

I wave her over. She's studied the hell out of my business over the past couple weeks, and I have the sudden need to have her by my side, to have her help answer questions and give her own hard sell to get these people interested enough to sign a contract with us. Maybe she doesn't care about my company, but she's getting paid handsomely to get us above water, and this is all part of it.

"This is Vivian Davenport, my colleague," I say to some guy whose name I've already forgotten. "She'd be happy to answer your questions."

Vivian looks surprised for a beat, but then she dives in. "Nice to meet you, Mr..."

She trails off, and I stare at her. Those perfect brown locks flow gently around her shoulders. She's all business, yet my dick hardens with an ache I need her to soothe as I stare at her.

"Woodley," the potential client fills in for her.

"Mr. Woodley," she says, flashing him a smile. Her face lights up with the smile, and I realize how little I've seen of it. I'm used to the lemon-puckered face of disapproval from her, so the smile completely throws me off balance. "What can I answer for you today?"

I force my gaze away from her once I see she's going to be okay and I focus on the next potential client in line. "Brian Fox," I say, holding out my hand.

"Dave Shaw from Booth Graphics," he says, and then he launches into questions about what my company can do for him. I focus all my attention on him and on our conversation, and by the time he leaves, I've practically got his contract drafted.

As the seemingly never-ending line starts to dwindle and more and more of these potential clients turn into probable clients, I realize I'm going to have a shitload of work to do this weekend.

I just hope a certain foxy brunette will want to hang around to help me get my work done, and if she does, I hope she's not just another distraction.

twenty-six

I gained at least thirty new contacts from the presentation, and my first order of business is organizing them by priority level when I get back to the office.

"Lauren, I need you to run a profile on each of these companies," I say, handing her the stack of business cards I collected. "And I need it as soon as possible." I glance at the clock. It's a little after one—plenty of time to get it done before quitting time at five. And if not, then she'll just have to stay late to finish. I hate to be a dick on a Friday afternoon with short notice, but I don't have time to waste with these qualified leads.

"Yes, sir," she says, and she sets to work as I head into my office.

I'm on the phone ordering a late lunch to be delivered when Viv walks into the office.

"Did you eat lunch?" I ask. She shakes her head, and I say into the phone, "Make that two."

"You didn't have to do that," she says when I hang up.

"I don't mind. It goes on my tab, and apparently my black card is unlocked again."

She shakes her head at me. "I see you never learn."

I shrug. "I'm still not over the roach motel," I say dryly. "Guess Mark will be paying for that a long time."

"That was my fault. He didn't say we had to go that frugal."

"But you're his proxy," I say, mimicking her tone as I glance through some of the notes I took during my one-on-one client conversations. She laughs, which I'm grateful to hear. I never know if she's going to take my teasing to heart or not.

"I am, and I have to say, Brian, it was amazing to watch you work that room this morning."

I glance up at her in surprise. "Thank you." I feel a little embarrassed, and I'm not sure why. Humility isn't really my strong suit.

"The presentation was impressive, the way you commanded that room. But it was the attention you gave each potential client afterward that showed me what a truly great businessman you are. Your communication skills, your confidence, your leadership—these are things that seem to run in the Fox family."

"You know my brother that well?" I ask.

She lifts a shoulder. "I was on the ground level of Ashmark when it launched," she says, referring to my brother's record label.

"I had no idea."

"I typically don't share client information, but Mark encouraged me to share that with you."

I've seen the fruits of my brother's company. It's a hugely successful label, and part of me wonders why she didn't tell me she helped him launch it. I might've given her more credence from the start rather than making her prove herself.

Or I might've seen her as just another one of my brother's groupies.

It's probably wise she waited to tell me until she earned my trust.

I clear my throat. "I have a confession."

She raises a brow as if to tell me to have at it.

"When you walked into that room, for a moment you were the only one in there."

it started with a lie

Her cheeks redden almost immediately, but it's not my intention to make her feel insecure.

"You've got my attention, Viv."

She shakes her head and averts her gaze to some papers on her desk. "Stop," she says unconvincingly. I do stop, though, because last night it was my vow to respect her wishes.

I'll take every opportunity I can, though, to let her know I want more than just a professional relationship with her.

* * *

While Lauren researches companies, I set to work on creating contracts for the companies I touched base with, and I have Viv work on the contracts for the ones she contacted. By the time five o'clock rolls around, Lauren's only about two-thirds of the way through the list of cards.

I'll be working all weekend anyway. I can take care of the rest. "Have a good weekend, Lauren," I say, and then she heads out.

"You want me to take half?" Vivian asks.

"You don't mind?"

She shakes her head. "I'll be going back to an empty hotel room. I'd rather stay and work."

I would, too, especially since she'll be here. Before I think of some witty response along those lines, Jason pops into the office.

"How'd the Con go?" he asks.

"Great," I say, nodding toward my computer. "I'd bet on twenty-five new contracts in the upcoming weeks."

"Twenty-five?" he asks, surprise evident in his voice.

I nod. We typically sign two or three per week, so this will be a much greater increase.

"Do we have the manpower for that?" He glances over at Viv and crinkles an eyebrow when he looks back at me.

"We'll take it as it comes. We may need new members on our support team. Viv here volunteered to help me sort through the contacts. Wasn't that nice?"

His brows draw down as he glances at Viv again. "What did you say you do again?"

Viv glances up at me. "I own a small consulting business," she says. I can't remember if she ever told him what she does.

"What sort of consulting?" he asks, suddenly interested.

"Mostly small business strategies, that sort of thing." She lies so smoothly I can't help but think she rehearsed it just in case.

"Is having our client list a conflict of interest?" he asks.

"Jason, stop," I say. "We can trust her."

He holds up both hands in surrender. "I didn't mean anything by it. Just making sure our work is protected."

It's protected because she's the one protecting it. I fail to mention this to my partner, though.

"It is," I say thinly. "Where are you off to tonight?"

"Tess and I are going to dinner and a movie."

A dart of dread passes through me as I realize I was supposed to have plans with Tess tonight. I never followed up with her after her frantic phone call two nights ago—I've been too busy between today's conference and thinking about Vivian.

"You kids have fun," I say, and Jason laughs as he heads out.

As soon as he's out, I text Tess that our plans are off. Permanently.

I just need to get FDB out of the red. Once we're back in black, my time with Viv will be done, our fake relationship will be over, she'll go back to Los Angeles, and I can stop lying to my friends.

I'm just not sure why the thought of her leaving has me feeling more than a little disappointed.

twenty-seven

I waltz into the office late Saturday morning. I actually have a glorious home office, but I like the idea of being in the place where Viv is during the week. I like the idea of sitting at my desk and wishing she was here with me.

Imagine my surprise when I find the object of my thoughts herself sitting at her desk and tapping away on her computer when I walk in.

"What are you doing here?" I ask.

She jumps in her chair, startled, and her hand flies to her chest. "Oh my God, you scared me!"

"I'm sorry," I say, watching as the blush creeps up into her neck and onto her cheeks. "I didn't mean to."

She sucks in a deep breath. "I wanted to finish the client profiles we didn't get to last night."

I glance at her desk. Neat rows of file folders sit there, and I wonder how long she's been here.

She hands me the first stack. "These are the highest priority level."

"You didn't have to do that," I say, taking the folder from her. Our fingers accidentally brush in the process, and a little thrill darts through me.

"I've told you, Brian. I'm here to help. Besides, I couldn't sleep and I wanted to sort this stuff out."

"Why couldn't you sleep?" I ask as I head over to my desk.

She doesn't answer as she resumes her tapping. "Let's just get through these, okay?"

I nod and take a look through the first folder. The information there is organized and exactly what I need to write up a proposal for the company. I set to work and send it off a few minutes later. At this rate, work that would usually take me at least a week to get through should be done by this evening, and it's all because of whatever system Viv has in place.

And I hate that it makes me even more attracted to her.

It's time for a plan, and last night I came up with the perfect one as I thought about her.

I'll catch her interest as we work together. I'll focus on getting to know her and making her feel how much things have changed for me. I'll let her know I'm interested just in case I haven't made that clear yet.

I'll get her back to Miami with me next week, but I won't try anything. Except maybe another kiss. I need another kiss.

I crave another kiss.

But when I get her back here and we head to the charity event together?

It's on.

"This is incredible, Vivian," I say as I hold up the folder. "So thorough."

"They don't call me *The Fixer* for nothing," she says, waving a flippant hand in the air.

I chuckle. "I never thought I'd say this, but I'm glad my brother hired you." I blow out a breath as I allow my vulnerability to show—something I rarely, if ever, do. The only recent times that come to mind when I've allowed this side of myself through, it was all an act, part of a manipulation. This, though, is real.

it started with a lie

When she glances up and her eyes meet mine already laser-focused on her, hers are wide with surprise. "You are?" she asks.

I just press my lips together in a tight smile and return my gaze to the papers in my hand.

We work in comfortable silence for a while, Viv sorting through the company profiles as I email the contacts I made with personalized documents showing what FDB can do for them. Some companies receive immediate proposals from me based on the conversations I had with them at the conference while I draft others and save them to send after I get their replies.

My phone interrupts our rhythm with its loud notification.

Jason: *Did you hear back from Beck on bringing the Schneider models in-house?*

Since I got an email from Becker letting me know he's on board, I'm confident in my next text.

Me: *It's a go.*

Jason: *Can you run interviews today?*

Me: *I'm already at the office.*

Jason: *Great. I'll meet you there. I have three prospects and all are interested in talking today.*

Me: *Let's do this.*

"Jason set up some interviews today for the design team to move the Germany work here," I say to Vivian. I feel like she should know what's going on.

She nods. "I see the long-term potential of hiring someone to head it up, so I will approve one new hire."

"Jason said we'll need at least three," I remind her. "One to lead the team and two support staff."

"You don't have the budget for three."

I clear my throat. After the nice morning we've had, I don't want to ruin it by being an asshole, but I need to make my point. "Make it work." My voice is direct and firm, but apparently I'm no match for her.

"I can't pull money out of thin air, Brian. I'm telling you that you don't have the budget. Move current staff into support roles. I can approve small wage increases, but the salary and benefits of a new hire are out of the question until I see these huge payments you supposedly have coming in."

I blow out a frustrated sigh then grit my teeth together. "What am I supposed to tell Jason?"

She shrugs and gives me a pointed glance. "The truth?"

The heat of anger creeps up my neck, and just when I'm about to say something nasty, I stop myself.

God, I want to fuck her.

I don't reply. I let her think I'm backing down, but I'm not. She can use words like *approval* and *budget* all she wants, but I'm still going to do what I'm going to do. It's her job to figure out how to pay for it.

I turn on the radio behind my desk and tune it to my favorite station. A Vail song happens to be on, and when I glance up at Viv, I notice her bobbing her head absentmindedly in time with the words my brother sings. She looks more carefree than I've ever seen her even though she's deep in concentration as she gazes at her laptop screen.

Her eyes edge over to mine after I've been staring at her for a full thirty seconds.

"What?" she asks. She runs a self-conscious hand over her hair.

I shake my head as my lips tip up with a smile. "Nothing."

She narrows her eyes at me. "What?" she repeats.

"Are you a Vail fan?"

She lifts a shoulder. "Isn't everyone?"

I roll my eyes because it's the same thing I always hear. "I guess."

it started with a lie

"This song is just so catchy."

She's not wrong, but it does throw up a major red flag. Wanting someone who's a fan of my brother is never a good idea given my history, but it's nearly impossible to find someone who doesn't like Vail, which means it's nearly impossible to find someone who might actually like me for me.

Not that Viv likes me. In fact, I distinctly remember her telling me she *hates* me.

"Are you close with your brother?" she asks quietly.

I think back to our quiet conversation about her siblings on the pier that ended with me kissing her. "We're some combination of best friends and total enemies."

"Sibling rivalry?"

I huff out a chuckle. "Something like that. Why do you ask?"

"Just curious." She's quiet for a beat, and then she adds, "You just don't seem to care about spending his money."

"I don't."

She looks surprised by my admission, so I feel the need to explain myself.

"When Vail's first album went platinum, he took care of my parents. He paid off all their debt—including their mortgage and our college loans they said they'd take care of. When he booked his first headlining tour, he took care of Lizzie and me. He sat us down and told us if we ever needed anything financially to just let him know. I took him at his word. He was fully supportive of Jason, Becker, and me leaving our old company in Chicago to start up FDB, and he told me he'd continue to finance us as long as he could come on as a silent partner. So that's what he did, but now he's cutting us off."

"Because you're blowing through his money and asking him for more." She has a point. "How many times have you done that since you opened your doors?"

"Asked Mark for money?"

She nods, and I shrug.

"A handful of times."

She folds her hands in front of her, showing me she's fully vested in our conversation now. "So he gave you startup capital, you cut the ribbon, and in three years you've asked him for additional money somewhere around five times?"

It sounds pretty bad when she says it that way. Before I have a chance to answer, she says, "No bank would approve those loans, and I don't blame Mark for drawing a line in the sand. There's a big difference between spending responsibly and spending—" She cuts her sentence short when Jason appears in my doorway.

"Hey guys," he says. He glances at Viv before he looks at me. He gives me some sort of meaningful look, but the actual meaning is lost on me. "The first interview is in thirty minutes. Can we go over the questions beforehand?"

I nod. "Give me a couple minutes to wrap up what I'm working on and I'll be right in."

His eyes edge over to Vivian again before he looks back at me. His brow furrows. "I'll be in my office."

I nod, finish drafting the email I was working on before Viv asked me whether I'm close with Mark, and try to think of something witty to say to Vivian. I come up short.

"I really should be in on these interviews," she says. "But for your sake, I'll sit out. Just please consider only hiring one new employee. I'll help you figure out how to move people internally if that'll change your mind." Her voice has an edge of desperation, and I realize the situation I've gotten FDB into is more dire than even I've allowed myself to admit.

twenty-eight

"I thought for sure she'd be tailing you in here," he says once I shut the door behind me and slide into one of the chairs across from his desk.

I lift a shoulder. "We've gotten close."

"That's great, Brian. I'm happy you've found someone. Just be careful, okay?"

I narrow my eyes at him. "What do you mean?"

He shakes his head. "It's nothing."

"Tell me."

He blows out a breath and focuses his gaze out the window. "It just seems like she's always here."

She is. That's why it seems that way. I don't say anything.

"And the other day when I walked in and you weren't there, it looked like she was studying FDB financial reports."

Fuck. The lie comes out of my mouth before I can stop it. "I gave her those. She has experience in finance and we were talking about how to maximize profits."

"Do we need those suggestions from someone not on our payroll?"

More than I can even say, apparently. "Every extra cent helps, don't you think?"

"Whatever, man." He shakes his head. "I hate to tell you this since clearly you're in love with her, but I just don't like it."

"Clearly I'm *in love* with her?" I'm not *in love* with her. I barely even know her. I'm attracted to her, and I want to sink my dick into her all the way down to my balls, and I think about her every second of every day...but love?

I don't do love. I stopped doing love years ago because it was the only way to protect myself.

I can count less than a handful of people I've actually fallen in love with. Kendra, for one. I started to fall for Reese, my brother's wife, but I stopped it as soon as I realized the actual feelings I was having. I couldn't fall for someone I was only using. I thought I loved some girl back in my late teen years, but I was too young to know what love was. And now, I'm older and wiser. Now I know it's a myth. Now I know it's not for everyone. Not even close.

"I've barely seen you without her for the past three weeks. I'm glad she makes you happy, but I'm starting to wonder where my friend went."

"I'm right here, man." I realize as he says the words I've been largely avoiding him without meaning to. Between sleeping with his ex and lying about the company, I've purposely kept myself too busy for our usual single guys nights out where we play wingman for one another and find women to bring home.

He narrows his eyes at me for a long minute, and then he passes me a sheet of paper and changes the subject. "Here's our standard interview questions. I added a few at the bottom pertaining to this role in particular. Look them over and let me know if we're missing anything."

I read through them, and as usual, he's done a thorough job. "This is fine," I say. "Let's focus today on finding our lead. Once we hire leadership, he or she can put together a team."

"I have three interviews set up. I figured we'd choose the lead from those three and the other two would come on as support."

"Are you that confident in all three?" I ask.

He nods. "I've worked with all three on different projects. I have my pick of who I think would make the best lead, but I'd like to get your feedback through these interviews. You've got a keen sense when it comes to people skills."

I nod. "We'll talk to all three and regroup at the end, though I do think it would be in our best interest financially to wait to hire the team until we've established the lead."

"Why? Are we in trouble financially?" he asks.

This is my chance. He's giving me the open door to confess, to give him the truth that's put a burden on my shoulders.

But I find I can't do it. There are too many lies surrounding the one big one at this point, so I keep up the act if nothing else to protect him from myself.

"We're fine. It's just smart business to hire a lead and let him put together his own team."

Jason studies me for a few seconds then nods. "Okay. We'll hire the best of the three and go from there."

I don't let him see me sweat, and I don't let him see my breath of relief—but I have a good feeling I just got myself out of some real trouble with Viv.

Each of the three interviews Jason set up lasts about forty-five minutes. We discuss each candidate for a few minutes in the conference room before Jason brings in the next one, and by the time we're done, I have no idea who to choose. They each come highly recommended, and I can see each fitting into a leadership role within our company.

"Which one tops your list?" I ask Jason.

He shakes his head. "You tell me yours first."

"I actually don't have a top. I liked Ben's vision. I thought Zach had the technical know-how we're looking for. But I love the idea of bringing a woman into a leadership role, so I can't rule out Dana, either." I wonder what Vivian would think of each one, but I can't exactly say that.

He nods. "I agree on all counts. Ben has the least experience."

"Which may keep him from being jaded," I add.

"True. Do you see why I want all three working for *us* and not for our competition?"

"Absolutely." I glance down at my notes. "But I'd still rather get someone into the role and let him or her determine the type of support they'd need."

"Let's go over our notes on our own for a bit," Jason suggests. He glances at his watch. "Meet me back here at five and we'll talk it over."

"Deal." I pick up my papers and head back to my office. I'm usually not this indecisive, but I'm really curious who Vivian would choose. Maybe someone with a business sense as strong as hers could see things I'm missing, and if she's truly been sent here to fix my company, perhaps she has insight I've chosen to ignore thus far.

If she's still here, she can help me decide.

I'm not surprised she's still working when I get back to my office. I drop my notes on her desk. "Read them over and give me your opinion."

She glances up at me in surprise. "You want *my* opinion?"

I nod. "I'm meeting Jason in the conference room in an hour with my decision, and I'd like to look at it from all angles. Jason will tell me technically who is the best fit, and I have my own opinions, but I'm curious as to who someone with your background might choose."

The surprise on her face turns incredulous. "I thought..." She stops herself as I sit at my desk.

"You thought what?" I ask.

"I thought you hated me," she admits. "I thought you hated having me here."

I shake my head and lower my voice. "Maybe I did, but things have changed."

"What changed things?" she whispers.

I press my lips together in a tight smile. "A kiss on a pier."

Her tongue darts out to wet her bottom lip as she forces her gaze away from mine and down to the notes from the interviews. She doesn't reply to my words, but the red creeping into her cheeks tells me they've hit her where I wanted them to.

Nearly a half hour passes before she breaks the silence, and in that time, I've come to my own decision.

"It has to be Dana." She says it without hesitation.

"Why Dana?" I ask. I lean back in my chair and fold my arms across my chest as I gaze at her.

"Three reasons. She's got the best history, she's a woman, and she comes the cheapest."

I raise my brows. "Can we talk about reason number two for a second? Why should I hire her because she's a woman?"

"Your company is severely lacking in female leadership, but it's not just that. She's got the fewest years' experience but with much bigger companies than her competition. She'll be able to provide a perspective the men around here don't always have, and she'll take a lower salary because she hasn't been in the field as long as the other two."

I nod as I avert my gaze to some papers on my desk. "I don't disagree."

"Is that your facetious way of saying you actually agree with me?"

I chuckle and glance up at her. "Yeah. I agree with you."

She rewards me with a rare and unexpected laugh that brightens the whole room. She shakes her head as her laughter slows. "I never thought I'd see the day."

"Yeah, well, me either."

I'm greeted with more laughter, and I stand and grab the papers from her desk before I do something dumb like push all the work off her desk, toss her on top of it, and kiss her like I did on that pier.

When I return to the conference room early, Jason's already there. He raises a brow at me. "So?" he asks. He seems guarded, but I brush it away. It's surely just my conscience playing tricks on me.

"Let's both pull the resume of our top choice and toss it in the middle," I suggest.

"Deal." He pulls out a paper, and I pull Dana's resume out as well. We both toss our chosen paper into the middle of the conference room table, and I find he has chosen Zach.

"Zach?" I ask at the same time he says, "Dana?"

"Why Zach?" I ask.

"Experience."

"In years, but not necessarily quality. Compare his history to Dana's. He's got five years on her, but she's worked at MTC since she interned there in college."

"So? Zach's been in the field longer and with more companies," Jason says.

"Exactly the problem. Dana's proven her loyalty by being with the same company for twelve years."

Jason nods thoughtfully. "Loyalty is going to be essential in this position given the fact that we're pulling models that Schneider has worked on for three years."

"Not that Zach wouldn't be an excellent candidate as well, and Ben, too, for that matter," I say. "I just feel Dana has some qualities essential to this new position."

"Okay," Jason says. "Dana it is."

"You're sure?"

He nods. "She was my first choice. I just wanted to see why you chose her over the others."

I laugh as I realize Jason has his own poker face, too.

Which leads me to a big question.

Did he overhear my conversation with Vivian, and does he know I asked for her opinion on an FDB matter? Because if he did, he might be closer to learning the truth than I realize.

twenty-nine

Jason calls the three people we interviewed with the news, and I head back to my office. It's already after six, and even though the pile of work is never-ending, I'm ready for a change of scenery.

I stand in the doorway for a minute and watch her work. I finally break the silence. "I'm heading out for an early dinner. Would you like to join me?"

She glances up at me and lifts a shoulder. "I don't think that would be a good idea."

I stride across my office and sit at my desk, puffing up my chest despite the slight rejection. "Why not?"

"We've already spent the entire day together."

"And it hasn't been so bad, has it?"

She lets out a soft giggle. "No."

"Do you have dinner plans?" I press.

"Yes, big plans to change into my pajamas and order up room service while I veg out with a rom com on Netflix."

My first thought is I want to be there with her.

I clear my throat as an image pops into my head of me on the bed beside her—nothing sexual for the moment, just lying around together watching a movie and eating room service. The image cuts painfully into my consciousness, and as it fades away, it leaves behind a strange ache of longing and loneliness. "You're welcome to come by my place and veg out with a rom com on Netflix."

"That would be a *really* bad idea." Her answer is firm and immediate, and this time the rejection stings a little more intensely.

"What's so bad about it?"

She blows out a breath. "I'm going to be really honest with you right now."

I nod. "I hope you're always honest with me."

"Transparent, I mean. Things in my head I wouldn't normally voice aloud."

I raise a brow, and her eyes dart toward my office door. I glance that way, too, wondering for a beat if Jason is still around. It's quiet in the office, but this feels like something he probably shouldn't overhear.

She gets up and closes the door, and my heart pounds as I wait for her words. She walks to the edge of my desk and sets her palms face down on it, leaning over to look me in the eye.

"I've already told you once. I can't get involved with you. We have professional lines we can't cross because I'm here as your boss."

"Don't tell me you don't feel it, too," I say softly.

She straightens and goes over to the window, crossing her arms over her chest as she stares out at the Strip. "Of course I feel it. The air in the room is always full of tension when we're in it together, and at first I thought it was because I hated you. And then you kissed me, and now I know it's not because I hate you. It's because I'm ridiculously attracted to you." I open my mouth to voice my surprise at her words, to tell her how much I feel it too and how I think we should both stop fighting against it...but then she continues softly, "I can't think about you like that."

"What about once your three months are over?"

She turns to face me again and shakes her head. "This will never happen, Brian."

it started with a lie

I stand up and walk around the desk. I walk into her orbit but I don't touch her. I don't reach out a finger to trace her jawline, don't lift a hand to smooth down her hair, don't lean forward to press my lips against hers. I just stand close enough that she can feel my heat and read all the pent-up need and desire in my eyes. "Why are you fighting this so hard?"

"Because I have to."

"That's not a reason," I say, my voice a clear demand for more.

"It'll have to do." She ducks around me and returns to her desk, where she starts packing up her things.

I'm desperate to find a way to prolong our time together. "Just go to dinner with me. We can talk business and you tell me how to do my job better and there won't be any pressure. Just two colleagues going to dinner."

She blows out a breath, and just as she opens her mouth to probably reject me once again, there's a knock at my office door.

"Come in," I say.

Jason opens the door. "Sorry to interrupt, but at least you've both got clothes on."

I laugh and Viv turns red.

"Dana is coming by tomorrow to get the ball rolling. Becker and Jill are back and I invited them to dinner with Tess and me tonight. Can I count you both in?"

"Absolutely," I say without even thinking twice about it. It's probably the single way to get Viv to go to dinner with me. So what if it isn't just the two of us? I glance over at her, and she gives me a look that's hard to read, but I'd label it somewhere between annoyed and resigned.

"Fine," Viv says with a sigh.

Jason's brows furrow down. "Everything okay in here?"

I nod and give him a tight smile. "Just let me know when and where and we'll meet you there."

Viv clears her throat. "I need to stop home first."

"Of course, babe," I say. "We can do whatever you need."

She raises a brow at me that Jason doesn't catch.

"I was thinking we could meet in an hour at Catch," he says, referring to one of the hottest new seafood restaurants in Vegas. "Can you pull strings to get us in?"

I nod. Having a brother as a rock star has its perks.

"See you there," Jason says, and he heads out.

I make the call and get us an easy reservation once I explain who I am, and when I hang up, Viv looks at me with daggers in her eyes. "*Babe?*" she says. "After all that no pressure talk?"

"Part of the act," I say. "And sorry you have to cancel your date with your bed and Netflix."

"They'll understand," she says dryly. She finishes packing her things. "I'm going to head to my hotel for a bit."

"Do you have a car here?" I ask.

She shakes her head.

"Then let me give you a ride. I have nowhere to be."

"That's okay. I like the walk. It's just down the road and it's nice out."

"It'll be hotter than hell in another month," I say.

"I know. That's why I want to enjoy it."

"Let me walk you, then," I say, trying my best to be gentlemanly. "There's some sketchy characters out there."

"I've walked back and forth from my hotel every day I've been here. I don't need some shadow acting like my security guard."

"Fine," I say, though what I really want to say is that she's stubborn as hell and, frankly it's totally exhausting. "I have some shit to wrap up here anyway. I'll pick you up in forty-five minutes."

"Fine," she says, and then she heads out the door.

I blow out a heavy sigh of frustration as soon as she's gone. So she's attracted to me, but it'll never happen?

We'll see.

* * *

It's not the night I imagined for us, but as I pull into the familiar driveway of the Westin, I think to myself it'll have to do.

I didn't bring flowers for my date. I didn't bring chocolates. I brought something else, something less cliché and more my style.

Viv opens the door and slides into the passenger seat before I have a chance to get out and open the door for her gallantly. She takes my breath away. It took her less than an hour to transform from the woman I work with to the woman I want to be with. She's still herself in another demure outfit, this time a black top paired with jeans and black heels, but somehow the look is utterly perfect on her.

"You look beautiful," I say, and then I lean over the seat and kiss her cheek as she leans down to buckle her seatbelt.

Her head whips toward mine when she feels my proximity, putting her mouth centimeters away from mine since I haven't moved. She doesn't say anything, doesn't react except for the surprised whip of her head, and God do I want to crush my mouth to hers, to bruise her lips unforgivingly, to take her mouth before I take her body and claim it as mine.

I pull back.

I need to lay the groundwork tonight, not jump the gun. Besides, I've got a whopper of a surprise planned for dinner.

She clears her throat, and I reach into the backseat, grab the envelope, and hand it to her.

"What's this?" she asks.

"Open it." I start driving because even though I want to gauge her reaction, we have a dinner we need to get to.

She pulls out the piece of paper inside the envelope. "A reservation?" she asks.

I nod and grin proudly. "For two on Wednesday night at Viv in Miami."

She shakes her head as she crams the paper back into the envelope. I sneak a glance over at her, and a little smile plays at her lips. "So we'll be back in Miami on Wednesday?"

"Yes, and I figured this time we might as well just plan on dinner together instead of me getting mad and storming off to eat alone."

"Yeah, that was pretty immature of you."

I have a nasty comment ready to fall off my tongue, but I manage to stop it.

It's yet another turning point for me, another line in the sand that makes me realize my feelings for her have started running deeper than I thought they did. I never stop my nasty comments. My brain seems to lack the filter required to do so, but with Viv...everything's different.

Everything.

"I saw that restaurant when we were headed back to the airport last week. I have to take Viv to Viv, obviously."

"Why do you call me Viv?" she asks. It's not the question I was expecting.

I lift a shoulder. "Why does anyone call anyone anything?"

"That's not an answer."

"I don't know." I think about it for a second. The real reason is probably because it annoys her. It slipped out the first time and just sort of stuck for me when I saw her reaction. "I guess I just like the way it feels leaving my mouth."

"Is that really why?"

I shake my head. "I do it because you hate it. Why do you hate it?"

"Why do you purposely do things that annoy me?" she shoots back. She's feisty tonight, and I like it.

I glance over in her direction, and I find her gaze pinned to me. "I'm just trying to get your attention," I say softly, and then I force my eyes back to the road.

My words are met with a sigh. We travel in silence a few more minutes, and then I'm pulling into a space at the restaurant and the short moment of intimacy we shared as I gave her my vulnerable words passes us by.

"Ready for our fake date, girlfriend?"

She slaps on a fake smile. "Ready, boyfriend."

We get out of the car and I take her hand in mine. Hers is cold again—it's always cold—and my bigger, warmer hand covers hers. I stroke the back of her hand with my thumb reflexively, absentmindedly, and when I look down at her, she's looking up at me.

A needy ache passes between the two of us, something I'm positive she feels as strongly as I do, and that's my window in. That's my *go* signal. It's that single look that tells me she'll eventually let go of her stubborn need to keep work and pleasure separate—some old principle I've never subscribed to.

I look away first. I have to, because if I don't, I'll give into every single emotion I'm feeling, emotions both unfamiliar and terrifying yet at the same time emotions I want to cling to and hold close and try to understand.

I spot Becker first at a big, round corner booth. I let go of Viv's hand and guide her by the small of her back through the narrow aisles to the table where my closest friends sit. Tess looks across the table at me with a curious gaze as her eyes edge over to the woman with me.

"This is Vivian," I say to Becker and Jill. I turn toward Viv. "And this is everyone."

Introductions are made and everyone scoots around the booth so we can sit. I love round tables for social events—they work better than rectangles for conversation, and they force me closer to my date. My knee brushes Viv's as we settle into our seats, and I leave mine there.

She moves hers immediately.

I'm getting seriously conflicting signals from her. Her words and her actions say one thing, but the way she looks at me like she's a starving animal about to devour a steak leaves me with a completely different impression.

I have to go with my instinct. I allow my leg to fall closer to her again, and when my leg brushes hers again, she leaves hers for a beat this time before pulling it away.

"How was Italy?" I ask the newlyweds. Becker launches into a recap of their trip while Jill peppers in additional details, and I'm only half-listening as I think about what I'm going to do. I'm biding my time and waiting for the perfect moment.

We order drinks and then dinner. Jill and Tess catch up on some gossip on one side of the table as Jason and I fill Becker in on things he's missed at FDB, including our new hire. Viv listens intently beside me, surely analyzing every detail we discuss to find cost cutting solutions. She manages to keep her mouth shut, which I find both surprising and endearing at the same time. She's really going all in on our act, which only bodes well for me.

When the dessert menus come, we're all too full to even consider it. We always find room for an after-dinner drink, however. We order another round, and then the conversation moves to relationships as Jason asks, "So what's married life like?"

it started with a lie

I glance at Tess, who shifts uncomfortably beside him. They just got back together. He can't really be ready to move to that step yet, can he?

"Pretty much exactly like before, but now I have the hardware to prove it," Becker says, holding up his ring and drawing a laugh from Jason and me—not so much from Tess or Viv.

Jill elbows him in the ribs. "And the sex has pretty much stopped, just like all married couples," she jokes.

"Which is exactly why I never plan to get married," I interject with a laugh, and I feel Viv's eyes turn toward me. I decide to meet her gaze even though all eyes on the table are on us. This is my moment. "I'm not opposed to changing our living arrangements, though."

Her brows draw down as she realizes nearly immediately what I'm doing.

"Viv, will you move in with me?"

Her jaw drops open when the words leave my mouth, and a blush of red creeps up from the little peek I have of her chest, into her neck, and finally into her cheeks.

"What?" she squeaks.

"Move in with me. We spend practically all our time together anyway. It'll just be more convenient."

I can tell she has no idea what I'm doing, and so I soften my eyes at her. It's part of the act in front of my friends, but it's also not. It's something I've thought a lot about over the last couple days.

Why is she staying at the fucking Westin and spending my brother's money for a hotel every night when I have a huge house with extra space?

I'm dead serious about her staying with me, and I figured asking in front of my friends, the same people she agreed to lie to, was my best bet in terms of getting her to say yes. I just don't know whether the yes will truly mean yes and she'll leave the hotel to stay with me for the remainder of her time at FDB.

But I do know one thing.

If I can get her on my turf, if I can get her to spend more time with me...then I can get her to fall for me in just the same way I'm finding myself inexplicably falling for her.

I feel Tess's eyes burning holes into me, but that relationship was so fleeting I can't even call it a relationship. It was two people having fun in secret a few times. Nothing more.

"Oh my God, say yes!" Jill squeals.

I've gotten to know Jill over the years she's been dating my best friend. It took a long time for her to warm up to me after I used her best friend, Reese, in my attempt at revenge on my brother. She still doesn't fully trust me—and probably never will—but we've sort of settled into the roles of two people who tolerate each other because we have to. I'm not going anywhere as her husband's business partner and lifelong friend, and she's not going anywhere as Beck's wife.

But this is the first time since everything went down with Reese and Mark where I've actually seen her as a cheerleader in my corner rooting for me.

I laugh nervously, again as part of the act but also not, as I stare down at Viv. I raise my brows at her, hoping my eyes tell her to say yes in front of my friends.

"Okay," Viv says quietly.

"Yeah?" I ask as I match her tone.

She nods, and I can't help it. I lean down and press my lips softly to hers. Whether or not this is part of the act remains to be seen, but I need to feel her lips under mine.

She breaks the kiss quickly and plays it off like she's embarrassed to have a public display of affection in front of my friends, but I kiss her cheek anyway and throw my arm around her shoulder. I act like I would if she really was my girl and I really did just ask her to move in with me, because what other choice do I have at this point?

We order one more round in celebration, and then we bid my friends goodnight.

Then it's time to head *home*.

thirty

"What was that?" Vivian hisses at me once we're in the car.

"Dinner with friends." I start the engine and back out of my space.

"I thought it would help ease our professional relationship if I earned your trust, so that's why I agreed to play along with your little lies. But what you did in there crossed the line, Brian."

"I wasn't trying to cross lines," I say. Despite my defensive words, I feel in control of this conversation. "I was simply trying to put on the act in front of my friends."

She huffs out a mirthless chuckle, but she doesn't say anything as she shakes her head in apparent disgust.

"And I was trying to save my brother some money." I chance a glance in her direction, and her focus whips from the window toward me as she lets out a loud and startling laugh.

"Ha! Right. Like my agreement to *live with you* was based in any sort of reality."

"Sort of has to be considering my friends are over all the time." I'm bluffing, but I'll get her on my side. "You signed an NDA that said you'd play along."

"Provided you'd treat me better."

"And I have. I'm offering you a place to stay free of charge. I'll even let you borrow one of my cars to get you to and from the office if you don't want to carpool."

"How incredibly gentlemanly of you," she spits out, her voice laden with sarcasm.

"Let's just give it a try. It's temporary, anyway. My house is big enough we don't even have to interact."

"Weren't you the one throwing a tantrum in Miami just a few days ago because you couldn't seem to get away from me?"

I lift a shoulder. "I've already told you, Viv. Things have changed."

"I feel like you're not giving me a choice."

"There's always a choice." I decide it's time to appeal to her good business sense. "But if you're really trying to save both FDB and my brother money, you can easily see where this makes sense. The Westin doesn't come cheap, nor do your meals when you're eating out for three months straight."

"What will you tell Mark?" she asks.

"I don't have to tell him a goddamn thing."

She leans back on the headrest and turns her head to stare out the window. The lights of the Strip are bright in the darkness of night, the glow magical as it always is.

"Take me back to the Westin," she says softly as she releases a breath, and while I sort of knew it was coming, it doesn't stop my heart from dropping anyway. "I need to get my things."

I don't say anything at all as my heart lifts back up and a smile tips my lips.

She tells me to wait in the car, and she disappears into the hotel for a good fifteen minutes. I scroll through email on my phone while I wait, and I find several replies to the proposals and emails I sent earlier today. Apparently weekends are fair game for business in this town.

Three of the proposals I sent have already been signed, one has a few amendments, and I have two companies interested in learning more about what we do. All in all, it's a good few minutes and I'm excited to share the news with Vivian.

it started with a lie

But then I realize these are the exact things that will keep her from me. Getting FDB out of the red and back on track is the goal, of course, but the faster that's done, the quicker she'll leave.

And that's not something I'm ready for just yet.

So rather than share my excitement about the green light to move forward with some of these companies we worked together on over the past two days, I decide to keep my mouth shut for the time being.

I put my phone down while I wait, and when I see her inside the lobby with two suitcases plus another large bag slung over her shoulder as she waits to be addressed by the clerk, I head inside to help.

As soon as I get close, I notice the fresh and slightly more powerful scent of roses and I realize she freshened up.

For me.

"I'll get your luggage to the car," I say.

"Thank you."

I nod and take both bags from her. She only had one in Miami, so she must've stored one here since she checked out and checked back in. I get both her bags into my trunk, and minutes later she's strolling toward my car. I open the passenger door for her and she slides in, and then I shut it and walk around to my side.

She fidgets as I get into the car, and before I start it up, she says, "I've been fighting with myself ever since I got out of your car."

"About what?" I turn to look at her rather than starting the car. It's dark here, but her face is lit by the flashing sign across the street from us advertising some cheap late night buffet.

"About what to do. I see where you're coming from and I agree it'll save money, but I just don't think this is a good idea."

"Now see, that's where you're wrong. I'm convinced this is the best idea I've had in ages."

She allows a small chuckle, and while it chips away at the ice between us, it doesn't break it. She lets out a long sigh. "I just think we want different things."

"I'm sure of that, but what's life without a little excitement?"

She purses her lips as she gazes thoughtfully at me, and then she nods. "Okay. Bring on the excitement then."

I laugh and start the car. When I chose my home, one of my top priorities was being close to the office, so it's only a ten-minute drive from where we are. I punch in the code to my gated community and the heavy iron gates open. We wind through the streets, and I can tell she's impressed when we pull into my driveway.

But then I realize it's not necessarily *me* she's impressed with. I as much as told her my brother bought the place for me, and she's well-informed of my current financial situation.

"What's your place in Los Angeles like?" I ask.

She stares up the driveway at my house. "It's modest compared to this. Three beds, three baths, a little over two thousand square feet. I love my backyard. It has a pool and it's just the most relaxing thing ever. And I have a custom-built wine room in my garage."

"Are you a big wine drinker?" I ask.

"Not huge, but I love a nice glass of pinot noir."

I shake my head. "Red wine drinkers," I mutter.

"What?"

"Nothing." I pull into the garage. "Come on in."

We step through my laundry room first and then into the kitchen. I gauge her reaction as she glances around, but she's hard to read.

"This is actually exactly how I pictured your home."

"You pictured my home?" I ask, sort of surprised she admitted to thinking about me.

She lifts a shoulder. "Sure. I love looking at houses." She leans in a little like she's about to reveal a secret. "I'm an HGTV junkie, especially when I'm in hotels. There's always something interesting on."

I'm already learning new things about her and she's only been in my house for ten seconds. "So what about this is how you pictured it?"

"The dark woods. The navy blue. The extravagance. It's all exactly your personality."

I narrow my eyes at her. "How?"

She leans a hip against my counter. "This countertop. Is this quartz?" She glances at me, and I nod. She runs a fingertip over the surface. "Did you pick it out?"

"With a designer's help, but I personally approved every detail of my house."

"Navy quartz. I read somewhere dark blues cut through clutter. You tend to do that as well, especially at work." She glances around. "You have lavish details, but only when you look closer." She nods toward my kitchen cabinets. "Those are high-end, as is the reclaimed wood paneling on this wall." She runs her fingertips over one of my favorite details of my home. "A darker wood is typically considered more luxurious, and from what I've seen, you enjoy life's luxuries. Plus your countertops are completely barren, which speaks to your Type A personality."

I raise my brows. "Well you've certainly got me all figured out."

She shrugs. "Homes say a lot about people."

"What would your home say about you?"

She lifts a shoulder. "Probably that I work too much. My plain white walls are barren. I don't have much time for home decorating, and I'm always traveling anyway. That's why I watch HGTV. I can decorate houses vicariously through others."

"Except for your wine room."

She nods. "Except for that."

"You know what that tells me about you?"

It's her turn to narrow her eyes at me. "What?" she asks.

"That you put a higher priority on alcohol than you like to admit."

She laughs and walks over to me just to mock slap me in the arm. I grab the spot of the offense dramatically.

"Show me the rest of your place," she says.

I take her on the grand tour, and she nods knowingly with each new detail I present to her. She's not at all shocked I have a room dedicated to my favorite sports team, and I'm reminded of the AceStar Gala when she distracted me from winning the signed Payton jersey.

I don't show her my bedroom, mostly because I don't want to take her in there unless we're planning to stay in there a while. Instead, I point down the hallway toward my room then lead her the opposite way toward my office and my guest rooms, ultimately ending up in the room where she'll be staying.

For now.

Until I can convince her she should be staying with me.

"Nicer than a hotel?" I ask as she takes a look around her room. Of course it's nicer than a hotel. The thread count is higher and it's a *home*. I set her suitcase next to the dresser.

"With the exception of someone who will come deliver my food for me, I guess it'll do."

I laugh. "Fox Estate will happily provide that amenity for you, but it comes with a cost."

"*Fox Estate*? I like it."

"I'll leave you alone to settle in. If you need anything, I'll be in my office."

My office happens to be the room directly next to the room where she's staying. I didn't plan that on purpose...except I totally did.

I hear her voice through the wall as I sort through a few emails and reply to the ones I saw earlier in the car. She must be on the phone. It's muffled, and I can't make out what she's saying, but just the hum of her voice reminds me she's here, and somehow that provides a sense of comfort I didn't expect.

I lean back in my chair for a minute and listen to the sound of her talking, and I realize even though this plan might've been out of left field, somehow it's working. She's here, and now that I've got unlimited access to her, it won't be long before she sees how great we could be together, too.

thirty-one

By Monday morning, I'm, as my sister would say, a hot mess.

I can't stop thinking about her legs.

I'm hornier than ever, and it has everything to do with the woman I invited to be my houseguest.

What a stupid fucking plan.

I didn't think it through, and now I'm paying the price. Yesterday as I lounged in one of the recliners in my football room just off the kitchen with a business magazine, she walked by in a pair of short shorts. Her pink top was as modest as ever, showing no cleavage, but her legs seemed to go on for days.

And she was *barefoot*. Fucking *barefoot*! I'm not a foot guy, but as my eyes were drawn to the bottom of those long stems of hers and the red nail polish adorning her toenails...well, maybe I became a foot guy in that moment.

I pretended to be invested in my magazine, but I was really watching her every move as she helped herself to a glass of orange juice.

Somehow even that became sexualized in my mind as I thought about all the sticky places I could trail orange juice along her body before I lapped it up with my tongue.

Hence the issue today with my aching balls desperate for relief. I gave the big guy some self-love this morning in the shower, and while it relieved some of the immediate pain, it came back quickly and with a vengeance. This is the sort of ache that only a woman can alleviate, and somehow I just know the only woman who can *really* take care of my needs is sitting in the chair across from my desk at the office, tapping away at her laptop.

She glances up at me and catches me staring. She gives me a polite smile and returns her attention to her computer. "What's the deal with Crimson Cloud?" she asks out of nowhere.

I'm snapped back to attention. "Crimson Cloud?" I ask stupidly.

She nods. "Their numbers don't add up. Eighteen months ago, they received analytics they paid for, but they've stopped paying their monthly service charge and you're still providing the service."

"Who's the CEO?" I ask.

She clicks a few buttons. "Vince Ridley."

I clear my throat. "Right. Highest bidder on a year of free services at last year's Vegas Business Con."

"Isn't that the event you presented at on Friday?"

I nod.

"Then it's been a year. Time's up and Crimson needs to start paying up."

"You're right. I had that on my calendar, but with last week's presentation and surprise trip to Miami, it slipped through."

She shakes her head. "We can't let things this big slip through. And you can't give away a year's worth of services for free. That's tens of thousands of dollars."

I shrug. "It got our name out there."

"But the winner was someone who's already a client. That makes no sense," she says, and her passion is yet another turn on. "He was already paying for his analytics, and you gave him a free pass. You offer freebies to catch new clients, not to retain the ones you already have."

"You think we shouldn't treat our current customers well?" I challenge.

She shakes her head. "You're missing the point. You treat them well, of course. But you never turn away a sure thing."

A sure thing.

Interesting.

I am a sure thing, yet she keeps turning *me* away. Rather than say that, though, I turn my attention back to some papers on my desk and say, "Let's just agree to disagree."

"No," she says, and her voice is so sharp my eyes whip toward hers in surprise. "I won't agree to that. I've agreed to a lot of things I'm not comfortable with, but my job is to fix what you've messed up."

My brows raise at her outburst. I feel the sting of her insult, but it doesn't matter. As much as I want to hate her, I just can't. Every single thing she does seems to make me even more attracted to her—seems to make me want her even more.

She forges ahead before I have the chance to defend myself. "And this is a definite screw-up, Brian." She taps some keys then looks up at me. "Thirty-six thousand dollars. That's what you lost. That's what your prize was worth. Thirty-six thousand. That's practically an entire new hire just from one company's bills for a year."

She's fired up, and her passion about my company just shows me what a great choice my brother made in her.

That thought is even more confusing than my sudden feelings for her.

My brother was right...and I'm admitting it?

Something is definitely wrong here. Something's in the water, or someone has drugged me. I'd never willingly admit to my brother being right about anything, and yet...

I'm glad Viv is here.

"You're right," I finally say. "And that's why Mark hired you."

She looks shocked by my words, but she doesn't get the chance to respond because Becker comes barging into my office.

"What have I missed?" He glances at Vivian sitting at her desk in the corner of my office. "Aside from the fact that you somehow found a woman to date you and she moved into not just your home, but your office?"

"Fuck off," I say with a good-natured roll of my eyes.

He chuckles and sits. "What's the latest?"

I glance through some notes on my desk I took specifically to fill him in. "I've written thirty-seven proposals in the last five weeks. Eight have signed and are in various stages of the contract, fourteen have indicated further interest, ten have declined, and I haven't heard back from five."

"Thirty-seven?" he asks. He raises his brows and lets out a whistle between his teeth. "Good work."

"The Vegas Con event really boosted that number. It's the single best event each year for us." I lean back in my chair.

"Meaning in about two months, we'll be rolling in the dough?"

I grin at my best friend. "Exactly."

"Excellent. Anything else I need to know?"

"We have a new hire starting today to bring the work we were outsourcing to Germany back here. She'll need a team, so we'll have to get back together in a few days once we determine her exact needs." I see Viv's sharp glare at me out the corner of my eye, but I choose to ignore it for now. She can yell at me when Beck leaves.

"I'll be sure to introduce myself," he says. He stands. "I tried to keep up with email while I was out, but I've got a lot to catch up on."

"Good to have you back, man."

He stretches lazily. "I wish I could say it's good to be back, but honestly, a month in Italy with my wife was pretty spectacular."

"Just go down to the Venetian for a few hours. It'll be like you're back there."

He lets out a loud laugh as he leaves, and Viv starts in on me as soon as he's out of earshot. "You didn't tell me those numbers," she says.

I shrug and sit forward in my chair, leaning my elbows on my desk. "I figured you knew since you have full access to everything."

"I only look at what I *need* to look at, and your email correspondence isn't one of those things." She looks a little offended, and it's sexier than I need it to be when she has already hooked my interest. "Frankly, I don't have the time to spy on you, and besides, stages of contracts don't come through on financial reports until you've secured the deal and they've made payments."

I steeple my fingers in front of my mouth. "Fair enough. I've got eight contracts coming through in the next few weeks."

"Brian, that's amazing." She looks at me with some degree of admiration—something I'm not used to seeing from her. "That might be enough to reverse this entire mess."

I hope it is for the sake of my company, but as soon as the mess is fixed, Viv will leave. And I'm definitely not ready for that.

* * *

"I've got an excellent proposal for you, Mr. Porter," I say. "I'm just confirming our meeting time tomorrow morning."

"Eight o'clock," he says.

"I'll be there." It's early for me considering we're three hours apart, not to mention the fact that I'm planning to make a move on Viv tonight...but I'll make it work. I've completed successful business transactions on far less sleep.

"Bring that lovely young woman with you again, would you?"

A twinge of anger pulses in my chest. Why does he want me to bring her again? My intuition tells me it's business-related—she took good notes that helped me draft the new proposal and she interjected some good ideas during our meeting—but the caveman in me tells me it's because she's a gorgeous distraction in a room full of men.

I have the call on speaker as I usually do when I'm talking with a client, and Viv glances at me and nods a confirmation that she plans to come with me again.

My heart leaps a little higher than it should as I wonder if somehow we can manage just a single hotel room to share again.

"She'll be with me."

"Great. See you both tomorrow, then." We say our goodbyes and I end the call.

"Lovely young woman?" I mutter.

She laughs. "I *am* lovely. You just haven't given me a second look to notice."

My eyes meet hers across the office, and I feel the heat of our connection from where I sit. "I wish you understood how wrong you are."

She doesn't say anything, simply returns her attention to her computer, but I know she's affected. I can tell in the pinch of red in her cheeks and in the way she holds her gaze as far away from me as she possibly can.

I wrap up what I'm working on mid-morning since I have to stop home to pack before I head to the airport—this time with Viv in my passenger seat. "You ready to head out?" I ask as I stand and slide my laptop into a bag.

"I'm thinking of renting a car when we get back from Miami," she blurts.

I raise my brows but don't say anything as I step around my desk.

"It's cheaper than a hotel, and I just think it's a bad idea for us to spend so much time together," she says. "I'm staying with you, working with you, and now I don't even get my own time on my commute?"

I lean against the backside of my desk as she throws up her defense. "I already told you you can borrow one of my cars. You were the one who agreed to travel with me today."

She sighs. "I just didn't expect all this."

"All what?"

She shakes her head. "Nothing. Let's go."

I walk toward her desk and lean forward. I set my palms on her desk and look down at her, and the predominant emotion I see on her face when her eyes meet mine is fear.

Fear.

Not that she's scared of me, per se. I'm sure she isn't. She's a fucking viper who could take me down if she needed to.

She's scared of what she's feeling for me when she thinks she has no business feeling it.

But that's where she's wrong.

"I won't accept *nothing* as an answer," I say, my voice gentle despite the strong words. "What did you mean when you said you didn't expect all this?"

She looks away from me and lets out a breath, but she doesn't answer, not right away. I wait her out, though. I keep my eyes on her, waiting for her real answer, and when I finally get it, her words pack such a punch I actually stagger back a step.

"I didn't expect to have feelings for you, Brian. Okay?" She stands up, and it comes across as a power move. She can't say her next words sitting down, and her volume increases as all the passion she feels spews out of her. "I didn't expect to want you when I can't have you. I didn't expect your hatred to come on so strong and to morph into something entirely opposite in a matter of days. I didn't expect the passion and the emotions and the confusion. I didn't expect to see you in a suit and tie every single day and feel so ridiculously attracted to you, to wonder what you keep hidden beneath it." Her eyes widen on that confession, but it doesn't stop her from charging forward. "I didn't expect to be going back and forth to one of my favorite cities with you and wanting you to kiss me again when you can't. *You can't.* I really didn't expect to be *living* with you and working with you and unable to escape your searing green eyes when I feel them all over me, inside and out and everywhere."

I don't know what to say to any of that. I want to argue and to tell her she *can* have me, that I'm here and ready to offer her more than just one fun roll in the hay, that I think we have potential beyond her three months here...but the way she crosses her arms over her chest when she's done talking and the way she looks away from me tell me she doesn't want a response. She doesn't want me to say anything at all, and even though it goes against every instinct I have, I don't.

Instead, I clear my throat, nod once at her as I press my lips together, and head for the door as she follows behind me.

thirty-two

The ride home was awkwardly quiet as she stared out her window for the duration of our trip. She beelined for the guest room the second we walked through the doors. I head to my own bedroom and change out of my suit, and I'm reminded of the words she spoke to me less than twenty minutes ago. *I didn't expect to see you in a suit and tie every single day and feel so ridiculously attracted to you, to wonder what you keep hidden beneath it.*

I want to fucking *live* in my suit and tie if that's the way she feels about it.

But, to be fair, I change into jeans and a casual black shirt. It's one less strike of ammo I have against her, one way to try to make her feel just a little more comfortable with me.

I knock on her door. "Viv? You ready to go?"

She throws the door open. "It's Vivian!" she yells at me. "Stop calling me Viv! It's VIV-I-AN."

I've never seen her like this. "Whoa. Sorry."

She heaves out a huge breath and shakes her head. "No—don't be. I'm sorry. I shouldn't have yelled at you. It's the stress of getting on a plane in a few hours. And beyond that, I'm sorry for what I said at the office. You just...I don't know. It's like you create this passion in me where I spew things out of my mouth I don't mean to. Those thoughts should've stayed in my head, but when you pin me with your eyes, it's like a truth serum."

I chuckle. "I promise not to look at you."

My words elicit a small giggle from her, and it chips away a little more of the ice between us.

"Can we just start over?" she asks.

"Nope," I say, shaking my head. "Because if we start over, I have to get past hating you for taking my company from me again, and I don't really want to go back there."

Her lips tip up in a tiny smile. "Agreed. Then can we go back to where we were before my word vomit at the office?"

"*Word vomit* may be the single most disgusting phrase I can think of."

"That's a dangerous game to start," she says, her eyes twinkling. "Is that a challenge?"

I laugh. "I've never seen this side of you, Viv-i-an," I say, purposely drawing out the syllables at the end of her name. "I think I like it."

"You're not allowed to like it. Or me." She turns around to grab her bag. "Let's just get through this Miami trip and take things one day at a time."

I nod. "Deal. Can I get your bag?"

"No. Don't be a gentleman. Things worked better when you were a jerk. I liked you less back then."

The ride to the airport is quick and painless, as is the check-in process. Soon we're sitting at the gate, and she takes a bottle of pills out of her purse.

"Time for the drugs?" I ask.

"It's the good stuff." She winks at me then pulls two pills out of the bottle. She swallows them down before I can grab her hand to stop her.

"What if I told you that you didn't have to take those?"

She lifts a shoulder. "I'd probably tell you you're nuts."

I laugh.

"It doesn't matter. They're already down, and they'll last me six hours. Hopefully I'll be awake by the time we land, and hopefully I don't use your shoulder as a pillow again."

"Hopefully you do," I murmur, and she gives me a look of warning.

She can warn me all she wants with her glares and her words. It's not going to change the way I feel.

By the time we board the plane, her sedatives have kicked in and once again, I have to escort her to her seat. Just like last time, we didn't book first class tickets, and some guy is already sitting by the window when we get to our row. He doesn't even acknowledge us as we slide into our seats. Viv is able to get her seatbelt buckled on her own, and as soon as we take off, her head hits my shoulder. I lean back and breathe in the scent of her hair close to my nose.

I relax into my seat and close my eyes for just a minute to enjoy the moment. When she's drugged up and asleep, she's not yelling at me. I can almost pretend for a minute we're not bitter enemies, that she doesn't really hate me that much, even that we're together and she wants to be with me as much as I want to be with her.

After her speech earlier today, though, I fear that even if she *does* want that, it can't ever really happen.

When I open my eyes, I realize I fell asleep for nearly the entire plane ride across the country. I *never* sleep on planes. It's typically the only uninterrupted time I have to work, yet I let nearly five hours slip through my fingers while I slept with my cheek resting on the top of her head.

The plane starts its descent. It'll be dinnertime once we land. I let Vivian choose the hotel where we'll be staying, and to my utter shock, she chose the Ritz. That means we'll be on my turf, and I can make choices that steer us in the direction of romance under the guise I'm just taking her to my favorite places in Miami.

Tonight, though, instead of meeting old friends or business associates, it'll just be Vivian and me. No matter how hard she's fighting against her feelings for me, I just know she won't stay cooped up in her hotel room when she only has one night in town.

And so I'll make it a night to remember.

I gently shake her awake once we land. It takes more than a few gentle shakes before she stirs and finally starts to move. She stretches lazily, and if she wasn't sitting right beside me, surely my eyes would fall to her tits. But I focus forward.

"Did I sleep on your shoulder the whole time again?" she asks, her voice raspy from sleep. It makes me want to kiss her.

I shrug and shoot her a small smile. "Maybe."

She twists her lips and runs her fingertips beneath her eyes. "Sorry."

I shake my head. "Don't be," I murmur. "Best five hours I've spent in a long time."

She glances away from me and doesn't respond as she pulls her purse out from under the seat in front of her. I notice she keeps herself busy when she doesn't want to face something I've said.

"Are those reservations at Viv still okay with you for dinner? We can go over the plan for tomorrow." I add that last part to make it seem as though it's related to the business purpose of why we're here.

She nods and yawns widely.

"It's Italian. Does that sound okay?" Viv is a little place that sits right on the water. It's got candlelit tables and oozes romance.

"Mm," she murmurs lazily, "pasta sounds perfect."

it started with a lie

Her *mm* sends a spike of need right through me, landing squarely in my already aching balls. I shake my head to try to get the sound out of my head, but it's useless. It's tattooed on my brain now, a gorgeous hum that'll haunt my dreams.

Once we're checked into the hotel—in separate rooms right next door to each other—we agree to meet up in a half hour for dinner. She wants to freshen up, and I want to jerk off.

Scratch that. I don't *want* to jerk off...I need to.

I obviously don't say this to Vivian, but I'll be a total asshole all night if I don't let go of some of the need building up inside me. I can't sleep with my cheek resting against her head, breathing in her scent, and expect not to wake up hornier than ever.

So as soon as I'm alone in my room, I sit in the chair by my balcony, open the door so I can hear the waves crashing onto the shore, unzip my pants, pull out the big gun, and set to work.

I stroke myself slowly at first then pick up speed as I think about her creamy tits always hidden behind such modest shirts. I think about kissing her on the pier the last time we were here. I think about wrapping my arms around her, and then I think about getting her naked on my bed back at home, a place where I can settle in every night and be reminded of what we did, where I can still smell the scent of roses she leaves behind.

It's that final thought, her scent still fresh in my mind mixed with her moan for pasta, that causes my undoing. I come on my hand with a grunt, grab a tissue, and clean up my mess.

And then I'm ready for a night out in Miami with Viv.

I knock on her door, and she answers a minute later. She's wearing a tan blouse and jeans, and she's barefoot. My eyes catch on that damn red toenail polish again. It's red and racy, everything she's not, yet it's there—a piece of her she keeps hidden away but she's allowing me to see.

She eyes me for a second before opening the door wider to let me in. I wonder what her look is all about, and then I get the strange feeling she heard what I just did in my room.

I don't know how she could have, and it's certainly not a cringe-worthy movie moment where the evidence is hanging off my face somewhere, but I feel like she knows. Beyond that, I feel like she knows I was thinking about her while I was doing it, and somehow that feels like a betrayal. Like if it's going to happen, it should *be* with her, not be me *thinking* about her.

"You ready to go?" I ask, breaking the silence.

She nods. "Let me just get my shoes on."

Her room looks pretty much exactly like mine, and then I see her balcony door is open. I was going after myself pretty hard there at the end, and I feel a little embarrassed I had to whip it out the second I got behind a closed door. In all honesty, though, it's her fault I'm a walking hard-on.

She doesn't ask and I certainly don't tell as she pulls on some heels that cover up the toes.

"Covering up the red toes?" I ask before I can stop myself.

She shrugs and brushes off my comment.

"Why red?" I press.

"It's my favorite color."

I wouldn't have guessed that. I lean against the wall and stare out the window only so I'm not staring at the bed and thinking naughty thoughts, and then we head out the door toward dinner.

It's a short walk to the restaurant, and there's a small line waiting outside the door. The hostess lets me know it'll be twenty to thirty minutes even with our reservation. She takes down my cell number and lets me know she'll text me when our table is ready.

Viv stands outside, her hair swaying in the gentle ocean breeze, and she is perfect in this moment. Her shirt is demure and simple, even crossing the line into professional territory, but the jeans give her back a casual edge. Her blue eyes glow in the twilight as the sun sets. It's so picturesque I actually want to take out my phone to snap a photo, but I don't. Instead, I memorize the moment.

"What?" she asks. She brushes her hair aside like something's wrong. "Why are you looking at me like that?"

I shake my head. "Nothing," I say. "You just looked so beautiful with the sun setting behind you."

She looks away from me without acknowledging my words. "How long of a wait?"

"Twenty to thirty. Want to check out the boats again?"

"No," she says. "That got me into some trouble last time."

Damn. "Okay. Want to take a walk on the beach?"

She narrows her eyes then points her finger at me in accusation. "No funny business."

I hold up both hands in surrender. "No funny business." There's absolutely nothing *funny* about what I want to do to her.

We walk a few feet apart as I fight every instinct I have to touch her—either by sliding my hand into hers or wrapping my arm around her shoulders. I give her the space she needs as my confidence completely bows down to her.

I thought I had it in the bag, thought I could easily seduce her into wanting me as much as I want her, but I was wrong.

We take off our shoes before we hit the beach, and as soon as she sinks her feet into the warm sand, she lets out what sounds like a sigh of relief.

"Feel good?" I ask.

"Feels like perfection," she says.

Sand between my toes isn't exactly how I'd describe perfection, but I don't say that. "Why?"

"I know I have dark hair, but I'm a California girl through and through. Born and raised minutes from the beach. It just always feels like home. When I'm not there, it's where I want to be."

"Didn't you say you don't live by the beach now?" I ask as we walk along the bumps and ridges of the beach.

She nods. "I did say that."

"Why not?"

She shrugs and turns her eyes out over the water. "The proximity to the beach wasn't convenient. I'd love to move back, though."

Her vague response leaves me feeling confused. I want to get to know her, but she's so guarded all the time. I have a feeling it has to do with the way I treated her at first. It's true I won't get the chance to make a new first impression, but I have no idea how to prove to her I'm not the guy I was at first.

Maybe because I *am* that guy. Maybe I actually need to change before she can see me differently.

I think about what that might entail.

Being honest with my friends—my business partners.

Thanking my brother for his help over the years rather than expecting yet another handout.

Treating women better in general instead of leading them on or using them to get what I need, whether that's a new contract for the company or a night of fun.

Each of those things individually sounds difficult, but together, they feel insurmountable.

Yet I suddenly know in order to earn Vivian's respect and for her to see me like a real prospect who can be a part of her future, they're the exact things I have to do.

And it's not even about *just* earning her respect. I need to do this for myself, too. I *want* to do this for myself. I want to be a better man, and I've never wanted that before. I've never cared enough and I've allowed myself to float through my entire life, relying on everyone around me to either help me clean up my messes or forgive me when I make them.

Vivian makes me want to be better...I just have no idea where to even start.

"What are you thinking about?" she asks.

"You." I turn to look down at her, and a flash of surprise crosses her pretty features.

She raises both brows as a hand flies to her chest. "Me?"

I nod and decide to go for broke. "I was thinking about why you won't give me a chance, and I think I figured it out."

"Brian, I..." she pauses then redirects her words as she stops walking. "You said no funny business."

I blow out a breath as I look over the water and then I turn to face her. "This isn't funny business. I'm not going to kiss you even though I want to kiss you so goddamn bad my chest hurts. I'm fighting against myself because all I want to do is hold your hand as we walk along the beach even though you don't want me to. I can't pretend like I don't have feelings for you when I do."

"I never said I don't want those things." Her voice is sharp and her eyes are angry. "Because I do. God, I do. I said I can't, and I need you to stop acting like this can happen when it can't. It won't." Her angry eyes fill with tears, and her words are laden with passion as they hit me square in the chest.

It can't and it won't because she can't be with someone who so easily lies and manipulates other people. It's so clear to me now, and if I want the girl, I have to find a way to man up to be the man she deserves.

thirty-three

She stalked away from me, and I let her. I watched her get her shoes up on the sidewalk and sit on a ledge while I stayed down on the beach and thought about what to do. She wants space, and I don't...yet I want to respect her wishes.

I stay on the beach and stare out over the water until I get the text that our table is ready. When I walk back to my shoes to put them on, I find her still on the ledge. "You ready to eat?" I ask.

She nods. "I—I'm sorry, Brian," she says.

I hold out hand to help her off the ledge. "Don't be," I say, and my voice sounds dejected even to me. "Let's just put it on hold and talk about our plan for tomorrow."

"I'd like that."

We sit at our table, a cozy booth overlooking the water. It's everything romantic I wanted for this night, but it just feels wasted.

I want to feel the same about every aspect of the time I've spent with Viv—but I can't really believe it's been a waste when she's on her way to getting FDB back on track and I've started experiencing feelings I thought were forever dormant. If nothing else, meeting her and feeling something other than the same indifference and boredom I've felt for years has been worth it.

At least I know there's possibilities now, even if I have to face the fact that those possibilities may not be with her.

We stare quietly out the window at our view, neither of us sure what to say anymore. When the waiter comes by and we order our drinks, she orders red wine, naturally, and I order whiskey...also naturally.

I steer the conversation toward the reason we're here. "I'm ready for tomorrow's meeting, but I'd like your opinion on something."

She turns to me and raises a brow. "Really?"

I nod. "Of course. You have an obvious knack for what you do, and I've already seen the ways FDB is benefitting from having you around."

Her mouth falls open just slightly, and before she has the chance to respond, our drinks arrive.

I sip slowly; she does not.

"What did you want my opinion on?" she asks once half her glass is gone. From the looks of things, she's stocking up on liquid courage to make it through this meal with me.

"I just want to make sure my calculations are on track for what we'll be charging Porter. I put the numbers in and I think they're fair, but I'm curious to know whether you think I'm either over- or under-charging."

"I'd be glad to take a look."

"You've studied this particular client, right?" I ask.

She nods. "I have a ballpark figure in my head, and now you've got me curious as to what you wrote in the contract."

I pull out my phone and tap around the screen until I get to the draft of the contract. I slide it over to her. The waiter stops by to take our order, and as soon as he leaves, she turns her attention back to my phone.

I watch as she scans the document, and when she gets to the section with the numbers, I watch as she nods.

She glances up at me. "Hm."

I arch both brows. "What does that mean?"

"The ballpark number in my head? It's exactly what you have on here."

I breathe a sigh of relief at her approval, something I've never sought from a woman in business before, particularly not when it comes to how I run my company.

"It's perfect, Brian." She slides my phone back toward me. "It's an immediate savings for Porter over the third-party in Germany, but it's future-forward. It's more money in your pocket as soon as the ink is dry. It's a smart enough number to get him to sign but ambitious enough that you can hire a team for Dana without concern."

"So no more hiring freeze?" I ask.

She laughs. "Provided Mr. Porter signs tomorrow, no more hiring freeze."

I grin.

"I meant to tell you how impressed I was that you talked Jason out of hiring three employees," she says.

I don't expect for her words to hit me in the chest the way they do, but I feel a bolt of pride dart through me at the thought that she was impressed with something I did. I shrug nonchalantly. "It was nothing. I just stalled him."

She signals our waiter for another glass of wine. "Well it worked, and I have to tell you, with the cuts we've made in just the past few weeks, the new contracts you've pulled in, and now bringing this third-party work to FDB...you're heading toward a record-breaking year."

"How are the books looking?" I ask.

"Between the money Mark gave you to cover payroll and everything I just mentioned, FDB will be back in black by the first of the month." She looks proud as she says it, and she should be.

"The first of the month?" I can barely contain my surprise.

She nods and her lips tip up in a smile.

"Seriously? It took you less than a full month to get us back on track?"

She lifts a modest shoulder. "I waved my wand and worked my magic."

"I'll say."

The waiter stops by with Viv's drink, and she takes a bolstering sip. "You weren't that far off, Brian. You just needed someone to step in and show you how to really run a company that has the potential to be extremely profitable. I just moved a few things around and made some suggestions. You're the one who took the necessary actions."

"God, I really could kiss you right now."

Her eyes widen, and I backtrack.

"Professionally, of course."

She rolls her eyes and drinks more wine. As her second glass turns into a third, something strange happens as she shovels forkfuls of spaghetti and meatballs into her delicate mouth and I watch over my own pasta dish.

She starts to loosen up.

She smiles more. She laughs more. She's not drunk, exactly, but she's also not so guarded.

"How long did you work with Ashmark?" I ask after we finish eating, referring to my brother's record label in some attempt to learn more about her.

"Just long enough to launch it and train some of the employees."

"You're a trainer, too?"

She nods. "I've dabbled in a little bit of everything."

"How long have you been doing this?"

"I've been in business since I graduated college ten years ago, but I didn't become known as *The Fixer* until a few years ago." She puts air quotes around her nickname.

"What happened then?"

it started with a lie

"I was a junior executive in the finance department at a major corporation, and it started tanking. I offered some advice in a meeting since it was my job to research finances, and the CEO took note. We tried some of my ideas out, and suddenly we weren't tanking anymore. The CEO said I fixed the company." She breaks for a sip of wine. "Someone mentioned it to the CEO of another company, and I was hired as an independent consultant outside of my normal work schedule. It sort of took off from there."

"Is that when you became a workaholic?" I tease.

She chuckles. "I think I always had it in me. I've always been ambitious and I've always put work first. You either do or you don't, you know?"

I nod because I totally get it. "Ever since I started FDB, I really believed I could never be in a relationship with a woman who didn't get that. You can't be committed to your job and be with someone who *isn't* the same way. They'd never understand sometimes work *has* to come first."

"Exactly! Some men just don't get that, either, and they feel the need to *always* come first." The way she says it with such wistfulness makes me wonder for a split second what sorts of relationships she's been in and what sorts of men she's dated.

It's just another thing that makes me feel a little closer to her, yet it also makes me wonder if anything could ever *really* happen between us. Is it fair if we both always put our jobs above our relationships, or might that be the indicator of a successful path for us?

"I dated a girl once who hated that I always had to dart out for business trips." I don't mention the fact I'm talking about my brother's wife...a woman I wasn't really invested in at the time even though I did end up developing real feelings for her.

She huffs out a laugh. "Been there."

"Yeah?" I ask.

She nods. "*How long will you be gone this time?*" Her voice is clearly a mimic of some dude, and I laugh at her impression.

"*Why do you have to go again?*" I mimic in response, and she laughs along with me, like she's heard it all before.

The check comes, and I treat—not on FDB's dime, but on my own. I still have some work to do to straighten out my own finances, but now that my company is back on track, my personal assets won't be too far behind.

And I have the woman sitting across the table from me to thank for that.

"You want to walk on the beach again?" I ask once the bill is taken care of and we're on our way out the door.

She glances toward the water with longing in her eyes, but when her eyes turn back to me, I sense her hesitation.

I decide not to give her a choice. "Come with me." We walk a few blocks back to the hotel, stroll through the lobby, walk by the pool, and end up at the poolside bar. I order the same red wine she's been drinking all night for her and get myself another whiskey.

She shakes her head. "I shouldn't have another," she says once the bartender heads off to fill our order.

"*Shouldn't* implies you're doing something wrong, and you're not. You're just having a drink with a coworker."

"Is that all this is?" she asks softly. Her eyes tell me the story I've been waiting to read.

I look away first because I have to if I'm supposed to be respecting her wishes. "It's whatever you want it to be."

Our drinks arrive, and I raise mine to hers. "To a successful meeting with Porter tomorrow."

She clinks her glass against mine and this time I'm the one drinking faster than I should. I can hold mine, though—I don't know about her.

it started with a lie

She nods toward a couple sitting at the other end of the bar. "Think they're here on their honeymoon?" she asks.

Their heads are close together, and the man brushes his lips near the woman's temple. He whispers something to her, and she visibly squirms in her chair. "Yeah. If not the actual honeymoon, then some sort of honeymoon phase. That state of bliss can't be anything else."

She laughs. "Have you ever been like that with a woman?"

I lift a shoulder, surprised at her question. "Just once," I say as Kendra flashes through my mind. I've been like that with other women, I suppose—but not because it was truly what I wanted. It was part of some scheme or lie, some act I was either putting on to impress the woman or to show off to someone else. Not because I truly felt something or wanted to be there.

I don't say any of that to Viv, though.

"What happened?" she asks.

I clear my throat. "Turns out she was using me to get to my brother."

"Oh," she says softly. "I'm sorry."

"It is what it is. Or rather, was what it was. She broke my heart and I hated my brother for a long time because of it."

"And then he hired me to boss you around." She takes a lazy sip of her wine, clearly trying to nurse it slowly.

"Yeah, but a lot of other stuff went down between those events. It's not like we both haven't paid for our sins at this point," I say absently.

"What does that mean?"

I take a bolstering sip of my whiskey. I didn't think grabbing a drink before taking a walk on the beach would lead to deep confessions about my history. "Long story. Suffice it to say I was bent on revenge for a long time."

"And how'd that pan out?" She takes another sip of wine, this one coming faster than the last.

"There's two ways to look at it. On the one hand, here I am, single and committed to my company with my brother's bankroll to fall back on when I need it. On the other hand, here I am with you by my side as the person my brother sent to fix what I've fucked up." I take another sip of whiskey, this time to cover up my real expression as I think about the fact that my brother is the one who stepped in to save me when I couldn't stop looking at it like a power play.

"You know what I think that means?" she asks.

I arch a curious brow.

"I think it means your brother loves you and whatever came between you is in the past where it belongs." She nods resolutely at the end of her proclamation, and I smile.

"I think you're right."

We sip our drinks as we move onto lighter topics, and once both our glasses are empty, I stand. Viv scoots her stool out to stand, too, and when she does, she wavers a bit—maybe from the four glasses of wine. I reach out my arms to steady her, and once she gains her balance, I lead her over toward the sand.

We leave our shoes where the sidewalk leads to the beach and walk down toward the water. Viv dips her toes in first at the shallowest point where the water just barely reaches us, and I stand beside her as I allow the cool water to lap gently at my feet. We both look out over the moon's reflection on the water, here together yet totally separate, and I wish I knew what was going through her head.

A bigger wave moves in, crashing against the shore in front of us, and we both take a step back so our pants don't get wet. We walk down the beach a few steps, the waves crashing to our right as we stay just out of range.

Viv stumbles on a seashell or some seaweed or just the wine, I'm not sure, but I reach out to steady her like I did back by the bar. Somehow my arms end up wrapped around her waist as she clings to the fabric of my shirt against my chest.

My eyes fall down onto hers, and all I see is pent up need and desire as she gazes up at me. I pull her a little more tightly against me, and she clings harder to my shirt.

I can't help it.

It's something about being here in Miami with her after a romantic dinner as the water rushes over our feet.

My mouth moves toward hers, but this time it doesn't crash down. This time I move slowly. I press my lips to hers, soft and sweet just like the moment is for us, but all the passion between us is no match for me trying to be slow and careful with her.

She opens her mouth to mine, and her tongue brushes mine. She pulls harder on my shirt, her hands fists around the fabric, like if she pulls the shirt harder somehow our bodies will be closer. My hips move closer to hers automatically, like my dick is trying to find a way to get to her, and she bumps her hips back toward mine, like she wants it, too. I tighten my arms around her as she deepens our kiss, our mouths dancing sensually together as we stand in the cold ocean water. A wave rushes around us, and I don't know if we're moving or not and I don't know if my pants are soaked now or not but I really don't care.

Nothing could ruin this moment between us.

She's finally giving in to what we've both wanted for weeks, even though we haven't been ready to admit it at the same time.

She moans lightly into my mouth, and my dick hardens painfully. God, I want her. I've wanted her for a while now, but I've never had to work like this for a woman. I've always had the advantage of a famous brother or a worthy business or my charming good looks to get me by.

But with her, none of that seems to matter.

With her, it's just *me* and what I have to offer, and suddenly I wonder whether I'm good enough for her.

The answer is no.

I'm not.

I'll never be intelligent enough or attractive enough or rich enough. I'll never be *enough*. But that doesn't mean I can't try anyway.

She finally unballs her fists and lets go of my shirt. She doesn't push me away, but she does break the kiss. My arms are still wrapped around her, but she leans back and looks up at me.

"Dammit," she whispers before she looks away, and it marks the first time I've heard an actual curse word fall from her lips.

"What?" I ask softly, the rush of water around us the only sound in the air between us besides our panting breath.

"That shouldn't have happened. I—" she cuts herself off then starts again. "*We* can't do this."

"Because we work together?"

"That's only part of it, Brian. I—I can't. I have to go." She looks around wildly for a beat, and then she pulls my hands off her hips and runs up the beach before I get a chance to ask her why.

thirty-four

Me: *Meet me at six in the lobby.*

I stare at the text without hitting send. I've typed about a hundred texts, deleted them, and restarted them over and over, and nothing seems to sound quite right.

I'm sorry I kissed you again.
Why did you run away?
Why can't we kiss on the beach?
What more is there?
Fuck your rules. I want to kiss you again.
Stay the night with me.

I finally send the business professional one and keep the personal stuff to myself. As much as I want to know why she ran from me, why we "can't do this" and what other reasons she has stored up in her mind, the fact is it's a conversation we shouldn't have over text message.

My message shows as delivered. I watch as the little bubbles show up on her end indicating she's typing me back. When the bubbles disappear, I wait a full minute for the text to come through before I admit defeat.

She didn't say anything back.

I toss my phone on the nightstand and stare up at the ceiling as I try to figure out when the hell this got so goddamn complicated. I've kissed her twice now. She's stopped our kiss twice now.

But that was all it took.

Maybe it's because I've always wanted what I can't have. Always. It's just part of my nature.

But at the same time, this feels like so much *more* than the petty shit of the past. I'm thirty-two, yet this feels like it could be my first real, adult relationship. The stuff with Kendra seems like nothing more than a childhood crush on a pretty girl compared to what I'm feeling for Vivian.

Except it's completely one-sided, and I don't know how to fix that when she keeps running away from me every time things start to heat up between us.

I finally grab my phone and slip out my balcony door. I slide into a chair. I set my feet up on the railing and listen to the waves roll in as I look out at the moon's reflection on the water for a while. A wall divides my patio from hers. It looks dark next door, and I wonder if she's sleeping. I wonder if she's curled up in bed with her phone as she reads my text message and tries to figure out how to reply. In my imagination, she's wearing nothing but a skimpy pair of panties and a matching bra, things I could easily remove with my teeth or a simple snap of fabric.

I shake my head to clear out those thoughts when my phone starts ringing. I glance at the screen and find it's my brother calling me.

"To what do I owe the pleasure of a phone call from world-renowned rock star Mark Ashton?" I answer.

"Just checking in on my little brother."

I roll my eyes. He knows I hate it when he calls me *little*. "I'm fine."

"Are you?" His voice is condescending, and it hits a nerve.

"What's that supposed to mean?"

"It means I've gotten messages from your boss telling me things are fine, but I don't believe her. I may be a musician, but don't forget about that little degree in psychology I also have."

it started with a lie

I blow out a breath and don't answer. He loves to rub my nose in the fact that he has a master's degree. He acts like he knows the motivation behind every person's actions just because he studied psychology.

I refuse to admit he might be right.

"I knew it," he says.

"Knew what?"

"Things aren't all right, are they?"

I don't answer again, but at least the salty ocean air is keeping me calm during this conversation that might otherwise be striking more than a few chords in me.

"Look, I'm just trying to line up all my ducks before Reese goes into labor."

"She still didn't have that baby?" I ask, deflecting as usual.

"Her official due date was three days ago, but the doctors say it's common for the first baby to come late." His words are filled with anxiety that only someone who knows him as well as I do might detect.

"Shouldn't you be off rubbing her feet or something?" I ask.

"She's sleeping. Well, she's attempting to sleep. She's lying in the recliner in the family room with a box fan three feet away from her turned on high."

"Sounds sexy." I'm teasing him, which is how it should be. What happened with his wife and me is three years in the past now, and while some of the scars still show, we've done our best as a family to put what I did behind us.

"Honestly, the woman who's about to deliver my child any second is the sexiest thing I've ever witnessed."

"Hotter than that threesome you told me about in Paris?"

He laughs. "Yeah. Way hotter. Now tell me what's going on with you and Vivian."

"It was just a kiss."

"Wait...what?"

Oh shit. That wasn't what he meant. "Um..." I rack my brain to come up with some way to backpedal out of blurting what I just blurted, but I can't think of anything to say.

"You kissed her?"

I sigh. "Yeah, kind of."

"Jesus, Brian. Can't you keep your paws to yourself? I'm calling for a fucking update on how the two of you are handling my investment and you tell me you kissed her?" He sounds pissed, and it strikes me how moody he's been lately. The hormones coursing through his pregnant wife must be rubbing off on him.

"You can't throw temptation that looks like Vivian Davenport into my office and expect me to work three feet away from her without acting on my attraction." It's a weak defense, but I don't care. I pull my feet from the railing and set them on the ground.

"You shouldn't have kissed her."

"Fuck you." I stand from my chair as I continue looking out over the water. "You don't know anything about what's happened between us."

"It doesn't matter. She's your boss, and besides that, she's—"

"I think I love her." My words are short and terse as I interrupt my brother, and they're met with a beat of shocked silence.

"You...you what?"

I blow out a long breath, and when I speak, my words come out more desperately than I intend for them to. "I think I'm falling in love with her."

I hear some noise in the background that sounds like yelling.

"Oh shit. Shit! Reese's water broke! It's baby time! Holy fuck! I gotta go." He cuts the call, and I stand on my balcony for a minute.

I'm excited for my brother and Reese. They deserve happiness, and I'm finally in a place where I can admit that.

I think it has everything to do with the woman in the room next door.

I open my door to head back inside, and that's when I hear a door open on a neighboring balcony.

My heart races at the implication as I think about what I just said on my balcony to my brother without censoring my words. I don't know if the door was directly next door to me, and I don't know if someone is just coming out or just going in.

I do, however, fear that the woman who keeps running away from me overheard me admit I think I've fallen in love with her.

* * *

My phone wakes me at four with a text notification. As I flip over lazily to see who's texting me so early, I think to myself I really should turn my goddamn ringer off.

Mark: *Update: No baby yet but Reese is doing great.*

I roll my eyes. He texted me in the middle of my sleep to tell me nothing's new?

Me: *Text me again when the baby is here.*

I toss and turn as I try to fall back asleep, but it's useless. I'm going to be an uncle any time now, and I can't help but think back over the time I spent with Reese. That could've been me.

I never wanted it to be me, and yet these feelings I'm having for Vivian are bringing out some strange caveman mentality where I want to reproduce with her. I want to look into a child's eyes and see her bright blues staring back at me. I want to hold something we create together.

I shake that thought away.

I'm halfway between dreaming and awake, and clearly the dreams are winning. These images must be coming from my conversation with Mark right before I went to bed.

I'm still up when a text from Viv comes through at five.

Vivian: *Sounds good. See you in an hour.*

I wonder why she didn't write that back to me last night. Maybe it's because she typed out ten different messages like I did and ultimately couldn't figure out a good one to send. Or she might have waited until morning because she's playing a game.

I could be totally overthinking this, which tells me my feelings *must* be love. That's the only time people's brains turn to shit like this, isn't it?

I get out of bed early and take care of some administrative shit on my laptop. I head down to the business center to print the final numbers on the contract Viv approved last night, and then I run over to Starbucks to grab a coffee. While I'm there, I decide to get Vivian a coffee, too. Unlike my secretary who knows Vivian's Starbucks order, I realize I have no idea how she takes her coffee. Ultimately I just get her a black coffee and a muffin and I grab some sugar packets for good measure.

With breakfast and coffee in hand, I'm a couple minutes early, so I head over toward the chairs near the elevators and sit. When I see her get off the elevator a minute later, I'm positive this is love.

She simply takes my breath away as I look at her in a professional navy dress paired with nude colored heels. She tugs at the neckline of her dress, and then her eyes edge over to mine. I stand, but even from this distance I can tell something's off. It's the way she looks away from me as soon as our eyes meet, and it's the unmasked unease I saw there in the little glimpse she gave me.

I know immediately she heard what I confessed to my brother last night.

She knows how I feel about her, and I can't even think of an actual way to pretend like I didn't say it because that would be admitting I said it. And even though I admitted it to Mark last night, I'm in no way ready to say those words to her—certainly not when she's so averse to the idea of getting close to me.

"Good morning," I say.

"Morning," she murmurs.

I hand her the coffee, and our fingers brush. "I didn't know how you take it, so I just got you black."

"That was nice of you. Thank you." She avoids my gaze.

"I have sugar packets, and Starbucks is just over there if you want some cream." I nod over toward the store.

"I think I'll grab some cream." She steps away from me, and I hate the sudden awkward wall between us. Things seemed so much easier back when we just hated each other. Now there's all these complications, and we still have to work together for a couple more months.

God, I'm an idiot.

When she returns with her coffee doctored up to her liking, she says, "You ready?"

"We have a little time, and I'd actually like to run through our proposal once before we leave."

"Of course," she says. She nods to the chair where I was sitting. "Here okay?"

"Yeah." I follow her over, and I pull out the paperwork once we sit. "Is everything okay?" I ask before we begin.

"Fine. Just adjusting to morning after too much wine last night." She shoots me a tight smile that tells me it's more than that.

"My brother woke me up early with a text to let me know Reese is in labor."

She smiles. "How early?"

"About four."

Her smile widens, and even though there's all this weirdness between us this morning, it lights up her whole face. "How exciting."

I nod and launch into what I'm planning to tell Paul Porter an hour from now. When I'm done, our eyes meet for a brief second. I spot the admiration there before she glances away. "It's perfect, Brian. There's no way he'll turn it down."

"Let's hope." I stand and shuffle all the papers into a neat folder then place them in my bag. "You ready?"

She nods, and I extend a hand to help her up. She takes it, surprisingly, and the fit of her hand in mine just feels *right*. I don't want to let go, but I don't have a choice.

We grab an Uber since the car I usually arrange for myself in Miami is currently out of my price range, and we get to the Porter building fifteen minutes early. I'm not nervous, exactly, but there's something in the air pushing a pin of anxiety in the pit of my stomach.

I think it's Viv's perfume. It's the scent that's everything I want but exactly what I can't have. It's the scent that tells me my personal life is suddenly in shambles even though the business prospects are looking up. It's so much more than that, but it's also something I need to sweep under the rug for now so I can close this deal.

And so I do. I put my professional hat back on and ignore the burning need I feel for the woman beside me. I strip away

it started with a lie

the feelings and emotions as I focus on what has to happen over the next hour or two.

It's my only option, and it's hardly the first time I've done it.

The act is good, I guess. Or at least I think it is all the way until we're getting ready to walk out the door.

Paul Porter signs on the dotted line and writes a deposit check that's enough to get FDB out of the red for the rest of the month.

It's not until we're leaving that he pulls me aside. Viv is several paces ahead of me.

"I just need to talk to Mr. Fox a quick second," Paul says to Viv. "It was lovely meeting you."

She turns back to shake his hand. "You as well, Mr. Porter. I look forward to doing business with you again soon."

He smiles at her, and she turns to leave us alone for a beat.

"There's something I need to say to you," Paul says as soon as Viv turns the corner. We step back into his office.

"What is it?"

"I've known you a few years now, Mr. Fox, and I have to say, you're a different man."

I raise both brows. "I am?"

"You're always a consummate professional, but this girl you're working with has changed you."

"In what way?" I ask.

"You smile more. You're more relaxed than I've ever seen you, yet your ambition seems twice as intense. You look at her for approval and you don't even know you're doing it. I don't know if I would've signed if I didn't feel the utmost confidence the two of you can handle this transition."

I'm surprised he admitted he might not have signed, but I don't let that surprise show on my features. I reach out my hand to shake his. "Thank you, sir."

"Keep her around. She's not just good for you. She's good for FDB."

I press my lips together in what I can only describe as a professional smile as an ache spears my chest. I don't have the option to keep her around. She's leaving when her contract's up. She's returning to her life in Los Angeles, to her other jobs and family and friends and other men who aren't me that might want to pursue her.

I can't let that happen. I've got to figure out a way to get her to stay.

thirty-five

The meeting took far less time than we planned for, so we've got a few hours in Miami to kill. If I was by myself, I'd head back to the Ritz and use the business center to get some work done.

I'm not by myself, though, and I don't want to work right now. I want to find a way to get her to open back up. I want to find a way to tear down the wall that divides us.

"What's your favorite thing to do in Miami?" I ask as we stand on the sidewalk in front of the Porter building.

"How do you know I've been here before?" she asks.

"You once said something about not wanting to come to the most romantic city in America with a guy you hate so much."

Her lips twist in embarrassment. "I didn't mean that. I don't hate you." Her voice is soft.

"Don't you?" I ask as I match her tone.

She looks at me desperately for a half a beat before she slides on her sunglasses. "No, I don't." She starts to walk away from me. "And my favorite thing to do in Miami is walk on the beach, but you ruined that for me last night."

"Where are you going?" I call after her as she moves further and further down the sidewalk.

"Away from you."

I blow out a breath of frustration before I speed walk to catch up to her. I grab her by the bicep and pull until she turns to face me. "Stop walking away from me. Stop running away from me. Face this thing with me and just admit how you feel!"

Her sunglasses hide her eyes, but her sniffle betrays her emotions. She runs a finger under her eye beneath the lens.

"I can't," she says with a soft, trembling voice.

"Why not?" I yell, our tones completely contrasting.

"Because I'm—" My phone starts ringing, loudly interrupting our moment. She stops short in the middle of her sentence and looks away from me. "You should get that. It could be your brother with news about the baby."

She's right, and of course I want to know what's going on and whether everything's okay. But hearing her finish that sentence seems somehow more urgent.

I stare at her for a beat and let my phone clang loudly in my pocket before I pull it out. It's not my brother. It's my mom.

"Hey Mom," I answer.

"The baby's here! I'm a grandmother!" She's full of joy, and I want to feel as jubilant as her...but I can't, not when Viv and I are in the middle of something.

"Congratulations, Grandma."

I can practically hear her smile over the phone. "She's seven pounds, four ounces and twenty and a half inches of perfection."

"Did they tell you the name yet?" I ask. They've kept it a secret ever since they decided months ago.

"Ashton Rose."

"Ashton Rose Fox," I say. "I love it."

"She has these little pink cheeks and just the sweetest little wisps of dark hair." I hear the pride in her voice.

"I can't wait to meet her," I say, and I really mean those words. I've never cared about babies before, but this one is part of my family. She's my niece, and I can't wait to get to Los Angeles so I can hold her, so I can see my brother in his new role as a father, so I can see Reese be the wonderful mother I already know she'll be.

I mentally scroll my appointments for tomorrow and make a snap decision. "I'm in Miami right now, but I'll redirect my flight and be there by tonight."

"Oh, Brian, don't do all that. It's too much."

"I want to be there for this," I say. Maybe it's part of the new Brian—putting family first. "I better go so I can get to the airport. Send me a picture and tell Mark and Reese congratulations, but don't tell them I'm coming. It'll be a surprise."

"See you soon, honey," she says. "I love you."

"Love you too, Mom." I hang up and pull open my Uber app to grab a ride to the Ritz so I can get my overnight bag.

"The baby's here?" Viv says beside me.

"Yeah. I'm going to Los Angeles instead of back to Vegas. You want to come with me?" The invitation slips out, but I immediately realize what a great idea it is. We could both just take the weekend off. She can show me her home not far from LA. I can introduce her to my niece.

Jesus.

My parents will be there.

Am I really considering introducing a woman I'm not even dating to my *parents*? Am I really considering *taking the weekend off*?

Yep. I am.

She clears her throat. "I should really get back to the office," she says.

"Of course," I say as I mask my disappointment. "Let's share a ride to the Ritz."

We ride in silence back to the hotel, and soon we're standing in the lobby looking awkwardly at the closed elevator doors as we wait for a car to take us up to our floor.

"Congratulations, Uncle Brian," she says softly.

I press my lips together. "Thanks."

She clears her throat. "When will you be back?"

"I'm just popping over for the night to meet the baby and see my family. I'll be back tomorrow, probably late morning." The elevator doors open and we both step on. I press our floor number, and it's not until the car glides to a halt that she says something.

"Are you still planning to attend the charity thing tomorrow night?"

"You agreed to be my date," I say softly. "I wouldn't miss it."

She glances up at me with something akin to wonder in her eyes, and then we step off the elevator.

I wish she'd just come with me to Los Angeles. I don't want to part ways with her right now, not when things are so awkward between us and not when I'm sure she overheard my private conversation last night. But I also have no idea how to convince her to come with me, and so I don't.

"I'll see you tomorrow," I say, breaking the silence stretching between us once we get to our rooms.

She looks over at me for a minute, and something intense passes between the two of us. "Travel safe," she says. She disappears through her door, and I stare blankly at it for a second once it closes before I head to my own room to get my shit and get out of this town.

* * *

Before my flight takes off, I text my brother's best friend and the drummer of Vail, Ethan, to let him know I'll be there in a few hours. He tells me he'll arrange a ride to get me to the hospital, so at least that's taken care of. I head to the airport

it started
with a *lie*

gift shop while I wait for my flight and find a stuffed dolphin and a little pink frilly baby outfit that says Miami on it. I purchase both so I don't arrive empty handed, and it feels weird to be buying things for a baby. It's just not something I've ever done before.

I spend most of the nearly six-hour flight to LA thinking about Vivian, and by the time we land, I've made zero progress and no decisions.

Her comment on the elevator confused me. She simply asked me whether we were still attending the ball together, but the way she asked it made me think she *wanted* to go with me. It seemed like such a fight to get her to agree to go with me, yet she's the one who brought it up.

I'm sure I'm overthinking it. She may have just wanted to know whether our plans were still on so she could make plans of her own if they weren't.

This shit right here is why I haven't had any interest in getting involved with a woman for the past few years. I hate the guessing games and the wondering.

I have a text waiting for me from Ethan with my ride details, and I easily find the driver. Soon we're on the LA freeway headed toward Cedars Sinai and my brand-new niece. I text my mom on the way, and she meets me in the hospital lobby. We wind through a series of hallways toward the deluxe maternity suites, and my mom goes in first.

"Someone's here to meet Ashton," she says softly.

When I peek my head around the doorway, the first thing I see is my brother and sister-in-law sitting on the bed. Reese stares at the cradled pink bundle in her arms, and Mark's tattooed arms are laced around his wife.

It really hits me for the first time they're a *family* now. My brother has his own family, and while it's a part of our larger family, it's something that's just *his*. He made that with his love for the woman cradling his child, and for a second, an unfamiliar lump forms in my throat.

This scene almost didn't happen because of *me*, and all the ghosts from our past catch up to haunt me at the same time.

"Hey," Mark says softly so as not to disturb the baby as a grin spreads across his mouth. He waves me in. "Come meet my little girl."

I step into the room and walk toward them, but my mom stops me. "Wash your hands first," she whisper-yells at me.

"I just want to look. I'm not even going to touch her yet," I say.

"Don't even think about getting near her with dirty hands." My mom's hands are on her hips and she means business.

I roll my eyes in my brother's direction, and he just shrugs pointedly, as if to say I better just do what she says. I wash my hands in the little sink across the room from the bed then step over toward my brother. He gently takes the baby from Reese's cradle and stands to show her off.

"This is Ashton," he says.

I stare at her. I've never seen a baby less than a day old, and I'm sure Mark hasn't, either. Yet he's holding her like he has, like he's held millions of babies…like he was born to do this, and I don't believe I possess that same gene. Mom was right—she's beautiful. She has a tiny nose and little pink cheeks. Her eyes are closed and her mouth almost forms a smirk, something I'm used to seeing on her dad's face, like she's going to be a little smartass just like him. People always say babies look like their mom or their dad and I never see it. I don't see it here, either, but I do see a perfect little angel, and the feeling that *I want this* rolls over me like a wave.

"She's perfect," I say.

"Isn't she?" Mark asks. He glances at his wife, and my eyes follow his. Reese is leaning back on the pillow, eyes closed, as if she's completely exhausted and completely content—which she probably is right in this moment.

"You want to hold her?" Mark asks.

I shake my head nervously. "No—I...I mean, I..."

Mark grins. "Don't be scared. I'll help you."

He hands her gently over to me. "Keep your hand there to support her head," he says softly, and I follow directions. I'm standing at an odd angle, and my mom snaps a picture followed by a sniffle, and I'm pretty sure she's crying.

"I'm sorry," I blurt softly as I stare at her.

"For what?" Mark asks.

"For everything I did. For everything I've ever done." I shake my head as I start to drown in the ancient memories.

"It's behind us, man," Mark says. He pats my back bro-style but more gently so as not to rustle the baby awake, and another lump forms in my throat. "Over and done."

And just like that, I believe him. A small weight of guilt I didn't even realize I'd been lugging around with me lifts from my shoulders. I thought I could do whatever I wanted and never have to feel the burn of guilt, never have to pay any consequences because I pushed all the bad things out of my mind and held onto the belief that I didn't have a conscience.

But I do, and it takes holding my brother's baby to realize it.

I hurt people by my actions, but the very people I hurt forgave me. These people around me are so much better than I deserve, and it takes this moment for me to see I need to start living my life differently.

As I stare down at the sweet girl in my arms, I feel a need and a craving I've never experienced before. It's strong and it's powerful, and as I close my eyes for a beat, I see the image of a woman cradling a child and a man with his arms around her.

Only in my vision, the man and woman aren't Mark and Reese.

It's me and Viv.

I swallow down that damn lump in my throat that just got a little thicker as I lift the baby closer to me. She smells like fresh laundry as I breathe her in, and I press a gentle kiss to her forehead. "I'm your Uncle Brian, and I will always look out for you. You're not allowed to date until you're thirty. I'll kick any boy's ass that even looks at you."

Mark laughs just as my mom says, "Language!" somewhere behind me.

"She's perfect, man," I say to my brother. I hand her back over to him, and he gently pulls her from my arms.

He stares down at his newborn daughter, all the anxiety of impending fatherhood melted away now that she's here. There'll be a new set of anxieties every day, I'm sure, but for this moment, both he and Reese are beyond blissful. "I know."

thirty-six

My brother and I didn't talk a single word of business in the short time I was in Los Angeles. Instead, I ate dinner with my parents and held my niece one more time last night and again this morning.

Both my mom and my brother asked me if everything was okay. Both accused me of being quieter than normal. I have a feeling Mark sensed what was wrong after the confession I made on a balcony over the phone, but he was a little preoccupied with a newborn, so it never came up.

My flight lands a little after nine in the morning, and I'm exhausted from traveling across the country over the past two days. I don't have time to stop home, though. Instead, I head right for the office from the airport, and the exhaustion dissipates as I think about what awaits me there.

Vivian Davenport.

I'm excited to see her after my revelations in a hospital room yesterday, but I'm a little anxious, too. We left things in a strange place, but I finally decided tonight's going to be the night I say the words to her face rather than into the darkness as she listens quietly from the balcony next door.

As I get to Lauren's desk, she gives me a nervous glance.

"Good morning," I say, narrowing my eyes at her as I wait for her to spill whatever it is she doesn't want to tell me.

"Good morning," she says. "I processed the paperwork on the Porter deal and it's all set." I nod. Always start with the good news. She *has* been listening all this time. And then comes the bomb. "You've got a surprise waiting for you in the conference room."

"What sort of surprise?" I ask.

She clears her throat. "A German one. They just arrived about fifteen minutes ago."

"Who is *they*?" I ask.

"Stefan and Hans."

I nod and blow out a breath after she names the two top executives from the company we work with in Germany. I really should've been the one to break the news to Schneider Technologies that we were going to start pulling clients as contracts renew to shift the work to FDB, and I was going to. I just had to get to Los Angeles and then work sort of slipped away from my mind as other things started to take hold.

Other *more important* things.

Things like family and love and children. Things I never gave much thought to before, but things I want as part of my future.

My job is great, and it's important, but it doesn't have to be the only thing that defines me. Yet that's exactly who I am right now.

And now I'm ready to rewrite my own definition.

When I get to my office, Viv's already there. She's tapping away at her laptop, but she stops and glances up at me when I walk in.

"How's the baby?" she asks.

I can't help the smile that tips my lips. "Perfect."

"I've been doing some research on benefits and have three new plans I need you to review. They could save you thousands of dollars every year."

I toss my keys on my desk and fish my laptop out of the bag. I turn it on then plug it in while I wait a few seconds for it to come up. "Forward them to me and I'll take a look this afternoon. Right now I've got to get to the conference room."

"For what?"

"Didn't Lauren tell you?" I ask.

She furrows her brow and shakes her head.

"Of course not. Why would she? She thinks you're my girlfriend using space in my office."

Viv lets out a little nervous giggle. "What's going on in the conference room?"

My laptop is on, so I sit down and pull open a few files. I print them and then turn toward Vivian. "Some of the executives from Schneider Technologies stopped by. They're probably impatiently tapping their feet as they wait for an explanation."

"You don't owe them squat," she says.

"Squat?" I repeat, my lips forming a smile.

She laughs. "I just mean they didn't need to come all this way to confront you."

I lift a shoulder then collect my papers from the printer. I shuffle them together and stick them in my professional leather portfolio. "I get why they did, though. If clients started pulling from FDB, I'd want to know why."

"I'd like to hear what they have to say," Vivian says.

I nod because if I had my say, she'd come in with me. That idea strikes me as really odd. There's just one problem. "Jason will need to come in with me since he's worked closely with Germany in the past couple months. He may find it strange if you're in there with me."

"Oh," she says. She nods. "Of course."

"I promise to fill you in when I get back." I dial Jason's office line.

"Hey, Fox," he answers.

"We've got Hans and Stefan from Germany in the conference room," I say. "And the ink is probably still wet on the Porter contract."

"You didn't call them right after you had Porter sign?"

"No, I didn't. I've had a lot going on." It's a flimsy excuse.

He lets out an audible sigh. "Where were you last night?"

"Los Angeles."

"Los Angeles?" he repeats. "What for?"

"Reese had the baby."

"Oh." He doesn't say anything else, and I'm certain it's because of the history there. He knows less about what my true intentions had been with Reese when I dated her than Becker does, and I get the sense he feels bad for me that my brother ended up with the girl I "dated."

"How is she?" he finally asks.

"Reese?" I ask. "Or the baby?"

"I meant the baby, but both."

"Both are doing well. The baby is perfect. Ten cute fingers and ten chubby toes."

He chuckles. "All right. I'll meet you in the conference room in two minutes." He hangs up, and I get the feeling he wants all that, too. Maybe even with Tess, though honestly I don't see her as the motherly type.

"Chubby toes?" Viv asks when I hang up. I'm surprised she admitted to listening in on my conversation.

I smile wistfully then pick up my portfolio filled with papers. "The cutest, chubbiest little things I've ever seen," I say, and then I head over to the conference room.

* * *

Two hours later, Jason, Becker, and I are toasting in Jason's office, our tumblers filled with the expensive bourbon Jason keeps stashed in here.

"To new beginnings," Jason says, and I take his words to heart.

This is a new beginning for all of us, and as we celebrate what happened literally five minutes earlier, I think for a second about telling my best friends the truth—the truth about the company's bottom line, about Vivian, about Tess.

I think about it, but I'm not ready to do it just yet.

So instead I smile and toast and play the part I've always played, the guy always willing to have a good time, to talk about FDB, and to mix business with pleasure.

"So Germany just caved?" Becker asks.

I nod. "They even said they'd sell us their equipment at a fair price." I raise my brows. "I couldn't believe it. I thought for sure they were here to confront us about pulling our clients, but instead they were here to offer us the first shot at purchasing their analytics division."

"Can we afford it?" Jason asks, his eyes edging over to me. After the hiring freeze Viv mentioned, I understand his concerns.

But surely this isn't something Mark would deny us. The chance to get everything we need to bring third-party work in-house is at our fingertips, and we stand to make a ton of money in the long run out of this deal. The possibilities are endless—we'll probably even need to open a brand new division of FDB, and I know just the person I want to head it up.

I just have no idea if she'll agree to it.

"Yeah," I finally answer Jason. "We're fine." I hold up my glass in a toast. "We're better than fine." It's not precisely true, and it's another fib, but I'll figure out a way to make it work. My brother and I had a breakthrough last night, and I really think he'll be open to lending me the money to buy out Germany. If not, maybe a bank loan will work this time. After the way Viv got our finances back in order, I can't think of a reason why a bank would deny us if Mark does.

"We're better than fine, too," Becker says.

Jason and I both look over at him, and he grins.

"Jill is pregnant."

A beat of silence follows his words, and then the surprised exclamations of excitement and congratulations from Jason and me fill the room.

I'm happy for my friend, and, if I'm being completely honest with myself, I'm a little jealous. Everything has fallen so easily into place for him. He dated a woman for a few years, they got married, and she's already pregnant. They're happy and blissful and they have a bright future built on a solid foundation.

Is it really so bad to feel a little envious of that?

"Seems like we have a lot of celebrating to do," I finally say, and the three of us gulp down the rest of our bourbon college-style even though we're not college kids anymore.

We part ways and head to our own offices to wrap up the day so we can head home to get ready for tonight's ball. Vivian still taps away at her laptop when I walk in.

"How'd it go?" she asks.

"Better than I could've imagined. Viv, they offered to sell us their analytics division."

"Sell their division?" she repeats.

I nod and shut my office door, and then I sit on the edge of my desk facing her.

"Did you accept?"

I nod.

"What are the terms?"

"Let's not worry about it right now. Let's just celebrate."

it started with a lie

She shakes her head. "No, I actually think we really need to worry about it for a minute. How much, Brian?"

"A couple hundred thousand," I say. Her eyes widen, but I charge on before she can stop me. "Mark will pony up for it. It's too good of an opportunity to miss. We can have a whole division dedicated to creating the models of our system and it would all be *right here*, even in this very office. We'd need more space, obviously, and Viv, I want you to head it up."

"More space?" She's clearly stuck on those words. "We're barely out of the hole to cover your rental agreement for this month and you want to take up more space in this building? You had to pick the middle of the Vegas Strip, didn't you?"

"Did you hear what I said, Vivian?" I ask softly. "I want you to head up the new division. I want you to stay on with FDB. I don't want you to go back to Los Angeles when your contract with Mark is up."

"Head up the division," she repeats. Her eyes widen as what I'm asking finally sinks in. "Wait...what?"

I stay planted right where I am even though I want to go to her, to pull her in my arms and kiss her while I get her to agree to this. "Stay here. Stay with me. Don't go back to LA."

She begins to shake her head to decline my offer, but I hold up a hand. "At least think about it. We can table the discussion for now, but your business sense will be the perfect addition to our team."

She looks up at me with those lovely blue eyes of hers. I'm sure merriment and excitement is reflected back at her as I think ahead to all the possibilities—at the top of that list celebrating with her tonight.

"There's nothing to think about, Brian. I can't."

"We'll talk about it later," I say. Confidence brims inside me. I can do this. I can convince her to stay. Once she hears me tell her the words I confessed to my brother, she'll realize she loves me, too, and she'll figure out a way to stay here in Vegas. I walk around my desk to gather what I need for the weekend. "Right now, we need to get home and get Cinderella and her prince ready for the ball."

She laughs. "Need I remind you this is pretend?" she asks, waving a hand between the two of us.

I sling my laptop bag over my shoulder. "We'll see," I mutter just loud enough that she might've caught my words.

thirty-seven

Burgundy, wine, oxblood, dark red, maroon...whatever you want to call it, it's my new favorite color.

Vivian steps out of my guest room and into my kitchen wearing a burgundy gown. It ties around her neck and has a slit up her thigh higher than anything I've ever seen her wear and if I don't get her out of this dress immediately I might actually die.

That's perhaps a little dramatic but I'm looking at her gorgeous legs, and my dick hardens as an ache settles in the pit of my stomach. I want her with an intense craving that pierces my chest and blinds me to everything around me.

Actually, fuck that last thought about getting her out of it—I'll just bang her right *in* the dress.

I allow my eyes to trail down her leg to her heels. They're the same nude colored ones she's worn before, but somehow they make her look like a minx tonight.

"Do I look okay?" she asks, touching some of the curls twisted in an updo along the back of her head.

I blow out a breath as my eyes land on hers. She wears smoky shadow on her eyes and wine on her lips, yet her beauty is understated and elegant. The light scent of roses wafts to my nose, and I'm gone.

"Not a single lady in the room tonight will hold a candle to you."

Red creeps into her cheeks at my compliment, and she breaks our eye contact. She looks down at her hands as they sweep along her dress. "Is it too much?"

I shake my head. "It's perfect," I say softly. I hold out an elbow to escort her. "You ready to go?"

She nods and tucks her clutch under one arm as she links an arm through mine. "You look nice, too," she finally says softly. My lips quirk up but I don't respond as we head out to my car.

Silence plagues the car on the way to the event, mostly because I'm suddenly tongue-tied around this beauty beside me and certainly because she's thinking about our earlier discussion. I don't want to talk about it tonight, though. I want tonight to be about my feelings for her. I want her to understand where I'm coming from and what we could be together.

I want to hear her say she loves me, too, but I'm not banking on it.

I valet the car and as we step out, Becker and Jill are getting out of the car behind us along with Jason and Tess.

"Good timing," I say to Jason and Beck, feeling like I'm back on my turf with my best friends close by. I avoid eye contact with the woman I slept with not so long ago.

"Good to see you again," Tess says to Viv, and then she links an arm through Viv's like they're old friends, and I feel a little nauseous at the display. I'm not sure what game Tess is playing, but I'm sure I don't like it.

"I love your dress," Viv says to Tess.

"Let's head inside," I suggest.

It's pretty standard as charity events go: a live band playing, a few couples on the dance floor even at the early hour, lots of networking disguised as mingling, and a silent auction, which I avoid like the plague tonight as a way to earn Vivian's favor.

It's a charity ball, and we've already doled out the cash for the tickets, which didn't come cheap. We've attended this ball since we first moved the company to Vegas. I paid for six tickets months ago, which might be part of what got our bottom line into trouble—things I didn't give a second thought to until Vivian came around and my brother cut me off.

I schmooze on my way to the bar like I always do at these things with Vivian by my side the entire time. I introduce her as my girlfriend, and she continues to play the part. We get our drinks—whiskey for me and red wine for her, naturally, and then work the room some more. I spot my partners as they talk to different clients and make mental notes about who to make sure we hit while we're here.

And then it's time for dinner.

Somehow I'm seated between Viv and Tess, and I feel the sense of awkwardness as it settles into my guts. The woman I want to sleep with sits on my right, and the woman I wish I'd never slept with is on my left. Two beautiful women who are so completely opposite.

The weight of guilt settles on my shoulders when Jason catches my eye. He grins at me as if to say *what a couple of lucky bastards*. He's right—we are lucky. I'm lucky I haven't been caught yet, and he's lucky Tess hasn't spilled the beans.

I eye the margarita she picks up from the table and pulls toward her mouth as nervousness etches itself onto my already guilty conscience. What if she gets drunk? Everyone knows tequila is truth juice.

Will it always be this way? If the two of them get back together, will I always worry she might tell him when it should have come from me?

The answer to that question is crystal clear.

Tonight should be a night of confessions. I'll get Beck and Jason in a room, tell them the truth about Viv, tell Jason the truth about Tess, then get Viv home and tell her the truth about my feelings.

Tomorrow I'll wake up with a clean slate, a clean conscience, and the woman I love in my arms.

As I ponder this over my first of seven courses, it all seems so easy.

It's too bad it doesn't turn out that way.

"We need to tell him," Tess whispers when Jason's attention is on a potential client on his other side.

"Not now," I whisper back. Becker catches my eye on the other side of Viv, and it's pretty obvious he deduces what happened between Tess and me.

And if he knows about Tess and me, he might know this thing with Viv and me is a bit preemptive considering I slept with Tess at Becker's wedding a little over a month ago.

I draw in a deep breath as I consider my options. Beck is staring daggers at me and I know it has to be tonight.

"After dinner," I say to Tess under my breath. All the while, Vivian sits quietly beside me, seemingly oblivious to what's going on at this table—yet I know she's not. I know she's keenly observant of everything, and it's one of the things I've fallen in love with.

Dinner takes fucking forever. The secrets and the lies have caught up with me, and I just know tonight has to be the night I lay it all out on the table.

I'm just biding my time, waiting through each of the seven courses and praying no one asks the wrong question or shoots someone else the wrong look. To be honest, I don't have any clue how I've maintained these lies for so long.

"Need another?" I ask Viv, nodding to her empty wineglass sometime during the fourth course, a pasta that should taste better than it does considering the price.

She nods once. "I'll join you." She stands and the gentlemen at the table stand along with her. I hold my arm out to escort her, and I love once again how she feels right here beside me.

"What are you doing?" she asks once we're far enough away from the table that no one will overhear us.

"What do you mean?" I glance down at her as I wave a friendly hello to a client.

"Stop talking to Tess under your breath. Jason is going to realize what's going on."

I clear my throat. "Jason hasn't realized what's been going on since you got here." My snide tone earns me no favors with her.

"You two are making it really obvious," she says, her tone hushed. "Becker knows for sure."

"About Tess and me?"

She nods and we arrive at the bar. "Pinot noir," she says.

The bartender nods at me.

"Whiskey. Macallan if you've got some left."

He sets to work on our drinks.

"Of course he knows," I say. "Even if he hadn't just figured it out, he's married to Jill. Jill's best friend is Reese, and Reese knows."

She rolls her eyes. "Of course."

"I'm going to come clean about everything tonight," I blurt.

She touches a hand to her chest in surprise, but her eyes betray her. She thinks this is the right thing to do. "You are?"

I nod. "I wanted to warn you because you deserve that. They might not take kindly to you having played along with me when you're actually working with us."

She shakes her head. "It's been a long road of deceit." The bartender hands her the glass, and she immediately gulps some down. "I don't really know why I agreed to lie with you in the first place."

My mind goes one place when she mentions lying with me, but I push off the suggestive words on the tip of my tongue. "I think it's because you care about me, much as you don't want to admit it."

She gulps some more. "It's not that I don't *want* to admit it. It's that I *can't*."

"Why not?"

She looks away from me. "It's complicated."

My heart races as I feel the words on the tip of my tongue. It's my moment, and I'm grabbing it. "Viv, I—"

The bartender cuts me off. "And your whiskey."

I clear my throat as the moment passes me by. I look blankly at the bartender, toss a bill in his tip jar since it's open bar tonight, and close my eyes for a beat. I blow out a breath.

Another moment will come, and it'll be the right one next time.

We head back to the table. Viv's glass is half empty by the time we sit, and I almost wish I would've grabbed her two while we were there. Jill eyes the two of us with some mix of curiosity and accusation, but I focus on the fifth course, some sort of free range chicken.

By the time dessert comes—a bourbon cheesecake that's better than all the other courses put together, a sense of dread washes over me. It's so bad I'm not even enjoying the cheesecake.

If I'm going to come clean to my friends tonight, it has to be soon. Jill and Becker mentioned over dinner they're not planning to stay too late, and Jason is eyeing Tess like they're a couple of teenagers and he's ready to have a go at her.

In the middle of dessert, Bart Delnore takes the microphone with his impassioned speech about the homeless of the greater Las Vegas community and the organizations benefitting from tonight's ball. I'm trying to focus on his

it started with a lie

important words, but I can't. Instead, my eyes flick to my friends. I've betrayed one more than the other, but betrayal is betrayal any way you slice it. Neither is going to like what I'm about to tell them, but my hope at the end of this dark tunnel is that Vivian will. I'll be a man she can look at with respect because I took the hard road when I could've kept up the lying and manipulation.

I'll be able to look in the mirror with respect for *myself*.

I've never in my life wanted to be a better man because of a woman. I've never cared about who I'm hurting or the repercussions of my actions, and I've gotten by just fine that way. But I need this clear conscience to move forward in my relationship with Vivian, no matter what sort of debris the bomb I'm about to detonate may cause. It's that thought that gives me the realization I've already changed because of her. I've never had thoughts like these before.

Delnore finally finishes talking, and Beck and Jill stand. "We're gonna head out," Becker says.

"Can I talk to you and Jason a minute?" I ask. I think I feel the wind from Tess's head whipping in my direction as if to ask whether this is the moment I'm going to do what she thinks I'm going to do. "Alone?" I add.

Jill sits back down and Beck presses a kiss to the top of her head. "Be right back."

Jason kisses Tess on the cheek as he stands, and I look over at Vivian. I wonder what she sees reflected back at her. Fear, maybe? Because in this moment, despite the façade I'm trying to present like this doesn't affect me, I'm terrified.

I grab Vivian's hand and squeeze it, and somehow that gives me the strength to push to my feet. The three of us head out to the lobby and I think for the hundredth time how much we've been through. Becker and I have been best friends since we were kids, but Jason and I met at the company we worked for back in Chicago. Regardless, the three of us have been close for over a decade. They've stuck by me through my bad decisions and supported me when I needed them. But they've never been the recipients of my lies quite like this before.

The lobby is quiet with a random person or two walking by on their way to the restroom or out the doors for a smoke. Everyone else is inside as the announcement of the silent auction winners gets underway.

"What's up?" Jason asks, his blue eyes looking at me in concern.

I blow out a breath. "I haven't been completely honest with you two."

Beck raises a brow but doesn't say anything.

"Vivian is...uh..." I stumble over my words, something that nearly never happens to me. I try a different tack. "I was having some trouble with FDB's finances. I asked my brother for a loan."

"What does that have to do with your girlfriend?" Jason asks. Becker remains silent.

"Mark sent her in to help me sort out finances. I lied when I said she was my girlfriend. I didn't want you two to worry about the company when you were getting married," I nod to Becker, "and when you had other things to deal with," I say to Jason.

Jason's brows furrow. "So you and Vivian aren't really together?"

"It's complicated," I say. Becker's expression remains passive. "I think I'm in love with her."

I expect some sort of fanfare at my confession, particularly given my history with women, but I get none.

Jason clears his throat. "How are finances now?"

"Back in black with nothing to worry about, though my personal finances have taken a hit in the process."

it started with a lie

"You put personal funds into FDB?" Jason asks.

My eyes edge over to Becker, who has still remained quiet. I can't quite judge how he's taking the news, and it's throwing me off my game.

Jason runs a hand through his hair, but he seems fairly unfazed. "Why didn't you just tell us?"

I shrug. "Finances are my responsibility, and I biffed it. I had to sign over controlling interest to Mark in the process." The last part comes out unfiltered since the conversation is going so well.

"Wait a minute," Becker says. "You *what?*"

I clear my throat. "I signed over eleven of my twenty percent to my brother."

"So you have nine percent." Becker's voice is flat.

I nod.

"Let me get this straight," Becker says. Now that the silence is broken, he's on a rampage. "The three of us moved seventeen hundred miles across the country to start a business we own together and we don't even technically own it together anymore because someone else owns fifty-one percent?"

I rub the back of my neck nervously. "That about sums it up."

Becker runs a hand along his jaw as he struggles to control his emotions. "Look, Jill wants to get home, and I do, too. We'll talk at the office on Monday." With that, he turns to go back to his wife, and I don't bother to stop him. He'll cool down over the weekend and when clear heads prevail, we'll be okay on Monday.

"I actually want to talk to you about something else," I say now that I've got Jason alone. He quirks a brow, and I charge forward. "I just want to be completely transparent and honest with you."

"Okay," he says slowly, drawing out the *a* sound in the word.

Just as I clear my throat to make my confession, Tess walks out the doors of the ballroom. She stalks over toward us. "Did you tell him?" she asks, her voice an accusation.

"Tell me what?" Jason asks.

Tess sighs then glares at me like this was my job to do and why the hell haven't I done it yet. "Jason, I don't know what's starting up between the two of us again, but I like it. On that note, you know it's basically in my nature to fuck up relationships, so before we really get off the ground and get into something serious, I need you to know something."

"What?" Jason asks. He looks wildly between the two of us, and I watch as the lightbulb goes on. "Oh, no. Oh, fuck. The two of you?" He says it to Tess more than to me.

Tess nods.

"It only happened a few times," I say.

"When?" Jason grits out.

Tess looks uncomfortable. "Beck and Jill's wedding was the first time."

"And the second?" he asks.

"It doesn't matter," I interject before Tess starts talking about how Viv walked in on the two of us in my office or the time we went out on a double date with Jason and Vivian before the two of us fucked like drunk bunnies afterward. "What matters is it's completely over. Right Tess?"

"Right," she says. "I told him when he was in Miami that we couldn't keep doing this."

Fuck. I put a hand to my forehead like that facepalm emoji. I can't believe she just said that.

"Wait. Miami?" Jason's eyes dart over to me. "Weren't you just there last week?"

I press my lips together and nod, but I don't say anything.

it started with a lie

"You two were still fucking last week?" His voice is rising.

"Jason, calm down," Tess says. "No. I think two or three weeks ago was the last time."

"But after the two of us started seeing each other again," he says flatly.

She nods. "I'm sorry. I just wanted you to know. Everything on the table, right?" she says softly, as if they are words they've spoken to each other before.

"Right," he says.

"Brian, will you excuse us?" she asks. She laces an arm around his waist as she looks at me, and I want the two of them to work this out, so I give them the space they need even though I'd rather stand here and take Jason's full reaction.

I walk back into the ballroom and spot Vivian as she sits alone at the table. A few clients sit across from her, and Becker and Jill are approaching me as I stand by the exit. Everyone is focused on the stage and the announcement of the auction winners, so it looks like I haven't missed much.

I wait until the two of them are within earshot, and then I say to Becker, "See you Monday."

He presses his lips together without a response, and I stand for a minute as I try to gather the strength to make one more confession tonight.

thirty-eight

I slide into the chair next to Vivian and stare straight ahead. I don't really know what the repercussions are of my big confessions. Becker walked away and Tess shooed me away. I know I'll dread Monday from here to there, but there's not much more I can do than let my friends process what I just told them.

"You did it?" Vivian whispers beside me.

"It's done," I whisper back.

"All of it?" she asks.

I nod.

"Quick and painless?" she asks.

I shake my head. "As much as ripping off a bandage that's been glued to your skin for a decade."

"What did they say?" she asks. We're both looking at the stage and pretending to pay attention as we whisper.

"Nothing. Becker walked away and said he'd talk to me on Monday. Tess came out just as I was about to tell Jason about the two of us and she blurted what happened then told me to get lost."

"No fallout?" she asks, brows raised in surprise.

I shrug. "Not yet."

She sets her hand on my arm, and it marks the first time she's willingly touched me without being high on sedatives. "I'm proud of you, Brian."

I glance over at her, but it's more than a glance once our eyes lock. I see admiration and something more there, something I want to identify but can't, not yet. Maybe it's just something I want to see.

I set my hand over hers. "I have another confession to make tonight."

She raises a brow and squeezes my arm before gently tugging her hand away. She goes right for her wineglass, which doesn't surprise me. "Such as?" she asks as she hovers the glass next to her mouth.

"We'll talk at home."

Home.

I used to call it *my place* or *the house* or something of the like. But now that she's staying there with me, it's become something of a home for the two of us even if we aren't exactly living in it that way. For now.

She tips her glass back and finishes most of what's in there, and then she looks at me with twinkling eyes. "Intriguing," she says. She doesn't even know the half of it.

Since Beck and Jason took their dates home early, I'm left as the lone representative of FDB. I have a few more people to talk to, so I take Viv back to the bar after the auction as I'm plagued with a question. I blurt it out before I can stop myself. "Why are you still here with me?" She isn't obligated to be here now that the truth is out.

She lifts a delicate shoulder. "I guess because we showed up together. Maybe you were honest with your friends, but the public and the press don't have to know yet. Besides, you ditched me the last time at one of these, so I know what it feels like."

My chest burns with love for her combined with guilt over the things I once did to her. I'm honored she's here with me

it started with a lie

tonight, even more that she'd protect me and look out for me that way. "I appreciate that more than you know," I say.

"Now get me tipsy so I can get through the rest of this night."

I laugh at her words because they're so out of character, and then I proceed to do what the lady asked me to do.

It only takes one more glass before she loosens up and wants to dance during an upbeat Bruno Mars song.

And it only takes one second of holding her in my arms on the dance floor after the song switches to something slower to know beyond a shadow of a doubt we belong together.

The song talks about two people being meant for each other, and her eyes flick up to mine. As I look down at her, my heart squeezes. Every part of me wants to tangle my hands in her hair and brutalize her mouth with mine. It takes reminding myself we're in public not to do that.

But time passes along as it always does, and once the party's over and we've traveled safely home, we stand in my kitchen squaring off against one another. I rack my brain for some way to recapture the intimacy from the look that passed between two people on a dance floor, but I come up short.

She opens her mouth, surely to say goodnight, when I blurt, "Nightcap?"

"Uh," she stammers nervously. "Oh—okay."

I find a bottle of pinot noir in my wine cooler, and I pour myself a glass of whiskey after I've handed her the wine. She takes her shoes off and sets them near the hallway leading toward the guest room then wanders into my football room set just off the kitchen. She settles on the couch—an interesting choice considering the single-seat recliners in there. I take it as an invitation and settle in next to her. She shifts to get comfortable then massages one foot with her palm.

"Those shoes did me in tonight," she says, shooting a glare at the shoes from across the room.

I set my whiskey on the end table beside me. "May I?" I ask, reaching for her foot. I apply pressure with my thumbs to her arch, and she leans her head back and moans. I glance up at her, and my dick seems to get somehow harder.

"Oh my God, that feels so good." Her voice is breathy and soft, and she sips her wine then closes her eyes.

"Vivian, I told you back at the ball I had another confession to make tonight, and I'd like to say it now before I lose my nerve."

"Mm," comes her soft reply. I take it as my affirmation to charge forward.

"I've fallen in love with you."

Her eyes pop wide open. "You...you what?" she stutters, sitting bolt upright and spilling her wine clear down the front of her dress in the process.

"Oh shit," I say, and I run to the kitchen to grab a towel. I toss it to her and grab another towel. I run that one under some water.

"It's okay," she says. I wring the wet towel out in the sink. "The dress is the same color as the wine. You *what*?"

"The couch!" I yell. "Get the couch. The wine will ruin the leather."

She's mopping the wine from the couch when I return with the damp towel. I swipe it over the leather, which is mostly dry. Her dress took the brunt of it. I take the wine glass out of her hand and set it on the table, and then I kneel in front of her legs and gently swipe at the fabric of her dress with the damp towel as I fight her rose-scented aphrodisia.

"I can get it," she says softly.

"I know you can," I say, continuing to work despite her meager efforts to stop me. It's doing nothing to save her dress, but at least, as she pointed out, it's the same color.

She finally halts me when she grabs my wrist. I stop scrubbing. I look up at her, and I know I'm not mistaken this time.

Her eyes are filled with lust.

"You should really take that off and soak it in some water," I say quietly. I glance down at the hem and finger it with my free hand.

I glance up again, and her bottom lip is snagged between her teeth.

"Take it off, then," she says.

I raise both brows. "Me?"

She nods slowly, and I rise to my knees and move between her legs.

"What changed?" I whisper.

"I did."

"But why is this okay when you've been telling me no?" I'm not sure why I'm asking. I should just go for it. She's giving me permission, handing herself over. But I only want this if she's positive she does, too.

"Because I want you, Brian, and I'm so tired of fighting."

"How much have you had to drink?" I ask. I can't help but wonder why all of the sudden this is okay when she's been adamant this could *never* happen between us.

"Shut up," she says, placing both of her palms on my cheeks and inching forward until her lips touch mine.

I drop the towel somewhere on the floor, my mouth never leaving hers. How could I when she's finally giving me everything I've craved since the moment I figured out it wasn't *hate* I was feeling for her?

I sweep a hand along one of her thighs as the other comes around her waist to pull her closer to me. Her hands stay on my face for a beat as she opens her mouth to mine, her hunger for me evident from the way she brutalizes my lips the same way I've wanted to do to hers for weeks. Her cool hands breathe life into my skin as they run along the stubble of my jaw before settling on my shoulders. I half expect her to push me away, but she doesn't. Instead, her hands move over my shoulders before they link around my neck.

I take the opportunity to hook my arm under both her legs to literally sweep her off her feet. I pick her up easily into my arms and break from her long enough to ask one very important question.

"Are you sure about this?" I nip at her neck, and her scent overwhelms me with desire.

"Am I sure I want you to shut up?" she asks with a twinkle in her lust-filled eyes. "Yes," she says before I have a chance to answer.

I laugh and nuzzle her neck, drinking in the roses as my chest tightens with an erotic craving for her. I carry her to my bedroom and set her on the floor. With one sweep of my hands, I pull her dress over her head.

I clutch it in my fingertips for a beat as I stare at her before me in her simple black bra and matching panties. I've seen all sorts of women wearing all shades of expensive lingerie, in various stages of undress, even completely naked.

Not one of them even comes close to comparing to the beautiful creature standing before me.

She runs a hand along her flat stomach nervously as she looks at me. "What?" she asks. She typically oozes poise in her professional wear, but as she stands nearly naked in my bedroom, it's like the confidence came off with her dress.

it started with a lie

I clear my throat as I realize it's my job to give her that assurance back.

"Wait here," I say, and I take the dress with me. I need a minute to calm my dick down, because just looking at her and loving her so much has weaved a tangle of nerves in my chest and an aching throb in my balls.

I set the dress in my sink and run some water over it to prevent the wine from staining it while I take a deep breath and give myself a pep talk.

I can do this, and I can make it last more than thirty seconds.

God, it's been so fucking long since I've had sex.

I want her so much. *So much*, so deeply.

I grab a condom from the drawer where I keep my stash. I set my suit jacket on the counter and kick off my shoes while I pull off my tie, and then I return to the bedroom.

She's sitting on the bed when I walk in, perched right on the end like she might change her mind and bolt at any second.

"Before the wine spilled, I told you I've fallen in love with you. It's true, Vivian. I thought it was something else at first, but God, I can't imagine living another second without tasting your skin and holding your body and kissing your mouth. You're gorgeous on the outside, but you were made for me on the inside."

She opens her mouth to say something back, most likely some witty remark or some biting insult, but I swallow it up when my mouth crashes down to hers.

Tonight marks only the third time I've gotten to kiss her like this. As I gently push her back onto my mattress and hover over her, I know this won't be the last time. I feel it back from her, and I kiss her with all the reverence and love I've bottled up for too long.

I lean most of my weight on one arm as I let my body lightly mold to hers. I run my hand along her thigh, to her stomach, along her bra-clad breast, and up into her hair. She moans into me, and I take it as a signal. I thrust my hips against hers once, and when I'm rewarded with another moan, I buck against her again.

I trail my lips to her neck, memorizing the sweet taste of her skin along the way, committing the silkiness of her skin beneath my fingertips to memory so I can call it up any time I please.

I reach into her bra and pull her breast over the cup. I swipe my thumb across her nipple until I see it pebble beneath my touch, and then I can't help myself. I lower my mouth for a taste, and I have so much pent-up desire for her I feel like I'm about to come everywhere and I haven't even dipped inside of her.

Yet.

I suck her breast into my mouth and swirl my tongue around her nipple. I pull her other breast out and lavish it with the same attention, and then I lift her up to unhook her bra. Her quiet kitten moans push me into dangerous territory and I'm afraid I can't hold myself off any longer.

The bra ends up somewhere behind me, and then she reaches for the buttons of my shirt. She unbuttons them one by one, a slow process as I watch her nimble fingers work. I'm about to tear it off to speed up the process when she finally gets to the last one and pushes my shirt off my shoulders. She gasps at the sight of my abdomen mere inches from her face, and I'm thankful for the hours I've put in at the gym when I haven't been working or scheming.

She trails her fingertips along the muscles there as I watch her with bated breath, and then her hand dips lower to grasp my cock.

"Jesus," I say as I let out a low hiss. Her hand feels like a slice of fucking heaven and she's still on the outside of my pants.

I reach down and unbutton them, and then she dips her fingers in. They brush against me, and the steel hardens into titanium. I need to be inside her with an intense craving. When I look up at her face as she concentrates on what's inside my pants, the love I feel for her rushes through my chest. I press a sweet kiss to her forehead, something so out of character for me and yet so right in this moment.

She grasps me inside my pants, and a low grunt bubbles up from my chest.

"I want you, Brian. I want this." Her voice is a soft plea, and it's what I need to hear. I stand up and pull my pants off. She gasps when I reach for her and yank her panties off as I decide to skip the rest of the foreplay.

The last four weeks have been foreplay. It's show time.

She's a flawless naked vision in front of me and I can't get inside her fast enough.

I roll on the condom and toss the packet on the floor. I pull her to the edge of the bed so her ass is nearly hanging off, and then I align the head of my cock with her pussy and push my way in.

A low and sexy growl spills out of her as I drive all the way inside her, and then she grunts as I pull back. I warm us up by thrusting slowly a few times, my hands finding her breasts as she wraps her legs around my waist.

And then I drop the hammer.

I drive into her as deeply as I can, back and forth, in and out, keeping a mild pace because if I go too fast, I'll lose control and the moment will vanish. I'm not ready to let that happen when I want to stay forever inside her warmth and cocooned in her love.

The naughty girl inside her must've been practicing her Kegels, because her pussy clenches around me over and over, and then she lets out a series of louder moans as she starts to come. I buck into her a little more wildly, wishing I could draw this moment on forever but knowing it's about to end.

It doesn't matter, though. She knows I love her. She watched from afar as I did the things tonight that made me a better man. She consented to this and wanted this. Because of all that, if it goes fast now, it's okay. It'll just happen again in a few hours or tomorrow or the next day.

Another squeeze of her body around mine met with pulses and moans from her mix with those thoughts in mind, and I let go.

I come hard into the condom, grunting my way through my release as she continues her musical moans that I'm certain I'll hear in my ears for the rest of my life.

* * *

It had been a long night up until the time we finally had sex, and she was exhausted. She cleaned herself up, kissed me softly once more, and fell asleep.

I listened to her even breathing as thoughts rolled around my mind. The last thing I remember thinking before I fell asleep was that this is where telling the truth gets you.

I had a clear conscience and the woman I love beside me in my bed.

Life was good. Finally.

Except when I wake up in the morning, suddenly everything shifts.

In our haste to get into the bed together, I forgot to close the blinds. Sunlight streaks across my eyes, waking me at an ungodly hour. I'm not hungover since I didn't drink enough to get drunk last night, but I still wake with a sense of grogginess.

Vivian moves beside me, awake too as the sunlight streams in on us. She glances over at me then does a double take.

"Oh God, what have we done?" she says, squinting against the rays of sunshine filtering through the open blinds.

"I told you I love you, and then we had the best sex of our lives."

She clears her throat and closes her eyes. She tosses an arm over her eyes. "I was afraid of that."

"Afraid of what?" I lean up on my elbow to look at her.

"Afraid it was just a dream. Afraid it wasn't."

"Afraid it wasn't?" I ask. I don't get it. She's the one who kissed me last night. She's the one who told me she wanted this. She told me to shut up when I questioned her.

"We really shouldn't have given into temptation, Brian."

"Because we work together?" I roll my eyes when she looks up at me.

"No," she says. She shifts a little in the bed, pulling the sheet up higher over her naked chest. "Because I'm married."

acknowledgments

As always, thank you first to Matt and Mason for everything. From managing my business to chatting about plot details, you're both there for me for everything, and you both give the best hugs. Love you!

Thanks to my beta readers, Stephanie, Kelly, and Jen for the feedback and the support. Thank you to my ARC team for reading and reviewing my books and for being excited about reading Brian's story after what he did! You're the best!

Trenda London, thank you for being the best content editor in the world. I absolutely love how we work together. Thank you to Katie Harder-Schauer for the eagle-eye proofs.

Thanks to the Vail Tail Fangirls! What started as a support group for A Little Like Destiny (that I thought maybe two people would join) has become a Vail haven and I love it! I hope you found a way to forgive Brian. Thanks also to Team LS (my reader group) for the fun times and the love!

Thanks to my author buddies, especially the 30 Days to 60K group for the sprints, and thank you to the bloggers who work tirelessly to promote my books. Thanks especially to Give Me Books for the release blitz and ARC distribution.

Thank you to you. If you're reading this, I hope you loved the first half of Brian's story, and I can't wait for you to see how this all pans out...

Lots of Love!
Lisa Suzanne

about the author

Lisa Suzanne is a romance author who resides in Arizona with her husband and baby boy. She's a former high school English teacher and college composition instructor. When she's not cuddling baby Mason, she can be found working on her latest book or watching reruns of *Friends*.

also by Lisa Suzanne

A LITTLE LIKE DESTINY
A Little Like Destiny Book One

#1 Bestselling
Rock Star Romance

THE POWER TO BREAK
Unbreakable Thread Duet Book One

#1 Bestselling
Rock Star Romance